E.N. Beck

Distant Spring

Distant Spring

Chapter One

Lottie

Lottie Stephens was running late. She despised running late. Always chronically early, her armpits were drenched, and her hands shook as she searched for her keys. Why didn't she hang them on the hook when she came in last night?

But she knew why she hadn't. She'd been drunk. And angry. And, hmm, had she tossed them against the wall? Swooping under the hallway table, she searched.

Ugh, they're not here.

Her flickering memory was hinting that's where they'd be. Twisting her head under the table, she turned to see them dangling, stuck between the back of the table and the wall. Also wedged between the back of the drawer and table was a bent photograph. She grabbed the corner and tugged it free. The breath pulled from her body as she glanced at it.

David.

As she shoved the picture into her pocket, Lottie hit her head on the table as she stood. She clutched it and pulled the table away from the wall enough to let the keys drop. She scooped them off the floor, scuttled through the kitchen, swiped her purse off the arm of the couch, and flew into the garage.

Hopping into her car, she momentarily fantasized about the cup of coffee she never got the chance to make, hit the door button, and cursed it for raising so slowly. While she waited, she slid her hand into her pocket and pulled out the picture of David, sighing before curling it into the cup holder. She backed down the driveway and headed off to her dental appointment, hitting every red light along the way.

A blue pickup pulled behind her about a quarter of her way along and followed her, riding her ass. Fire grew inside her. "It's not like I can go any faster!" she screamed to the silhouette in the rearview mirror. "What do you expect me to do? There are cars in front of me." Lottie wished she had the guts to jump out of her car at the next light, open the truck's door, pull the man-shaped silhouette out, and beat the living shit out of him. But, as it was a him, it was not very likely that she would be the one giving the beating. And what if it was some sort of psycho who would have no trouble fighting a woman? The way he drove, it seemed more likely than not that he'd be just that kind of man. Instead, she opted to throw her middle finger up as she took off from the last light before turning into the dental office parking lot.

Panic swept through her as the blue pickup followed her into the parking lot. What if this was the kind of psycho who would follow a woman to her destination and pummel her for throwing the bird? She whipped into the closest space she could find and threw the car into park. She grabbed her purse and scurried to the office door, keeping one spying eye glued to the truck. It pulled into a space. She saw the driver's side door open as she ducked into the safety of the dental office.

Side-eying the entrance, she removed her coat and flung it on the hanger. It slid off immediately and fell into a crinkled heap. She wasn't going to take the time to try to rehang it. The psycho could come in at any moment. She scuttled over to the front window to check in. The hair on the back of her neck rose as she heard the jingle of the doorbell, the hanging of a coat, and the patter of footsteps walking across the carpet behind her. He was standing behind her. Oh, why wouldn't the lady at the front desk look at her already?

Quit looking at that computer screen and check me in, goddamnit.

As though reading her thoughts, the women with blue-rimmed glasses looked up. "Hello there."

She leaned in and whispered, "Charlotte Stephens. I have a nine-thirty appointment."

"You're all set." The woman smiled.

"Thank you." Lottie twisted and rolled around the man standing behind her.

She tucked herself back into the security of a corner seat near the front of the office by a large ficus plant.

Wait, is this a real ficus?

She rubbed a leaf between her thumb and forefinger.

Wow. Real.

Lottie allowed her eyes to drift up to the man standing at the window. That was definitely the one she'd given the finger to. She could tell from the shape of his silhouette—the way his hair was lightly spiking upward in the front and his shoulders were very broad.

"Grant Ryan," she heard him say. She quickly scooped a magazine off the corner table and shoved her nose inside. There was no way she was going to make eye contact. Her stomach swirled.

Why did I have to throw him the bird? This is just my kind of luck. I'm going to have to get a new dentist now. Ugh, but I really like coming here. No! He's the one that was wrong. He can get a new dentist.

Once again, a fire grew, perturbed at the thought that he was the asshole driver and now he was going to push her out of the best dentist office she'd ever been to. He took a seat catty-corner to her. She chanced an angry glance in his direction, but her eyes quickly shot away from his as they met. He'd been looking directly at her. His eyes darted away as quickly as hers had. Her heart pounded in her chest.

He knows I know he was staring at me. He didn't look angry, though. God, and he's cute too. Just my luck, he'd also be really cute.

"Hey, Lottie. I'm ready for you now." Kay, her regular hygienist for the last three years, smiled and motioned her back.

Lottie hopped up and scampered toward her.

"Oh, don't forget your purse." Kay pointed toward Lottie's bag, sitting by the side of the chair.

"Oops." Lottie's face flushed red as she spun to grab it, careful not to look in his direction.

The morning is complete. Now you look like an idiot in all regards.

"We're going in room four." Kay motioned Lottie to the room and followed quickly behind her. "You can set your things on that chair."

Lottie plopped her purse where she was directed and climbed into the dental chair as Kay donned her mask. "How've you been?"

"I've been better."

4

"Yes." Kay pulled down her mask and put a hand on Lottie's shoulder. "I'm so sorry, honey. We got the request for David's records to be sent on to Hickam Air Force Base."

Lottie's stomach dropped. Yes, the last time she came, she and David were still trying to work things out. "Thanks, Kay. It's for the best this way. I'm really all right with things now. I'm happy teaching at the school still. You know I love my students and this town."

"And we love having you here. You know, my granddaughter still goes on about how you are her favorite teacher. And she had you, what? Two years ago?"

"That's right. Sarah was in my first class. She's such a sweet girl."

"Thanks. She really is sweet. I'm worried you might not think the same when you get my grandson, Todd, next year." Kay laughed and picked up a scaler.

Lottie opened her mouth as Kay began her work.

"Todd's a sweet boy, but he can't sit still for a second. I swear, my daughter had no idea what she was in for with him. Sarah was such an easy child, and Todd's still giving her a run for her money. It's like she was a first-time mom with her second. Ah, I'm sure you'll be able to handle him in class. He's got a good heart. Just can't sit still is all."

Lottie smiled around the dental tool scraping her teeth. Kay worked away. Scraping and polishing. Silently and quickly. That's what Lottie loved about Kay. Cleanings with her were always quick, painless, and never filled with questions expected to be answered around a mouth full of metal scalers, mirrors, and curettes.

After finishing, Kay raised the chair. "Would you like to schedule your next appointment?"

"Sure. I'll be here."

"How's October 4th? Same time?"

"That'll work for me."

"Okay, see you in six months. I put your appointment card in with your new toothbrush and sample paste."

"Thanks, Kay."

Kay handed Lottie her dental prize bag as the dentist swooped in.

"And how does everything look today?" The dentist washed her hands, tipped the chair back, and looked into Lottie's waiting mouth.

"She was squeaky clean as always." Kay winked at Lottie.

Just as fast as she swept into the room, the dentist sat back, pulled her gloves off, and smiled at Lottie. "Everything looks great. No cavities today. Keep up the good work."

"Thank you." Lottie wiped away some spit that had swept across her chin.

Kay removed the bib from Lottie as the doctor waved and scuttled out of the room, ducking into the room next door. "Hey, Grant, and how are you doing today?" Her words cutting off as she disappeared inside.

Lottie waved at Kay as she scooped her purse off of the chair and left the room. With the dentist's hands in his mouth, there he was, the cute guy she'd given the finger to in the next room. She froze for a moment while pulling her purse over her shoulder. His eyes connected with hers before she quickly averted them and hurried to the front desk.

"Am I all set?"

"You're good to go, Charlotte. See you next time." The receptionist waved and quickly went back to her computer.

Lottie grabbed her coat from the hanger—someone had rehung it for her—before bursting through the door and half-running to her car. His mouth was full of the dentist's fingers, but for some reason, she was worried he'd soon be behind her if she didn't hurry. As she bustled out to her car, she glanced over at his blue pickup. A bone-shaped magnet was stuck on the tailgate that read "I ♥ MY RESCUE." Her mind drifted momentarily—as she pressed the unlock button on her bobble—wondering what type of dog he might have. A lab? Or maybe he looked like a German shepherd man. Pit bulls were the dogs that filled most shelters. Yeah, she could picture him with a gray pitty riding next to him in that old blue pickup. She shook her head and climbed into her car. No, he's a tailgating jerk, not some sweet guy who rescues pitties.

Why are you always trying to give jerks good qualities and imagine them to be anything other than they are?

Lottie buckled, took a quick glance in the rearview to make sure he wasn't coming out yet, backed out of the space, and headed off toward the school, wishing she'd taken the whole day off.

After a morning like this, school was the last place she wanted to go. Her energy levels already felt completely zapped. She turned onto Falcon and headed straight for the White Buffalo Coffee Bar, fumbling in her purse for her wallet as she neared. Grabbing it, she sighed as she looked inside, only spying repeats of Alexander Hamilton's handsome face. She hated to part with her tens. Why couldn't there be an Abe or Andrew on them instead?

Great timing. There was only one car in front of her, unlike whenever she'd try to swing by before school and hit the morning rush. Once it was her turn, she pulled up and ordered a large white buffalo mocha and an espresso. She took the hot drinks, carefully placing them in her cup holder, and handed the barista the ten.

"Keep the change." Lottie smiled, pulled off, and headed for the school. Before pulling out of the parking lot of the White Buffalo, she peeled off the lid of the espresso and sipped out the hottest little bit before turning the AC on full blast and pointing it at the open cup. She carefully pulled out onto the road, praying she'd sipped enough coffee out to avoid a spill, and headed toward the base.

She slowed and rolled down her window at the gate, handing the guard her ID. "Good morning."

"Morning, ma'am." The guard handed her ID back. She shoved it in her purse, rolled up her window, and drove by the "Welcome to Altus AFB" sign like she did every weekday morning, headed to Rivers Elementary School. Pulling into the parking lot, she was relieved to see an empty spot waiting for her. Until she realized there was a motorcycle hiding in it.

"Dammit! You really gotta take up a whole space with that thing, buddy?" Lottie picked up her espresso as she rolled through the lot looking for another space and took a big gulp. Ah-ha, another spot. A small spot, but her little silver Honda Fit could squeeze into a space half that size. She pulled in and unbuckled before downing the rest of her only slightly too-hot espresso. Purse in one hand, her white buffalo mocha in the other, she headed into the office.

"Lottie, you're back. I wasn't expecting you for another half hour." Maura pressed her glasses to her face and smiled before picking up the phone the moment it rang. "Good morning, Rivers Elementary. How can I help you?"

"I'll be in the teachers' lounge," Lottie mouthed as she waltzed by, taking a small sip of her mocha. She walked down the hall and stopped short when she saw streamers, balloons, and a sign hanging up in the teachers' lounge which read, **'Sayonara, Melissa! We'll miss you.'**

"Fuck." Lottie closed her eyes. She'd forgotten Melissa's goodbye party was today. She sank down into a chair and sipped her coffee, staring at the line-up of goodbye presents covering one of the lounge tables. So much for not writing things down. She kicked herself. She knew she forgot any and everything if she didn't write it down in addition to setting a reminder in her phone.

The bell rang just a few moments after she finished the last sip of her coffee and missed the trashcan when she tossed her cup at it. "Of course." Bending over as soon as she rose from the chair, she waddled over to pick it up. Lottie squealed and jumped when she got a firm smack to her backside.

"Hey, hot stuff. Make me work for it." Beth waggled her eyebrows at Lottie.

"Shut up, and keep your hands to yourself, ya old pervert."

"Never! You know I can't resist that sweet ass. Especially when you're presenting for me." Beth peered into the trash. "Mr. Cooley's trash lounge coffee not good enough for you this morning?"

"I needed something stronger. I've had the shittiest morning, and to top it all off, I forgot about Melissa's going away."

"I knew you would. I put your name on the card of my gift." Beth winked.

"Oh, you're the best, Ms. Grimes." Lottie threw her arms around her.

"Ah, you're welcome, sweetie. I knew you'd forget when I told you to write it down and you didn't. You really need to start listening to me." Beth rubbed Lottie's back before pulling away. "So, did you hear? They finally hired a long-term sub to finish out Melissa's class for the school year. He's supposed to stop by the going away party. Melissa invited him."

"Nothing like waiting until the last minute to hire someone."

"I know, but that's the way they roll around here. Better get to class or we'll get sent to the principal's office." Beth stuck out her tongue and headed off down the hallway.

Lottie stuck hers out and headed to her class, curious about who the new teacher would be.

Chapter Two

Grant

"You can close your mouth now. Grant? Grant!" The dentist waved her hands over his eyes, which remained locked on the empty hallway.

"What?" His attention turned to the dentist.

"You can close your mouth. I'm finished. Something out there got your attention?"

"No, not at all." Grant shifted in the exam chair. "Well, kinda. Who was that woman that just walked by?"

"I don't know. I was concentrating on that cavity you've got on your molar."

Grant sighed. "I've got a cavity?"

"Sure do. Maybe from now on, you'll rethink skipping dental visits."

"I didn't skip any…"

The dentist tilted her head to the side. "Don't even try. We got your records from Dr. Tillmooth in Tulsa, and I know you missed three visits. You need dental cleanings every six months. And you know if you don't show up for them, I'll call Nana Aileen."

"You wouldn't dare!" Grant raised an eyebrow at her.

"I guess you'll be making an appointment to have that cavity filled and to come back for your six months checkup. Liz will help you out. Won't you, Liz?" The dentist smirked at Grant as she removed her rubber gloves and dropped them in the trash on the way out.

Liz typed away on her computer. She stopped, twisted around, and smiled at Grant. "Charlotte Stephens is the woman you saw. I have an appointment on October 14 at 2 PM for your next cleaning. Will that work for you?"

"I guess so. I can call and change it if it doesn't."

"Better not cancel. She really will call your nana."

"Don't worry. I know she will. I haven't been gone long enough to forget how this town works. What do you know about her?"

"Who?"

"Charlotte."

"Oh. Well, I don't know much other than her name. She always sees Kay. She'd know more if you wanna ask her. Monday work for your filling?"

"No, I'm starting my new job on Monday."

"Don't worry. I got you set up with the last appointment of the day. 4 PM. I know you can make that one."

"Living in this town is like having a dozen mothers."

"I know. But I'd have to be a sister. I'm clearly too young to be anyone's mother. We're all here to take care of you." Liz handed Grant two appointment cards and his bag of goodies.

"Thanks." He sat up and strolled out into the hallway, stopping for a moment to glance in at Kay, who was readying the room for her next patient. He shook his head before heading off to grab his coat and climb into his truck. Once behind the wheel, he lowered his head onto it. "She'd never want to know you now anyway," he muttered before sitting up and starting the engine.

He headed toward Main Street and pulled into the parking lot of Happy Donuts, hopped out of his truck, and ran inside. He purchased a dozen and one special apple fritter. Pushing out through the door with his butt, he smiled and scooted out of the way of an old man scuttling through with a cane.

"Grant." The man lifted his cane to tip his hat. "Good to see you back in town. You stayin' a while?"

"Uh, yes, sir. I'm taking care of Nana."

"Ya always was a good kid. That Nana of yours is a pistol." He chuckled. "She'll be all right in time. All us old cocks have learned to live without our hens." He motioned to the group of old men sitting at the counter with their donuts and coffee.

"Yes, sir. Good to see ya."

The old man grunted his approval as he waddled the rest of the way into the shop. Grant tucked the donut box under his arm as he pulled the car door open, careful not to let the precious fritter in the bag on top slide off onto the wet pavement.

Placing the parcels on the seat next to him, he buckled and threw the truck into the reverse. A horn beeped from behind. He slammed on the brakes. His eyes popped up to the rearview mirror to see one of the other salty, old widowers in town flipping him the bird.

Grant shook his head, wondering just how much of the town's population would be flashing him their middle fingers before the day was out.

Waving as the car pulled into the parking spot next to him, he eased his foot off the brake and onto the gas, careful to check for other old buzzards before backing out of the lot and turning onto the street. The familiar sound of one of his all-time favorite musicians came over the radio. Grant cranked it up.

He pulled into the driveway of his nana's little yellow and brick house on Trail Drive. He'd remembered the yard so differently as a kid. It seemed so big, and the street to the playground—that could be seen from the front of the house—seemed to stretch on forever. Now, as he got out of the truck and looked on, it was just a short jaunt. Grant thought back to the way his papa and nana always walked him down to the park, holding hands. Papa Joe always had a way of looking at Nana as if she were the most precious treasure on earth. But Papa was gone now. And the life that had always danced inside Nana's dazzling blue eyes had disappeared with him.

Tears welled in Grant's eyes as he opened the passenger door to retrieve the donuts.

The last thing she needs is to see you upset and missing him, too.

As he slammed the car door shut with his hip, he sucked in a deep breath and painted on a wide grin.

Surprised to find the door already unlocked, he tucked his key into his front pocket and pushed his way in. "Nana, it's me." He stepped into the galley kitchen and set the box on the counter. Noticing there was no coffee made, he quickly set to making some. "Nana?"

The only noise that echoed back came from the television in the living room. Once the coffee machine began its work, Grant walked through the dining room and into the living room, where he found Nana Aileen staring blankly at the TV.

"There's my girl." Grant kissed her on the cheek. "Did you know your front door was unlocked? I'd feel much better if you'd start locking it when I'm gone."

"What does it matter?" Nana slightly waved her hand.

"Don't say that, Nana. You matter to me. Don't I count for something?" Grant squatted beside her chair and met her eyes.

A smile curled at the corners of her lips, and a momentary spark re-entered her blank eyes. "You're a dear boy, you know that?"

"And wanna guess what this dear boy brought you? An apple fritter from Happy Donuts." Grant winked.

"An apple fritter? Oh, that's my favorite. You know, Joe used to bring me one every Sunday."

"I know, Nana. I remember picking it up with him a few times. Papa told me that he couldn't resist the way you smiled when he brought you one."

Nana Aileen broke down into sobs. She buried her face in her hands.

"Oh, Nana. I'm sorry." Grant put his hand on her shoulder. "I didn't mean to upset you."

With her face still buried in her hands, she shook her head. "It's not you, sweetie. I just can't bear the thought of going on without him." She slowly lowered her hands and reached into the pocket of her pink housecoat, pulling out a white handkerchief with blue forget-me-nots in the corner. She dabbed her tears. "I know I was blessed more than most, Grant, but ya see, I'm greedy. I wanted more time with him. I lived my whole life being adored and spoiled by a wonderful man. He held my heart gently in his hand, fearful of hurting it. When they put him in the ground and threw dirt on top of him..." Nana returned her hands to her face and sobbed for a while before gathering herself to continue. "Well, he took my heart with him. It's the worst kind of injury when someone else holds your heart and they leave. I guess a smart woman would never have handed it over. She'd be able to go on stronger at my age. I was blessed, and now I'm cursed."

Grant took her hands from her face and held them. He didn't know what to say or do. He almost felt a little jealous. He was sure he'd never have that kind of love and that no one would ever ache over his absence in such a way. Horrible and beautiful at the same time. He wished for it.

His thoughts momentarily flashed back to the events of the morning. There was no way Papa Joe would have made such an ass of himself. No, he was always calm and always a gentleman, not one to ride the rear end of a lady. Normally, he wouldn't either, but he just couldn't stand the thought of being late. Nothing bugged him more than people who were habitually late.

Nana Aileen squeezed Grant's hand, shaking him free from his moment of self-loathing. "What's say we eat? That coffee is calling me." Grant could tell Nana was stretching a mask of fake strength over her face now.

"Sure thing, Nana." Grant took her hands and helped ease her up from the chair.

"You know, it's so weird. I'm an old woman, and my body is so fragile, but I still feel young inside. I knew I'd get old one day, and here I am, but I guess my mind is still in denial somehow."

"You're still the prettiest girl in Altus." Grant kissed her on the cheek as she eased into the dining room chair.

"Oh, stop. You're an old charmer like your Papa Joe. And you know you're the spittin' image of him."

Grant ran his fingers through his dark blond hair. "More and more as my hairline runs away from my face."

"Oh, pish. You still got a gorgeous head of hair. Exact same color as your papa's. But you know, you got my eyes. We're the only ones in the family with ice blue eyes."

Grant raced around the corner into the kitchen to retrieve the box and the bag with the fritter. He placed it on a plate, grabbed a plate for himself, and a stack of napkins. "I know, Nana. Everyone tells me that I look like Papa. I'm gonna get us some coffee. Half and half, right?"

"That's right, my sweet boy."

Grant poured two cups of coffee, both with more than a splash of half and half, and returned to the dining room, taking the seat next to Nana Aileen.

"Mmm!" Nana clapped her hands once after taking the first bite of her fritter. She leaned over and kissed

Grant on the cheek before licking the icing from her fingers.

Grant smiled, seeing the joy dance across her face. That was the reason that Papa Joe always got her a fritter.

"They don't call 'em Happy Donuts for nothin'." Nana took another big bite.

Grant shoved his Bavarian cream donut into his mouth, coughing once on the powdered sugar that got sucked into this throat. He gave a thumbs up.

"Always did take too big a bite, just like your papa in that way too. Well, I bet you couldn't find donuts this good in Tulsa. I guess I'd shove the whole thing in my mouth if it'd been such a long while since I'd had one. And Grant," Nana Aileen reached out and wrapped her arm around his, leaning her head on his shoulder, "I appreciate you coming to live with your ol' Nana. I know it's not hip for a young man to live with an ol' lady. But you never know, maybe you'll find someone to marry and start a family with in this ol' town. It's where I found the love of my life, after all."

"Actually, it feels good to be back. And you're not an old lady. You're a hip cat, and anyone would be lucky to get to live with you."

"Oh, stop, you ol' charmer." Nana kissed Grant's cheek again and took another bite of her apple fritter, dancing in her chair as she chewed. Grant looked at the wrinkles on her face and the dark spots resting on her paper-thin skin, but he could see her radiant beauty shining through from underneath. He smiled. She had the most beautiful heart of anyone he knew. She loved everyone just the way they were and never tried to change a hair on their head. If only he could be so lucky to meet a girl who could look beyond all his flaws the way Nana did, he'd be the luckiest man on earth.

After finishing her fritter and drinking her coffee, Nana leaned back in her chair and patted her flat stomach. "Well, I can't believe I shoveled the whole thing in, but I guess I don't have anyone to look good for anymore. May as well get good and fat. You'll have to roll me down the hall to my room, Grant."

"I don't believe you could get fat if you wanted to, Nana."

"Oh, stop." Nana smiled. "Well, I think I'll get my ol' butt up and head to my room. I didn't get much sleep last night, and with this full tummy, I just may be able to rest a little while."

Grant stood and helped Nana out of her chair and to the bedroom. He helped her lay down on the bed and covered her with a blanket. "You got plans for to-day, honey? Gonna see any of your old buddies?"

"I promised I'd stop by a going away party for the teacher I'm replacing. I don't think I'll know anyone there but Dan."

"Who's Dan, now?"

"Dan Cooley. He's the principal at Rivers, and he's the reason I got the long-term sub job."

"What?" Nana clapped her hands together and giggled. "That little rascal, Dan Cooley, is the principal of a school? Well, I don't believe it."

Grant chuckled. "Believe it, Nana. It's true."

"Well, I'll be." Nana clutched her sides as she gig-gled. "The only thing I ever saw him leading was a cell block riot."

Grant shook his head, smiling. "Well, I'm glad that gave you a good laugh." Grant kissed Nana on the cheek. "I hope you can get some rest whenever you finally stop giggling."

"Ooooh, you need to tell him to come by for dinner. I've got to see how that rascal looks all grown up. I can't believe I haven't run into him."

"Maybe you just don't recognize him. Sounds like you expect to see him wearing prison stripes."

"Ooooh." Nana clutched her ribs even harder as she giggled, shaking the whole bed. "Grant, you little devil. I never said that."

"You just did, Nana, not even a minute ago."

"Oh, I guess I did. Well, I'm gettin' old. I can get away with forgetting some shit from time to time."

Grant's mouth gaped open as he stared with smiling eyes at the old, giggling lady.

"Oh, honey, I'm gonna do what I wanna do and say what I wanna say from now on—even 'shit.'"

"You're a wild woman, Nana." Grant smiled. "I'm glad to see you laughing and smiling again."

Nana took Grant's hand in hers. "It's all because of you, my dear boy. I just don't know how I would survive without you here to lift my spirits."

"I'm really happy to be here. I love you." Grant kissed her one more time before closing the blinds, turning off the light, and closing the door behind him.

He slipped out the back door and eased into the patio chair.

"Charlotte Stephens." He sighed as he looked out over the little yard he once thought of as a grand play land.

Chapter Three

Lottie

Lottie stared at the clock. The red hand seemed to tick by as though the dial was stuck in molasses. The little third-graders' whispers filled her ears. She couldn't bring herself to remind them that class wasn't over yet.

Tick. Tock. Come on. Come on.

The bell rang out, and Lottie jumped up and quick-stepped to the door, offering her "see you tomorrows" and "have a nice days" as the children rustled passed with their backpacks and sprinted down the halls.

Eh, let the other teachers remind them to "walk, not run" today.

Lottie's energy and will to discipline for something she wanted to do herself were lacking.

Once the classroom was empty, she grabbed her purse and tote stuffed with papers that required grading and slipped down the back hallway, fumbling quietly inside for her car keys. She slid out the door and headed straight for the parking lot, only to find Beth, grinning from ear to ear, leaning against the driver's side door of her car.

"Going somewhere?" Beth tilted her head. "I don't know why you think you can get anything by me anymore."

Lottie dropped her purse to the ground and threw her head back. "Ugh, well, it was worth a try, warden."

Beth strutted over in a very George Jefferson manner and scooped Lottie's purse from the ground, placed her hand on Lottie's back, and turned her to face the school. "Now you get your little butt back in there, young lady. You're not missing this going away party."

"All right." Lottie stopped in her tracks. "Let me just say this one thing. I've had a horrible day, and I'm never going to see her again. It's not like we were close. What difference does it make if I go?"

Beth raised her brows and put her hand on her hip. "The difference it makes is that if you leave, I have to suffer in silence. Now get back in there and make this bearable for me."

Lottie stomped her foot. "Fiiiiiiine. You're a real selfish butt sometimes, you know that?"

"Yes, I know. But so are you. And that's why we love each other so much." Beth took Lottie's hand and dragged her into the school.

When the pair walked into the break room, they noticed everyone was crowded in one corner of the room.

"Let's go get in line to say our goodbyes." Beth pulled Lottie closer to the gaggle of elementary school teachers. She stopped when they reached the perimeter of the group. "I don't even see Melissa." She leaned from side to side to search around the group.

A tap on her shoulder caused Lottie to twist around. Melissa was standing behind her. Lottie hugged her. "Hey, Melissa. We were just waiting to see you." She pulled back, smiling wide with her best "I'm so happy to be here" smile.

Beth hugged Melissa too and motioned to the group with her thumb. "If you're right here, what the crap is going on over there?"

Melissa shrugged and shook her head. Beth took Melissa's hand and shoved her way through the group. "Hey, everyone, our honored guest is here."

The rumbling voices momentarily hushed before roaring up again with greetings to Melissa. Beth emerged from the crowd with a grin on her face.

"What's that look for?" Lottie shook her head. She knew that look. Every time she saw it, Beth was either already up to no good or plotting to be. Lottie thought about sprinting for the door, but there was something about Beth's shenanigans she never could quite resist.

"Melissa's replacement is here." Beth waggled both her eyebrows and her shoulders. Her tongue darted from her mouth like a snake. "Got a nice set of pheromones, that one."

"Oh my god, Beth. You know he can probably hear you." Lottie covered Beth's mouth but quickly pulled her hand away when Beth's wet tongue swiped the palm of her hand. She wiped her hand on her skirt. "Gross, what are you, five?"

"I learn the best tricks from my students." Beth grinned. "Seriously, you've got to come see this guy. He's a cutie. No wonder everyone's crowded around him." Beth grabbed Lottie's arm, but she quickly pulled it back.

23

"There are people talking to him. Why don't we just wait?"

"We'll be waiting a long time then. We've got to get in there. Most of these ladies are married. They don't need to be occupying his time. I didn't see a ring on his finger." Beth sang the last line.

"So what?" Lottie rolled her eyes. "I have one on mine." Holding up her hand, she reminded Beth of the silver band on her finger.

Beth pursed her lips.

"Technically. I'm not divorced yet."

"So? You've been separated for over six months, and I don't believe there's any rule that says you have to stay celibate until the papers are signed. You know David's not." Beth quickly cupped her own mouth. "I'm sorry, Lottie."

Looking down at her shoes, she took a deep breath. "No, it's okay. I know you're right. It's just still hard to believe it's over sometimes. My head knows he's cruel. It's my heart that's the fool. I can't do anything about it no matter how hard I try. I still love him."

"You need a distraction. And nothing works better for that than a hot piece of man meat. Seriously, Lot, wait until you see him." Beth walked backward a few steps and pretended to cast out a line to a fish.

Lottie shook her head and grinned, following her with heavy, begrudging steps. Beth turned around and squished her way through the small crowd, hip check-ing a few on the ladies along the way and sending out sincere-sounding apologies. "Hey, there. I'm Beth. It's nice to meet you. Have you met our other third-grade teacher yet?"

"Beth. Hello. I'm Grant. No, not yet," a deep voice said.

Lottie's stomach fluttered, and the hairs on her neck stood at attention at the sound of his voice and his name. She slowly started to back up.

"Lottie, get over here and meet Melissa's replacement, Grant." Beth reached and grabbed Lottie's hand, pulling her forward.

The awkward, pressed smile on Lottie's face melted away when her fears were fully confirmed. Her eyes now rested upon the man from the dentist's office. The very one who had ridden her ass that morning. Lottie gulped and looked down at her shoes. "Nice to meet you."

He placed a plate—overloaded with cookies—onto the table next to him as he struggled to get up from underneath all the treats the ladies wanted him to try. He finally stood. "It's nice to meet you too, Charlotte."

Her eyes flew up to his. Her lips pursed and her brows crinkled. "How did you know my name?"

"Your friend said it. Right?" He motioned to Beth.

"Uh, no. I said Lottie. Not Charlotte." Beth shook her head and grinned widely.

"Oh." Grant scratched the back of his neck. "I'm sure someone mentioned the name of the other third-grade teacher."

Lottie tried hard to stifle a smile. "Well, nice to meet you…"

"Grant." He stretched out his hand.

She took it briefly before pulling away "Grant." Lottie nodded and turned away. Running straight into Mr. Cooley. "Oops, sorry, Mr. Cooley."

"Where's the fire? I don't hear an alarm." Mr. Cooley held his hand to his ear as though listening for one.

Lottie forced a smile and scooted around him. She scuttled down the hallway, ducked into her classroom, and plopped down at her desk, resting her forehead on it.

After a few deep breaths, a tapping came at the door. "What?" She didn't bother lifting her head. She knew it was Beth by the sound of her shoes clapping on the floor.

"What the fuck was that all about? I've seen you act awkward around men before, but that takes the cake!"

"Ugh. Of all the men in Altus." She sat up and gripped handfuls of hair.

"Oh, I've got to hear this." Beth lowered herself onto the corner of the desk.

"It's nothing."

"You're not acting like it's nothing, and I'm not going anywhere until I find out what it really is."

Lottie scowled at Beth and kicked the corner of the desk. "Fine!" She dropped her hair and slapped the desk, taking a few deep breaths to calm herself. "I was running late for the dentist this morning."

Beth clutched her chest and gasped. "What? You? Running late? After all the times you vag-punched me for being late."

"Yeah, okay. So, you know how I hate being late. When I was driving, I hit every single red light in Altus. Then I had this super obnoxious asshole in a blue pickup riding my ass the whole way. I was so aggravated, I gave him the finger."

Beth laughed and clapped her hands. "You giving the finger? This is great. Go on."

26

"So, I get to the dentist and the truck pulls in after me. Apparently, we were both headed to the same place."

"And it was him?" Beth roared with laughter. "This is great. I wondered why you looked like you'd seen porn with butt stuff for the first time when you looked at him."

"I've never seen porn with butt stuff. God, you're gross."

"I wonder how he really knew your name." Beth waggled her eyebrows.

"Oh, shut up." Lottie reached into her purse and fumbled around for a mint. "You want one?"

Beth stretched out her hand, and Lottie plopped a mint on her palm. Beth put the mint in her mouth and smiled with it clenched between her teeth. "He's cute, though. You gotta admit that, and no wedding ring."

"So what?" Lottie shook her head and sucked on her mint, trying not to smile. "He's not going to want to have anything to do with the woman who flipped him the bird this morning."

Beth laughed but stopped abruptly at the knock on the door accompanied by the clearing of a throat. Lottie's mouth dropped open when she peered around Beth to see Grant standing there.

"Fuck," she muttered.

"Indeed." Beth made kissing faces and raised her brows at Lottie, who crinkled her face and waved frantically for her to stop doing it.

He took a step inside. "Hey, I just wanted to stop by and see if I could talk to you for a minute."

Beth turned to Lottie and grinned. "I was just going anyway."

Lottie glared at Beth with pleading eyes, but Beth quickly turned and trotted across the room. "Nice to meet you, Grant. I'm sure I'll be seeing you again." Beth waved as she walked out the door. Lottie gulped as Grant crossed the floor toward her, suddenly worried about the way her hair looked. Were there boogers hanging out of her nose? How was her breath? Oh, thank goodness for the mint. She almost choked on it when Beth popped back into view, humping the doorway and giving her the finger before ducking away again.

Lottie shifted in her seat. Once he was beside her desk, she tried to pop up, to stand and be polite, but she banged her hip on the desktop, causing her to flop back into her seat. She blushed and put her hand to her forehead. "This has been quite a day." Hiding behind her hand, she couldn't bring herself to look at him.

"I'm guessing that's partly because of me. Anyway, I just wanted to stop by and apologize for being so rude this morning. I'm usually not a dick driver like that. It's just, well, I was running late, and I hate being late."

Lottie's hand slowly slid from her face as she looked up at him. "Me too."

"So, I'm sorry. And I hope we can get to know each other a little better since we'll be working together, and I hope to have the chance to show you that I'm really a nice guy." He smiled. "Well, I'll let you get back to what you were doing, and I'll get back to the party." Grant turned and headed for the door.

Lottie pushed back from the desk and stood, clutching her hip. "I'm sorry, too."

Grant stopped and turned. "For what?"

"For giving you the finger."

Grant smiled and released a small chuckle. "It's okay. I deserved it."

"No, you didn't. I don't usually do things like that."

"No?"

Lottie shrugged.

Grant smiled. "Okay, what if we both agree to forget about this morning completely and start over. Friends?"

"Friends." Lottie smiled.

"Do you want to go back to the party with me?" he asked, holding out his arm for her to take.

"I'd like to go home. I hate things like this." Lottie crinkled her lip.

"Oh, come on. You can't leave me in there alone. You're the only friend I've got here. And besides, it's kind of like a rattlesnake pit. I was seriously waiting for a few of them to bite me."

"Bite them back." Lottie took his arm. "Rattlesnake tastes pretty good. I tried some at the roundup they have over in Mangum. Ever been?"

"Yeah, I've been lots of times. I grew up in Altus."

"You did?" Lottie stopped and turned to face him. "I've never seen you before. I've only lived here a few years, but this is a pretty small town."

"I've been living in Tulsa for the past twenty years. My dad moved us out there when I was sixteen for work. My grandpa recently died, and I moved back here to take care of my nana. She's taking it hard. I'm worried about her. Physically and mentally, she's still a very strong lady, but emotionally, she just crumbled."

"I'm so sorry to hear that."

29

"Yeah, they were married for sixty-one years. Can you imagine living with someone for that long and they're suddenly gone? And my grandpa adored her. He treated her like she was the most beautiful girl and he was seeing her for the first time every day. It was like something out of a movie."

Tears filled Lottie's eyes. She thought about David, unsure he'd ever felt that way about her. He'd always had a wandering eye, and she'd always wondered why those eyes had settled for her in the first place. She never felt like she was good enough. A tear spilled over and traveled down her cheek.

Grant reached into his back pocket and handed her a handkerchief. "Don't worry. There're no boogers on it. Nana insists I carry one. 'You never know when a lady might be in need of a handkerchief,' she says. She tends to always be right."

Lottie smiled, took it, dried her eyes, and wiped her nose. "Well, there might be some boogers on it now."

Grant chuckled.

"I'll wash it and return it to you." Lottie dabbed her eyes again and smiled.

"That's okay. You can keep it. Trust me, Nana's got an endless supply."

Grant held his arm out for her again. She tucked hers around his and followed him into the teacher's lounge and back into the party—now in full swing. Lottie blushed and shook her head when her eyes caught those of Beth, whose grin was so big, you'd think she was the one on his arm.

"Do you want anything to drink?"

"Maybe some water." Lottie smiled and wiped the remaining moisture from her cheeks. She watched him as he walked away. His shoulders were wide, and his waist was narrow. Blushing, she noticed his butt was round and his jeans fit snugly around it. His eyes were a cool, ice blue. His dark blond hair mingled with some white hairs at the temples. A short beard surrounded his square, masculine jaw, and full lips. Lips she was suddenly thinking about kissing.

He handed her the water. His finger brushed hers as she took it. She could barely mutter a thank you.

"Hey, Charlotte, since we've decided to put this morning aside and be friends, I have a confession to make so that we can start completely over with a blank slate."

"Me first. It's Lottie. I hate being called Charlotte." She smiled, wondering what his confession could possibly be.

He grinned and pretended to take a note on the palm of his hand. "Check. As for me, I knew your name because I asked at the dentist office. I thought you were pretty."

Lottie's cheeks flushed with heat, and even though she fought it as hard as she could, a smile slide across her face. Her green eyes locked on his and mingled there for longer than she usually found comfortable.

Chapter Four

Lottie

A rush slid up Lottie's body when she thought back to what Grant had said.

I knew your name because I asked at the dentist office. I thought you were pretty.

A smile flitted across her lips. He thought she was pretty. Pretty enough to want to find out her name. How could it be possible? How could a man with the kind of rugged good looks only seen in a vintage Stetson commercial think she was pretty enough to ask about?

Flicking her shoes off her toes and into the shoe basket by the front door, she skated down the hallway in her stocking feet, grateful the one thing she'd taken the time to do—despite running late—was to pull on her control top hose. Inside her bedroom, she pushed back the door to look herself over in the full-length mirror, placing her hand on her stomach and smoothing it down. It looked pretty good. Pretty flat, indeed. Until she let the blubber free from the sausage casing it was trapped in. If only her skin could be so taut without the hose.

Her eyes followed the line of her body up to her small breasts—nose crinkling a moment—before drifting up further to her face, freezing on the makeup-crusted zit on her chin. She'd forgotten about it. Surely, he'd seen it.

Pretty, but not beautiful.

A sigh escaped her.

I should feel fortunate anyway. If I were to pick a word to describe myself, it would be plain or even ugly. Plugly?

But a man wouldn't ask who that plain woman at the dentist office was, would he? Maybe he did think she was pretty. Maybe he normally wore glasses and had forgotten to wear them that day. He did say that he was running late.

A thunderous stabbing struck at her neck, and her head flew back.

Why can't I be anyone else in the world besides me? Not pretty enough. Ungraceful and definitely not gifted with charm or mastering the art of conversation.

She closed her eyes, shuddering again at the approximately two hundred and fifty million times in her life she'd stuck her foot in her mouth or tripped over her own feet. Like the time she told that lady her baby looked like Walter Matthau. Even though it was true, she should have known better than to say it. And the verbal diarrhea she regretted the most was telling David that if he thought he'd be happier with Veronica, he was free to leave. Perhaps if she'd never said that, he wouldn't have had his bags packed and been gone by morning. She should have begged him to stay. She should have found a way to forgive him and work it out. That was the biggest one. Hoping to someday

33

learn to think before she spoke had oozed out and disappeared from her body after that one. Why was it so easy to remember all the horrible things one says and all the stomach-kicking feelings that goes along with being an idiot? Would her life ever not be filled with should'ves?

Lottie flung herself onto her bed, ready to wrap herself in the covers and disappear into the hole of nothingness she'd so often wished would swallow her up and whisk her off to someplace where the realities of life couldn't reach her. Just as she pulled the comforter around her, blocking out all light, the sound of her cell rang out from the hallway.

"What now?" Although she was certain it was just another garbage call—as she'd named them—a compulsion to find out dragged her out of her bed cocoon and sent her racing down the hallway. Scooping up her purse, she slid the zipper open as quickly as she could and sifted through the pointless contents until she found it. David's smiling face standing in front of the C-17 in his flight suit was looking back at her. Her heart jumped. Her thumb flew to accept the call.

"Hello, hello? David?" She tried to pull back the desperation in her voice, but it had escaped.

"Hey, Lot." His voice was bathed in aggravation.

"What's going on? How are you doing? How's Hawaii?"

"It'd be a lot better with the rest of my clothes. I thought you said you were going to send them last week."

"Okay, I'm fine too. Thanks for asking." Lottie regretted answering, wishing she'd stayed wrapped up in her burrito of solitude.

"Sorry, but you said you were going to send them and they're not here. I don't want to go out and buy a whole new wardrobe, especially when I'm paying two mortgages."

Lottie's stomach sank. He'd bought a house for her —Veronica—in Hawaii. He was living with her in Hawaii and didn't want Lottie to have any of his things.

"It's not my fault you're paying two mortgages. I'm not living in the old house, and it's not my fault it hasn't sold. As for your clothes, you should've supervised the movers yourself. I didn't forget them on purpose. I have things to do here too. And I tried to send it out all week, but I just couldn't make it to the post office in time. Between staff meetings and late parents, I couldn't find the time. Oh, and there was a going away party after work."

Lie.

She'd never tried, but he didn't know that. The truth was, she was thinking he'd come back to her. Or want her to come to him and she'd bring it then. "I'll try to send it out tomorrow. I have a life too, you know."

"Yeah, well, I wish you'd move on with it already. Just send me my stuff. I don't want to have to keep calling you."

"Why? Does it upset Veronica? Your whore can't stand you talking to your wife?"

The phone was silent. He'd hung up. Lottie flung the phone at the couch, flinching for a moment when it nearly missed the couch and hit the wall instead. Lord knew she couldn't afford a new one. A tear spilled down her cheek. She felt stuck with her foot in her mouth again, having said the wrong thing, and surely, she'd pushed him away even further.

Lottie padded down the hallway and slid back into her burrito.

The way he treats me, you'd think I did something wrong. That's what I get for being a good wife. Left behind in Altus, Oklahoma, while his little slut gets taken to the beautiful beaches of Hawaii.

Her mind drifted back to Grant's story about his grandparents. How do people get lucky enough to find a love story like that anyway? Jealousy stabbed at her gut. When she met David, she was sure he was her one and only. But looking back on it now, she could see the signals just weren't visible to her then. She'd loved him so hard. Always hopeful for the return of her grand admiration. She never thought that when he'd return it to someone, it wouldn't be to her.

One day when she'd been shopping at the base exchange, she rounded an aisle and saw them picking out a pair of sheets together. The way his eyes danced when he laughed with Veronica had never happened with her. And yet, here she was, holding out hope that he would come back to her. Here she was, heart sputtering like a girl with her first case of puppy love when his photo popped up on her phone. And here she was, wrapped up in her burrito of solitude, wondering who was ever going to love her in that way. And questioning why anyone would even want to.

***

Grant

The doorknob turned easily, and Grant pushed the door open, sighing. "Nana, you left the door unlocked again."

He sat on the bench in the hallway and pulled off his boots. He was lucky Nana hadn't noticed he'd had them on earlier and hadn't made him mop the floor like she did when he was twelve.

"Nana?" Grant made his way into the living room and found Nana watching black and white episodes of some old comedy. "Hey, there's my girl." He kissed Nana on the top of her head. "You left the door unlocked again."

"Well, the mailman came by. He brought you two or three big packages. Well, I couldn't lift 'em, so I opened the garage door and he tucked 'em right inside."

"Thanks, Nana."

"Whatcha got in them big packages? A mail-order bride? They were so heavy. I wasn't sure Richard was going to be able to get them into the garage himself. Never was a strong boy. You know he had braces on his legs when he was little. Looked like a little marionette." Nana giggled. "Joe used to call him Peeni. You know why he called him that?"

"No, why?" Grant chuckled. Nana was giggling so hard, tears were coming to her eyes. It was good to see her crying from joy rather than pain.

"He called him that because he had them braces on his legs and he has that big long nose. Like Pinocchio."

37

Nana was laughing so hard she could barely get the words out. "And you know what else?"

Grant laughed and shook his head.

"Joe said his dad, Mel, has a micro-penis." Nana doubled over. Grant jumped forward to stop her from tumbling out of her chair.

"Nana," Grant stumbled over chuckles. "Did you just say a micro-penis?"

"Yup, I sure as shit did. Your papa used to go to the base gym, and Mel was always there, strutting around proud as a peacock with his little thing hanging out and no clothes on. More like a pea cock." Nana roared with laughter, holding up her two fingers with just the tiniest space in between. "Cuz it's the size of a little pea."

Grant wiped tears from his eyes as he chuckled and looked at the old lady, roaring with laughter and holding up her two fingers.

"Your papa said there's no way on God's green earth that any offspring of tiny Mel Collins was going to escape with anything over an inch or two. Like a little button."

The pair continued to laugh, each trying to calm themselves but starting up again when catching a glimpse of the other. Anyone walking in would think they were laughing at the old comedy on the television and not the micro-penis of the town mailman.

"I'm not sure too many people have conversations like this with their nana." Grant shook his head, putting his hand on her arm and giving her a squeeze.

"Well, why not? It's not like we become inhuman when we age. I still feel exactly the same inside, and you know your Papa Joe gave it to me on the regular."

"Okay, Nana. That's a little too much information. New subject?"

"Oh, Grant, stop blushing. I am a woman, after all." Nana calmed herself from giggling as Grant squirmed. "Okay, my sweet boy, what should we talk about? Well, how was that party you went to at the school? Seem like you're gonna like it there?" Nana pulled a fresh handkerchief from her pocket and wiped away the tears that still streaked her face.

"That's kind of a long story. I'll start back before my dentist appointment this morning. I was running late. You know how I hate to be late."

"You take after me on that."

"Anyway, I drove like an asshole behind this car. I was tailgating. I'd normally never drive like that. I just had that pit in the stomach anxiety over being late. Anyway, the car in front of me turned into the dentist office as well. I couldn't just miss my appointment and not go in. Nana, when I got inside and she turned around, I saw the most beautiful woman I've ever seen in my whole life. It was like my breath was just sucked from my body and I couldn't remember how to get more. Well, as you can imagine, she avoided all eye contact with me, and when she finally did look in my direction, I was staring right at her. She looked away immediately, probably thinking I was some gross pervert." Grant took a deep breath. "So I'm at the going-away party and there she is. A friend of hers introduced us. It was obvious she wanted nothing to do with me. She couldn't walk away fast enough."

"Well, who is she dear? Anyone I would know?"

"No, she's not from Altus, originally."

Nana huffed and shook her head.

39

"What is it? There's plenty of good people that were born outside of Altus, you know?"

"Dear, I know that. But if she's not from Altus, and she's working as a teacher on the base, then most likely, she's married to someone on the base. Did you ask her if she was married? Or check to see if she had a ring on?"

Grant searched his memories for answers. "No, I didn't ask. But I don't recall seeing a ring."

"Honey, you need to find out if she's married. You don't wanna head down that road even an inch if she is. I can tell you're already ready to give this girl your heart." Nana crunched the handkerchief to her face and let out a few tears and sniffles before she was able to straighten herself out again. "I'm gonna tell you something not many people know about."

"What is it?"

"One of them sluts that worked as a maid at the base lodging tried to come between your Papa Joe and me. They had an affair, Grant. Her name was Flor. Can you believe that? Like floor. Well, it suits her. She was a dirty ol' trollop. They met cuz Papa was the services officer, so he was over to check on the lodge quite often. I found out about it because SSgt. Tim Wetmire, who worked for your papa, told me. He took a big risk telling me, was afraid your papa would discipline him. But Tim was my good friend too, so he told me anyway. Couldn't stand that your papa was making a big fool out of me. You know, he would tell me he was working late, but he'd really be taking that trollop to Lawton for steak dinners and dancing. Can you imagine? Wasting good steak on someone named after a floor."

Mouth hanging open, Grant could do nothing but force a blink or two and shake his head.

"After I found out, I packed up my things and I left. Your dad was only two at that time, so he doesn't remember. I was gone for about a month, back to Kansas with my parents, when he comes driving up full of tears and apologies. Said he realized what a mistake he had made and begged me to come back. I wasn't sure if I wanted to, but I eventually forgave him. He spent the rest of his life trying to make it up to me. And he was so careful never to hurt me again. And he never did. I never told anyone that, and all anyone remembers is the way he was with me afterwards. I guess I didn't want anyone to know that our love story wasn't perfect. But that's the truth of it. I'm only telling you this because I don't want to see you go through any pain. You're a treasure, Grant, and when you do find that special someone, I know you won't be making anything up to anybody because you'll love them right from the start."

Grant, still speechless, learned forward and kissed Nana on the cheek. They sat in silence and watched the old black and white comedy, but the laughter had stopped flowing. Grant searched his memory for the sight of a ring on Lottie's finger and crossed his own that it hadn't been there.

Chapter Five

Lottie

The sunlight cast an angry red light across her lids. The blinds were closed, but one asshole corner had been caught up. With a certain person on her mind, she was a little distracted and hadn't noticed when she turned them closed the night before.

Lottie pulled the covers over her head and flung them back off again after two minutes, muttering, "I hate stale air." She pulled down the sock she wrapped around the alarm clock to block out its obnoxious blue light, and it read 6:58. "Way too early."

Turning on her side, she took her second pillow and placed it on her hip, to block the sunlight that was still too brightly beaming through the window. Smiling, she closed her eyes and sighed, ready to sink back down into the illusions of her dreams. Maybe she'd fall back into a sexy dream. Like the reoccurring one she often had about the Russian Submariner who was only able to speak two words in English: "beautiful" and "more." Or even the one she occasionally had about the Italian mobster who was heartless and cruel to everyone but her.

"Ugh," Lottie kicked off the covers, her bladder mocking her all the way to the bathroom. There was no going back to sleep now. Sure, she could knock that corner of the blind down where it belongs and try to get back to sleep after she peed, but there had already been too much physical activity, and her mind had already begun to drift to the events of the day before. That wretched morning followed by that unexpected and flattering afternoon. She washed her hands and slid out of the bedroom, padding down the hall to her little galley kitchen. She grabbed the French press and filled it with coffee. Reaching over, she pulled her lime green teapot to the sink to fill it with water. She sighed and looked out the little front kitchen window.

Why would anyone get up this early on a Saturday if they don't have to?

Apparently, no one on her street did. It was like a ghost town. A crow hopped along the middle of the street, almost as if it were celebrating the fact that the roads were not bustling yet. It almost looked like fun. What would the neighbors think if they woke up and found her hoping in the street and randomly shouting like the crow? "Caw caw caw." She grinned.

Maybe when I'm an old lady and can use senility as an excuse, I'll give it a try.

The stove knob for the front right burner was missing. It had been since she moved in. She'd asked the landlord about it, but he said he'd get her one and never returned. Always avoiding confrontations, she didn't have the nerve to bring it up to him again.

I can do without it.

Lottie picked up the pliers and turned it on. It wasn't her landlord's fault that she insisted on using the front right burner. Lottie returned to the window, looking for the crow who had been so happily hopping, but he was gone. The red Vespa of the old man who lived on the corner came zipping down the street. The bird crowed from the telephone pole above as though he were cursing the thing. Lottie caught herself wishing the bird would dive-bomb the old man's head. He'd had that Vespa for sale when she'd moved in three months ago. They'd agreed on a price of $1,800, but he changed his mind as he held her check and was supposed to hand over the keys. Millimeters from her hand. Millimeters! And he quickly closed his fist tightly around them and placed her check back in her waiting hand.

She unlocked the window and slid it open partially. "Next time he's standing under a tree, do me a favor and shit on him, would ya?" Lottie smiled up at the crow and gave it a thumbs up. The crow cawed back a few times as though replying with a ha ha.

The tea kettle screeched out as though judging them in disapproval. Lottie grasped the pliers and twisted the burner off. She picked up the tea kettle and poured the water over the grounds. The glorious, sweet aroma of the coffee filled the kitchen. Lottie sucked in a deep breath.

Yes! This almost makes getting up worthwhile. Welp, maybe. Okay, not really.

She twisted the little kitchen timer—that looked like a pineapple—to set it for four minutes. A frown took up residence on her face as she set it back down. The memory of buying it was one of the last happy memories she had of her life with David.

He had called her from work to say he'd found out their next duty station. Joint Base Pearl Harbor/Hickam in Hawaii. She'd jumped up and down and squealed like a piglet. He asked her to meet him at Roma's for dinner because he wanted to talk about something important.

Of course, she thought she knew what he wanted to talk about—the next logical thing for them to do—start a family. Excited, she'd dashed out of the house the moment she got off the phone and headed straight to Walmart. She bought a rattle, and as she was waiting to check out, she'd spied the little pineapple waiting to be purchased impulsively. And it worked. How could she resist its sweet smiling face, complete with rosy cheeks? Especially when you consider that she'd just found out she was moving to Hawaii—the land of pineapples.

The appetizer order of Mussels Marinara had just been placed in the center of the table when David looked straight up from the plate, to her eyes, and blurted out, "I'm in love with someone else."

She's still not sure how much time had gone by before she was able to speak. He continued, perhaps taking advantage of the silence. He had fallen for another C-17 pilot, Veronica. Who was named Veronica anyway? She got assigned to Hickam as well. They were going to get a place together, near the beach.

Near the beach? She still couldn't figure out why he would feel the need to add that little bit of information. To twist the knife? To fill dead space? Lottie couldn't do anything but stare at him. Who was he? He looked like the man who'd only five years earlier promised to love, honor, and cherish her until death do them part, but clearly, he wasn't. Blinking, she stood. He quickly stood with her.

"I'll wait in the car," she muttered.

Lottie got up and bolted out of the restaurant without looking back at him or any other living soul. And after fumbling through her purse through teary eyes, unable to find her keys, she leaned against the door of the car, her hand touching the rattle inside her purse. She groaned at it as she pulled it out and chucked it across the parking lot. Reaching back in, she clutched the pineapple, pulled back to throw that too, but stopped. Lowering her arm, she looked at the pineapple's sweet, happy face and tucked it softly back inside her purse.

The ride home had been silent. David insisted she was too upset to drive and that she should ride back with him. They'd pick up her car the next day. He looked over every few seconds as though he were fearful of a—well-deserved—sucker punch to the nads. Probably smart on his part, but she hadn't thought about doing anything to hurt him. She wasn't even sure she was thinking. It was more like she was trapped in a space of nothingness. Was time going faster or slower? Was the car moving? Had he really said he was in love with someone else? Someone named Veronica?

Lottie's head snapped to the timer, which sounded the four minutes were up and her coffee was ready. A sliver of the ache she felt that evening was drawn out of her memories and hung around her the rest of the morning until almost noon when she had to put on her work-out clothes and meet Beth for their Saturday afternoon walk around the reservoir. Today, she really wanted to skip it but realized it was probably the kind of day in which she'd need it most.

Begrudgingly, she pulled on the spandex pants and sports bra, questioning why she even bothered. She didn't have the type of breasts that flapped when walking. She pulled on one of David's old Air Force Academy t-shirts and her brand-new pair of walking shoes. She filled a bottle with water—no ice. The weather was a prefect seventy-two degrees. She hopped in her car, wishing she was hopping onto that red Vespa instead. She stuck her tongue out at the old man's driveway in the rearview mirror. She left the windows down and turned the radio up, arriving at the reservoir before two songs could finish.

She pulled up next to Beth's green Jeep Wrangler and hopped out. Beth was sitting in the driver's seat with her leg dangling out the door, listening to the same song Lottie had just turned off. She held up a finger. "We can't start until the song's over."

Lottie nodded and walked over to where a woman and her small son were feeding bread to some ducks. She smiled at the mother who only looked up from her cell phone for an instant, too preoccupied to smile back or notice the fact that her son had just picked up a duck turd. Lottie shook her head.

"Not my job," she muttered as she looked out over the water.

I wonder if there are any dead bodies in there. Maybe.

She'd seen enough beer cans and used condoms as she walked around the reservoir to know that it wasn't always the beautiful, angelic place that it was during the daytime.

Only the sounds of the begging ducks remained when Beth flipped off the Jeep's engine once the song wrapped up. She joined Lottie and clapped her hand. "You ready for this?"

"As ready as I'm gonna be."

"Let's get to it then, lady." Beth slapped Lottie's ass and charged over to the paved walking trail like some kind of psychotic drum major.

Lottie sighed and followed after her with heavy steps. "You know I haven't lost a single pound since we started doing this. You said I'd lose twenty."

"I never promised anything. You have to stop making all those trips to Happy Donuts. I lost seven pounds." Beth motioned for Lottie to catch up with her.

"Yeah, well, you lost it all in your boobs."

"Jealousy! At least I could lose seven pounds of boob and still have some. If you lost seven pounds of boobs, I could use you for my cereal bowl and coffee mug." Beth stuck out her tongue.

"That's true. Veronica has huge boobs."

Beth stopped in her tracks. "Oh, honey, stop. You know I was just joking. I'd love to have your perky little tits any day. Mine are starting to look more and more like oranges dropped down into a pair of pantyhose."

"Men love big boobs. It's just another one of my many shortcomings. I'm surprised David married me at all, to be honest."

Beth wrapped her arms around Lottie. "David is an asshole. A stupid asshole. I don't know why he would leave you for that ugly twat, but Lottie, if I were into eating fish taco, I'd hold you tight and never let you go. You're a treasure."

"Sometimes I wish we were both into that. Because I know I'd be happy with you."

Beth kissed Lottie's forehead. "Let's get back to our walk. Standing here feeling sorry for our fondness of dick isn't going to help us find you any."

"I'm not looking for new dick."

"You should be. Nothing will get your mind off the old one faster. What about that hottie, Grant? He's definitely into you."

Lottie tried her best to stifle a smile. "He said I was pretty, you know?"

"No! You didn't tell me that. How dare you withhold information like that from me for nearly a whole day?" Beth swatted Lottie's ass again.

"Are you sure you don't like cooters? You sure can't stop touching my ass today."

"I'm sure. I just like to spank it when you're bad."

"You are so weird."

"So? You gonna go after him? Man, if I were single, I'd fuck the shit out of him. That scruffy beard and gray peppered in at his temples. Damn!" Beth wiped imaginary sweat from her brow. "You know, I love Michael, but sometimes, I just want to take a different dick for a little test drive."

Lottie rolled her eyes and shook her head. "You would never cheat on Michael. He's the sweetest guy on earth, and he adores you. You're really lucky, Beth."

"I know, hon." Beth took Lottie's hand and pulled her along on the track. "Michael really is the best. I have nothing to complain about. You know, that Grant seemed pretty sweet."

"Yeah, well so did David at first, and look how that turned out. Besides, he's an Altus local."

Beth laughed. "Really? I've never seen him around town before, and I'm pretty sure I would have noticed him."

"He just moved back from Tulsa to help his grandma out. But he was raised here."

"Oh my god. That is so sweet. To help his little ol' granny? Only a real sweetheart would do that. Who cares if he's an Altus local? Don't tell me you wouldn't let him dirty you up a little bit."

Lottie blushed, opened her water, and took a long drink, avoiding eye contact with Beth.

"That's what I thought." Beth slapped Lottie on the ass.

The water bottle shifted and poured down Lottie's shirt. "You butthole!"

Beth sprinted away, turning to stick her tongue out. "You'll never catch me, slowpoke."

"I'm not even going to try, douche bonnet. I hate running more than I want to get you back."

"Ahh, boo!" Beth slowed and waited for Lottie to catch up. "Let's just jog a lap. We need to get your stamina up for blue eyes. You don't wanna be sweating and panting like a pig when you're riding him like a mechanical bull."

Lottie ran forward and punched Beth in the shoulder. "Would you shut up about that already?"

"Probably not." Beth pumped her arms like one of the old people at the Central Mall in Lawton.

"You look ridiculous, you know?"

"No, I don't. I look like a professional power walker with a gorgeous ass. Now come on. Let's burn some fat."

Lottie sighed and shook her head before mimicking Beth, shaking her ass and pumping her arms as they walked around the reservoir, giggling the whole way. Beth loudly announcing her "good afternoons" to everyone they passed along the way. If acting like idiots burned calories, Lottie was certain that they'd be the two skinniest girls in Oklahoma. Her heart sank as the thought crossed her mind that it would soon be time for Beth to leave her and move on to a new duty station.

Chapter Six

Grant

Grant straightened his tie and nodded at the mirror on his bedroom door before leaving. He strolled into the dining room where Nana sat at the table. She glanced up at him and did her best attempt at a whistle—she never could whistle—letting out a high-pitched, "Woooooo-wooooooooo."

He chuckled, "Thanks, Nana."

"Well, you sure do look dapper when you slap on a tie and a nicely pressed pair of slacks."

"And thank you for ironing them. I would've done it this morning, you know?"

"I know. Last night I had a dream that your Papa Joe was still alive. When I woke up, I was so broken hearted I couldn't go back to sleep. I do miss him, you know? Despite the secret I told you, we did have a happy life together. It was a small blip in our time together, and I wouldn't base all my memories on the one big, big mistake he made."

"I know, Nana." Grant put his hand on her shoulder and gave her a squeeze.

She patted his hand. "I made you some dough dodgers. They're still warm and waiting for you on the counter."

Grant's eyes widened, and he raced into the kitchen. He bent over the plate, closed his eyes, and breathed the scent in. If he didn't know better, he would've believed he was a kid again. He opened them again and grabbed the plate holding eight delicious dough dodgers and returned to the dining room. "You're an amazing lady, you know that, Nana? I haven't had these since I left."

"Did you honestly think your nana wouldn't remember how much you love 'em?" She pulled the butter dish from the middle of the table and handed him the butter-coated knife that balanced on her empty plate. "Eat all you want. I've already had two."

Grant spread butter over the top, watching it melt and drift across the surface. He quickly scooped it up and took a huge bite, moaning with delight as he chewed. With a full mouth, he leaned over and kissed Nana on the cheek.

Giggling, she wiped her butter-kissed cheek with her napkin and waved him off. She slid a cup of coffee—with the perfect amount of half and half already added—his way. After chewing, he took a sip, swallowed, sighed, and stared at Nana, shaking his head with a huge grin. "I hope I find a girl just like you."

"Oh, go on." Nana waved her hand at him again and smiled. "I'm sure any girl you find will be capable of frying dough."

"Not the way you do. Or as thoughtfully as you do. I was pretty nervous about starting my new job this morning, but now I feel like this is going to be a great day."

"If she loves you, she'll do things like that for you. Thoughtfulness comes easy with love."

Grant paused his chewing and searched his mind. "I guess none of the women I've dated loved me too much then. Loved themselves a whole lot, though."

"Then they didn't deserve you, honey. You were smart to wait. Someday, you'll find the perfect girl for you." Nana swiped a dough dodger from the plate. "Maybe one more."

"I don't know how such a tiny woman can pack away so much food." Grant shoved another bite into his mouth.

Nana did the same.

After devouring three more dough dodgers, Grant glanced at the large clock over the living room mantle and jumped up. "I better get going. This is a good morning, and being late will shift it."

Grant went into the kitchen, filled a thermos with more coffee, darted back into the dining room, and kissed Nana on the top of her head. "See you later!"

"Have a good day! I can't wait to hear about it when you get back."

Scooping up the old leather briefcase that had belonged to Papa Joe, he headed out the door. "I'm locking the door. Remember to re-lock it if you open it up today."

"You're not my dad!" Nana called after him.

Grant grinned. She was getting her spunkiness back. He slid the key into the lock of his old pickup and opened it, never tired of the fact that his truck still had to be unlocked the old-fashioned way. No fancy fobs for him. No computers required to run his truck. Would kids today have any idea how to unlock his truck? He'd have to remember to ask his students.

***

Lottie

Lottie woke up early that Monday morning—earlier than usual. Her eyes popped open a full thirty minutes before she had to get up. The fluttering in her stomach hinted at the fact that a dream had been the reason for her waking, but as hard as she searched her mind, she couldn't remember any details. All she was left with was a feeling, and that feeling told her that the dream was about Grant. A smile raced across her face. He had said she was pretty. Or had she dreamt it? Confusion lurked in the wee morning hours when one was trapped between two worlds. Lottie tilted her head from side to side as though the movement might shake the memory free.

Once she was satisfied that it had been a fact of the waking world, she practically sprang out of bed and headed into her closet. She picked out her most flattering dress, even though she didn't enjoy wearing it because lunch always made the waist fit just a little too tight. She'd gotten so many compliments on it, though, she knew it was worth it. Especially today. The weekend had given her crusted-over zit time to heal, and she planned on spending a little more time on her hair and makeup than she normally did.

Lottie laid her outfit out on her bed and headed into the bathroom for a shower. While conditioning her hair, her wedding band slipped from her finger and fell near the drain. She reached down and pulled it up, examining the plainness of it. She didn't have an engagement ring. David had proposed with a wedding band. He said his reasoning for doing so was that he was going to take her to the jewelry store to pick out any engagement ring she wanted, but he never got around to it. She'd reminded him once or twice after they were married, but he'd just shrugged and said, "What's the point now?" or "But we have a matching set," and he'd hold up his finger. Not wanting to be ungrateful, she'd always just smiled and gone back to whatever it was she was doing.

Huffing, she flung the ring in the soap dish and finished her routine, doing an extra good job shaving to ensure she didn't miss that strip on the back of her calf that she had mistakenly let grow for too long from time to time. Beth teased her once that she was going to French braid the long-missed hairs and start a trend.

Dressed, primped, and ready for work, Lottie headed to the front door, grabbing her keys, and still about fifteen minutes ahead of schedule, thought about stopping at Happy Donuts to grab a couple dozen for the teachers' lounge. Once in her car, she cranked the radio and rolled down the windows before looking at her hair in the rearview mirror and immediately rolling them back up to preserve the perfection of it. She put the car in reverse and began to back out, slamming on the brakes when she realized she had forgotten her wedding band in the shower. Her heart began to pound, and her stomach flipped. She'd never left the house—even one single day since David gave it to her —without it on her finger.

She slid the car back into park and stared at the front door. Then looking at her quaffed hair and painstakingly perfect makeup, she gave her head a little shake and put the car back in reverse. Sucking in a deep, hitching breath that squealed on the way out, she grinned and shook her head.

I can't believe I'm doing this.

Walking down the halls of the school, she kicked herself for forgetting the donuts until she walked into the lounge and spied about seven full trays of cookies left over from Melissa's going away. Suddenly, she was delighted she hadn't shown up with dozens of donuts and ended up feeling like a fool for bring sweets with so many already scattered around.

"Hey, there, Lottie."

She jumped and turned to see Grant sitting on the old, lime green sofa that she was sure had been in the break room since the school was built. He stood, took a step forward, and reached out his arm. She had moved in, thinking he was offering a hug but was too far away to complete it. Instead, she awkwardly grabbed his forearm with her hand. So he wrapped his hand around hers and shook it.

Lottie blushed and pulled her arm back. "I don't know why I did that."

"Hey, it's cool. I hear that's a good way to avoid germs. Not that you have germs." Grant scratched the back of his neck. He sat back down on the sofa, which promptly let out the same type of sound a whoopee cushion emits. "That wasn't me. I swear."

"Suuuuuure." Lottie sat down next to him. "That never happens when I sit on this sofa." Lottie smiled and pinched her nose. Beth and she always called it the farting couch, but she wasn't going to let Grant know that. The farting couch had—for the moment—taken away the embarrassment of her Julius Caesar forearm shake and shifted it to him.

"You're here early." Grant glanced at the clock above the coffee maker.

"So are you."

"I was a little nervous about my first day, to tell you the truth. This is my first time teaching."

"You're not a teacher?"

"No. I mean, I'm a certified substitute. I got lucky. Dan's an old friend of mine, and when I told him I was moving back to take care of Nana for a while, he offered me this job, providing I took the certification courses."

"What did you do in Tulsa?"

"I'm a firefighter."

"So why the teaching, then?"

"I wasn't sure how long I'd be here. And since I'm just moving back to take care of Nana, I knew the schedule at a firehouse would still leave her alone for long periods of time." Grant relaxed back against the back of the sofa and sighed. "She's a tough woman, but I'm not sure she's ever going to get back to her old self."

"I'm sorry about your grandpa. It's really sweet of you to move back for her. You might enjoy teaching. At least you know how to handle chaos." Lottie grinned.

"It's not that bad, is it?" Grant over-exaggerated a gulp.

Lottie laughed. "No, it'll be great. Third grade is the best grade to teach, in my opinion. Although I might be a little biased."

Beth swooped into the room and made a bee-line for the coffee machine, poured some, and turned around, raising her cup to her lips. Her eyes landed on Lottie and Grant sitting together on the sofa. Lottie could see the smile hidden by the cup and a twitch of her right brow.

"Well, hello there, you two," Beth said after her first gulp.

"Morning, Beth." Lottie lips pursed, and her eyes pleaded with Beth not to embarrass her.

Beth returned her look with a wink. "Mmm, nothing like a cup of Cooley's crap to start the day. The line at the White Buffalo was insane, and I didn't finish grading papers last night, so I have to settle. Have you tried this crud yet, Grant?"

"No, I haven't. I had my coffee before I left the house this morning."

"Uh, Beth. Grant and Dan are old friends. Did you know that?" Lottie subtly shook her head.

Beth lowered herself onto a chair across from the farting sofa. "No, I didn't not know that. Did I say this coffee was crap? I meant that in the best possible way." She smirked at Grant.

"I'm not going to say anything." Grant waved her off.

"Good, or Lottie would give you a swirly. She's ruthless." Beth took another sip of the coffee. "Mmm, it's good."

Grant turned to Lottie. "Is that a fact? You'd give me a swirly?"

"Yeah, and I'd hang you from the flagpole by your underwear." Lottie raised her brow at him and crossed her arms.

59

"Well, I better keep my mouth shut."

"You will if you know what's good for you." Lottie shoved her arm into his.

A few more teachers trickled into the room. She noticed one whispering to another and looking at the two of them on the couch. Lottie's smile fell from her face. She cleared her throat and quickly stood. "Well, I better get to class." She headed straight for the door and down to her classroom, not stopping once to greet anyone along the way.

Inside her room, she sat at her desk and spun away from the door, worried tears might find their way onto her cheeks at any moment. Her heart seemed to be racing in her stomach. She took a few deep breaths, trying to calm herself.

"What the heck was that about?" Beth's footsteps drew nearer as Lottie slowly turned to face her. "You two were so cute together. He was clearly flirting with you."

"Yeah, and you weren't the only one that noticed."

"What are you talking about?" Beth lowered herself onto the corner of Lottie's desk.

"People were looking at us. And I'm a married woman."

Beth rolled her eyes. "Look, Lottie, your current marital status isn't a secret to anyone. It's not like anyone thinks you're being a ho. David isn't even in the same state. He left you. You don't owe him anything, and you deserve to be happy."

Lottie nodded. "But I am still married. Officially."

"Well, I don't see a ring on that finger." Beth winked. "And I'm glad."

Lottie rubbed the empty spot on her finger. "Grant probably thinks I'm a freak."

Beth moved around the desk closer to Lottie, squatted next to her, and rubbed her back. "Oh, honey. You are a freak."

Lottie smiled and shoved Beth, who almost fell.

"Hey, if you make me spill Cooley's crap coffee on my crotch, I'll sue you for millions!"

"Get out of here, butthole. Students are going to start arriving in a little bit."

"I'm not leaving until I get a smile that says you're all right." Beth tilted her head and once again sat on the desk in front of Lottie. "Come on. Let me see it."

Lottie painted a wide, toothy grin across her face. "Happy?"

"Oooh, yes. Happy." Beth kissed Lottie's cheek. "You need to learn to stop giving a shit what other people think. That guy likes you, and if you blow it because of David, or any of the stupid, jealous twats who were looking at you, I'll sneak into your house and put my dirty underwear in your pillow case. Okay?" Beth backed out of the room. "Okay?"

"Fine!" Lottie shouted. "Get out of here already."

Beth blew a kiss before walking out the door.

Grant passed by at that moment on his way to his classroom. A flush of heat rushed through Lottie's body.

Chapter Seven

Grant

Grant sat at his desk. Then leaned against the wall. And stared at the clock.

The students would soon be arriving. He regretted his decision to try to teach. What did he know about kids? He didn't even have any nieces or nephews. His last experience with kids was when he was one. He picked up the marker and wrote his name on the board, "Mr. Ryan."

Do teachers really do that? He'd written it in cursive. Do kids read cursive anymore? His throat went dry as the first students started to trickle in. They immediately went about their business. Unpacking their lunch boxes, hanging their backpacks, and taking their seats. They sat quietly and stared at him as though waiting for him to say something.

"Hey, there." Grant's voice cracked like it hadn't since he was thirteen. He cleared it and repeated himself. "Hey, how ya doing?"

"Are you our new teacher?" A boy with spiked hair crinkled his nose at Grant.

"Yes, I am."

"A boy teacher?"

"Yup."

The little boy crinkled his face up even more. "I never saw a boy teacher before."

"Aren't there any others in this school?"

"No. Just janitors."

"Well, I'm not a janitor." Grant walked to the front door and looked out at all the students pouring in through the side door. Down the hallway, he saw Lottie in her room, sitting at her desk and taking a piece of paper from a little girl. She glanced at the paper and hugged the girl. Clearly, she had an ease with the students that he wasn't sure he'd ever develop. He didn't know what to say to them. As the girl left her desk, Lottie glanced over and their eyes locked. Instantly embarrassed for staring, again, Grant backed away and nearly knocked over a boy who was entering the room. "Sorry, buddy." He patted the boy on the head and swiftly scuttled into the seat at his desk. He pulled his briefcase up onto the table and pulled out the lesson plan. He shuffled and fumbled through it until the bell rang. He avoided eye contact with all the children who were watching his every move. They almost appeared suspicious that he could be a good teacher. Could they smell his fear? He pretended to throw an imaginary object into the trash, but it was just a ploy to sniff his armpit. Was he beginning to sweat and stink?

The spiky-haired boy seemed to be smirking at Grant when he looked up from his sniff check. Grant's cheeks flushed. He rubbed the back of his neck and jumped when the second bell rang. Springing to his feet, he grabbed the dry erase marker and scribbled his name on the board, chuckling nervously and grabbing the eraser after realizing he'd just written it for the second time.

"Just writing it in a more eye-friendly color." He erased the name previously written in green. "As you probably noticed, I'm Mr. Ryan, and I'll be your teacher for the rest of the year."

The boy with the spiked hair raised his hand.

"Yes?"

"Are you sure you're not a janitor?"

Giggles poorly hushed behind little hands trickled forward. The little boy clearly enjoyed the raucous he'd caused, and it was obvious to Grant that by the look on his face that this was going to be a reoccurring question from this boy in a bid for attention.

"I'm sure I'm not a janitor. But to be honest, this is my first time teaching, so I'm going to need help from all of you."

"Your first time?" The spiky-haired boy's eyes grew wide. "But you're so old."

"I'm not that old. I'm only thirty-six."

"Thirty-six! That's older than my dad. And you have some gray hair."

"People can get gray hair at any age. I knew a boy that graduated high school with some gray hair. And I don't have that much." Grant ran his fingers through the gray hair at his temples. "Anyway, I was a firefighter before this."

The kids seemed to all lean forward at once, hands shooting into the air. The boy with the spiky hair didn't even bother raising his hand. "A real firefighter? That's so cool. Did you ever rescue anyone?"

Grant smiled. The mood in the room seemed to shift. No longer was he suspected of being a janitor but was now a real-life superhero. "Yes, I've pulled a number of people from fires."

"Did you get to drive the firetruck?"

"No, I didn't drive. I just rode on it. What's your name?"

"Martin." The boy with the spiky hair spat out his name, ready to ask another question.

"Martin, why don't you let some of the others have a chance to ask a question?"

Martin smiled and shook his head, raising his hand in the air, happily doing what the cool, non-janitor asked of him.

The rest of the morning slid by quickly for Grant, and it wasn't long until it was time to send the kids to lunch and recess. Grant checked his schedule. This quarter was not his to monitor the lunchroom. The class's former teacher, Melissa, had done that chore. "Thank you, Melissa." Grant pulled his lunch out of his briefcase and sighed. Though the morning had quickly improved from the way it had started, he was glad to have a break. His lunch was packed in a brown paper sack with his name scratched shakily across the front. Nana had packed his lunch the night before and put it in his briefcase early that morning. The night before, she had asked him what he'd like in his lunch, and while he told her he would pack it himself, she insisted that she needed to do something to feel useful now that she was no longer cooking for Papa Joe.

Looking at his name lovingly scribbled across the bag, he smiled and rose, walking over to the door. He peeked down the hall to Lottie's room, wondering if she was there. He spied her at her desk, opening a container and getting ready to eat. He returned to his desk, grabbing his lunch sack, and headed across the hall. He was worried he'd be invading her space. She'd rushed off so suddenly that morning, but she seemed to be enjoying herself before then. Maybe she had forgotten something suddenly? His pit check earlier told him that it couldn't have been his smell that offended her.

Grant softly tapped on the doorframe. Lottie looked up and smiled. His body flooded with warmth, and he smiled back. "Hey, Lottie. You mind if I join you?" He held up his sack.

Lottie nodded. Grant walked over and pulled a student chair over to her desk and sat down, placing his sack on the desk. Lottie giggled and rose. She walked into the small broom closet and rolled out another large swivel chair. "You might be more comfortable in this."

Grant grinned. Quickly sliding the student seat back, he turned. "Thanks. I felt like a bit of an ass in that tiny seat."

"I hate sitting in them. I always feel like they're going to break."

"I didn't even consider that." Grant opened his lunch and pulled out a sandwich followed by a note.

Have a good first day at school. I love you, Nana.

Grant folded the note and tucked it in his pocket.

His cheeks flushed. He rubbed the back of his neck, suddenly feeling like a little boy again. The way Lottie was smiling, he knew she'd seen the note. "So? My nana loves me."

"I think it's super sweet." Lottie smiled. "I wish I still had my grandma around. She died when we were stationed at McChord."

We? Grant's eyes shot to her left hand. There was no ring on her finger. He forced his eyes to return to hers.

"Where's McChord?"

"It's near Seattle."

"Is that where you're from originally?"

"No, I grew up in Michigan. I was in Seattle on vacation visiting a friend of mine when I met David." Lottie's eyes dropped.

Grant almost didn't want to ask the next question, but he knew he had to. He could tell from the way Lottie shifted in her chair that she knew the question was coming.

"Who's David?"

Lottie took a bite of her salad and chewed, smiling and swallowing hard before picking up her water. "My husband." She took a drink.

Grant's eyes drifted back down to her bare finger. "Oh." He unwrapped his peanut butter and jelly sandwich—with the crust cut off—and took a bite. His stomach suddenly felt too full of his dropped heart to allow the bite of sandwich; he forced it down anyway.

"We're not together anymore." Lottie tucked her hair behind her ear and put another bite of salad in her mouth. "He's living in Hawaii now."

"I see." A mix of emotions flooded through him. Relief that she was not married and guilt for being grateful for that. "Do you have any kids?"

Lottie shoved another bite of salad in her mouth. She shook her head.

"Do you?" Lottie asked once she'd finished chewing.

"No. No kids. Never been married."

Lottie smiled at him. Their conversation stalled, and Grant could hear nothing but the sound of his chewing. Was it extra loud? He swallowed. It seemed so loud that he looked at her to see if she'd noticed or been grossed out. He wondered if her ex-husband had been an obnoxious chewer. He had so many questions about this man who had a girl like Lottie and lost her. It was clear from the awkward way Lottie's body had shifted and the way she now suddenly became focused on her lunch that she didn't want to talk about it, so he wasn't going to ask. His mind searched for a subject to switch to that would lighten the mood.

"So, you grew up in Michigan?"

Lottie nodded. A smile flitted across her lips, clear she was happy with the subject change. She took a drink of water.

"I always wanted to live someplace with snow when I was growing up. It only snowed a couple times, and when it did, the snow didn't last the day. Do you miss winter?"

"No. I prefer the heat."

"Well, you get plenty of that here."

"The summer heat doesn't really bother me. The only thing that I don't like is the threat of tornados. I mean, there're no basements, and I don't have a storm shelter. I'd have to run over to my neighbor's house."

"Eh, don't worry about that. The white buffalo protects us here."

"If you believe in that sort of thing." Lottie shook her head.

"I do. I grew up here, and I believed it all my life. I mean, we still got in the storm shelter when a warning went off, but nothing major has ever happened, and that's saying something for tornado alley."

"I guess, but I have bad luck. I probably brought it with me."

"I don't believe for a second that you're bad luck." Grant smiled.

Lottie tucked her hair behind her ear, smiled, her cheeks flushed pink. "So, how's your first day going?"

"Pretty good. It started out a little rough. One kid kept insisting I was really a janitor. Once I told them that I was a firefighter, things turned around pretty quick."

"I'll bet. Kids love firefighters. Smart of you to bring that up."

"It wasn't any strategy on my part. I was just deflecting their insults. First, I was a janitor. Then I was too old to be a new teacher. Those kids were ruthless. It didn't help that I wrote my name on the board twice, and I think one kid saw me sniffing my armpit."

"Sniffing your armpit?" Lottie giggled. "What were you doing that for, weirdo?"

"I was so nervous, I was afraid I stunk. I thought I was being sly about it, but when I looked up, a kid was staring right at me."

"They notice everything at this age. They're so funny. You're lucky you impressed them with your firefighter hero-ness or you'd end up with a nickname all year. Like Mr. Pitsniffer."

"Oh, yeah? Did they ever give you a nickname?"

"No, but I'm a perfect teacher." Lottie raised her chin and straighten her back.

"Well, I can believe that." Grant took a bite of his sandwich and spied another smile pulling up the corners of Lottie's lips as she took bite of her salad. He liked seeing her smile. She had a beautiful smile. "I haven't actually done any teaching yet today."

"You'll get around to it. It's good to take the time to get to know the kids and let them get to know you too. I'd do the same thing. There'll be plenty of time to get caught up on the lesson later."

"I guess I'm better at this than I thought." Grant straightened in his chair.

"You're going to be great." Lottie winked at him.

"How long have you been teaching?" He leaned his head on his hand and turned his attention to her completely.

"Six years. This is my third year here. The first couple years I worked as a sub. It was easier to find work when I graduated, and it was hard to get hired when I was going to be moving in a few years, so I didn't really try once I moved to Seattle. I was lucky to get a position when we moved here. Teachers leave often, as you know, and so there are vacancies opening, and the base school is more open to hiring teachers who may not be around for their entire careers. Welp, the bell is about to ring." Lottie began packing up her lunch.

Grant did the same. It was obvious that Lottie was uncomfortable with the direction of the conversation again. Grant returned his chair to the broom closet.

"Would you like to have lunch with me again tomorrow?" He picked up his brown paper sack and rubbed the back of his neck.

Lottie looked up from their desk and smiled. "I'd like that."

"Same place?"

"I'll be here."

"Great." A shiver of excitement slid up Grant's spine. He couldn't wait to get home and tell Nana about his day.

"Great." Lottie smiled and waved.

Grant turned and headed back to his class. Once inside, he threw his paper sack in the trash and sat at his desk. The image of her tucking her wavy, blonde hair behind her ear and that smile sliding across her lips entered his mind. David had to be the world's biggest idiot, but he was grateful that he was. He couldn't imagine meeting someone as sweet and beautiful as Lottie only to find out she wasn't available.

Chapter Eight

Lottie

Once Grant was out of the room, Lottie let out a breath she felt she'd been holding since the moment he walked in and asked to join her. Her mind raced through the conversation. Had she told him she was still officially married? She had been so concerned with avoiding the subject of David that she wasn't exactly sure what she revealed. She glanced at her bare finger. Maybe she should've worn her ring and avoided all the awkward silences. A smiled tugged at the corner of her mouth. Part of her was tickled that she hadn't worn it. David was happy with someone else. Why should she be branded and marked by him?

A tickle in her stomach re-swirled and gave her a shiver. Grant did like her. Didn't he? It was obvious. Wasn't it? Not just wishful thinking on her part? Of course, it'd been so long since she'd been interested in any other man's attention that it was very possible she was misreading things. Where else was he supposed to have lunch? Maybe he's just lonely and looking to make friends. She was the only other third-grade teacher, after all. Her mind skipped to thoughts of

Grant in a firefighter's uniform, and her face instantly flushed with heat and her pelvis began to throb. Picking up a stack of quizzes on her desk, she fanned herself. She had to get her thoughts under control before the children started filtering back in. The last thing she needed was to be all hot and bothered when they returned. Kids that age did notice everything, and she didn't need them asking why her head was all red.

For the rest of the afternoon, Lottie found herself drifting over to the classroom door as she taught, peering at Grant's classroom, hoping to catch a glimpse of him. She never did. Laughter trickled down the hall on more than one occasion, though. He certainly was doing a good job of winning them over. She was curious what he was doing to get them laughing so hard and so often. Hopefully, they were laughing with him and not at him. But he had such an easy way about him, she was sure it was the former and not the latter.

When the bell rang at the end of the day, Lottie packed up quickly and lingered by the doorway in hopes of running into Grant. Not seeing him emerge after waiting for what felt like an awkward eternity, she closed her classroom and locked the door. She jumped when she turned around. Beth was standing right behind her.

"You scared the shit out of me!"

"Language! There are still children present." Beth clutched her chest with wide eyes.

"Oh, shut up! The kids are all gone, and you have the worst potty mouth of anyone I've ever met."

Beth tilted her head and smiled, pulling both hands to her chest. "Really? Ever? I'm so honored. You like me. You really like me!"

"God, you're an obnoxious nerd. You know that?" Lottie rolled her eyes and slung her bag over her shoulder. She glanced at Grant's door.

"Whatcha looking at?" Beth turned to look at the door.

Lottie shook her head and smiled. "Shut up."

"Let's go see how Mr. Ryan's first day went, shall we?" Beth twirled and walked toward his classroom.

Lottie grabbed her hand. "Don't! I don't wanna bother him."

"How is asking how his first day went 'bothering' him?" Beth marched into the classroom. "Well, hey there, Grant. How was your first day?"

Lottie lingered outside the classroom, shook her head, and peeked in. Beth was sitting on the corner of his desk. Spying Lottie, she waved her in. Lottie drug her feet and stood next to Beth. She smiled at Grant, gave a quick wave, and tucked her hair behind her ear.

"Hey Lottie." Grant smiled.

She chewed her lip when his eyes met hers. Her legs felt like spaghetti. She casually stepped back and took a seat on the edge of one of the student's desks.

"I had a great day. As I told Lottie at lunch, it started off a little rough, but it wasn't long before we were all havin' a pretty good time in here. I guess tomorrow I'll have to do some teaching. I didn't accomplish much."

"Getting comfortable with the kids is accomplishing a lot." Lottie smiled. "You don't want them to think of you as a substitute, and treat you like one, all year."

"Or like a janitor." Grant chuckled.

Lottie giggled. Beth raised an eyebrow at Lottie. Uh-oh, she could tell that Beth was going to grill her to find out what all that was about.

"So, Grant, do you have any big plans for the weekend?" Beth kept her eyes on Lottie before turning back to him.

"No. I'll probably need to rest. Even though it was a good day, I can tell I'm going to be tired by the end of the week."

"Eh, you'll get used to it." Beth grinned. "Listen, Lottie and I meet up every Saturday afternoon to walk around the reservoir to burn some calories. Would you like to join us?"

Lottie's heart began to slam in her chest. Her mind quickly formulated plans on how to murder Beth for asking him along. She didn't need him to see her in her skank clothes with her hair pulled into a ponytail wearing practically no makeup. She gulped, unable to speak as a lump formed in her throat. He's surely in good shape, and he and Beth would probably decide to jog the reservoir instead of walking it. He'd see her struggling to breathe and moving slow as molasses while her thighs slammed together in protest. Oh yeah, she was definitely going to murder Beth.

Grant nodded. "You know what, I think I'd like that." He rubbed the back of his neck. "Would you mind if I invited Nana along? She could use some exercise, and a walk around the reservoir might do her a world of good. I'd also like you to meet her."

If he brought his Nana, he wouldn't want to be jogging around the reservoir. Yes, Lottie was sure she'd be able to keep up with an elderly woman. She perked up in her seat. "I'd love it if she came along."

75

"Yeah," Beth agreed. "Bring her. The more the merrier."

"Let me write down my phone number for you." Grant pulled out a pad of sticky notes from the desk and scribbled his number on it. He handed it to Beth. He smiled at Lottie and wrote on a second. "May as well give it to both of you."

Beth took the second sticky, walked over, and stuck it to Lottie's forehead. "Put that in your phone." She walked back over to the desk and swiped the sticky pad. "Here's my number and Lottie's." Beth scribbled the numbers down. She turned and raised her eyebrows at Lottie. "Welp, I better get home. Michael has a night flight tonight, and I wanna spend a little bit of time with him before he's off."

"Yeah, I better get going, too." Grant stood, picking up his briefcase. "I've got to get to a dental appointment. Filling." He frowned.

Lottie pulled her bag up to her shoulder, tucking the sticky note safely inside her grade book. The trio walked into the hallway, pausing while Grant locked his door, and headed off down the hall together. Dan Cooley waved at Grant from the office and motioned him to come inside.

"Looks like you're stuck here a little longer." Beth waved to him as he headed into the office.

"Bye, ladies." Grant waved.

"Bye." Lottie smiled and waved.

Once outside the door, Lottie turned to Beth. "Why did you invite him to the reservoir? I'm not sure if I'm going to poison you or mail you pipe bomb, but it's probably going to be one of the two."

"Because you like him, and he likes you. And I know you, you'll never make a move. You need a little encouragement to get things going."

"But the reservoir? I don't need him seeing me without make up and a sweaty red face right away. That's going to do anything but help me."

"Oh, shut up. You look pretty with no makeup."

"No, I'm hideous. I have the worst skin on the planet."

Beth stopped in her tracks and turned to Lottie, grabbing her shoulders. "Then you don't see what I see."

Lottie's eyes stung and tears quickly threatened to spill from the rims. Beth pulled her in close and hugged her.

"I just want you to be happy, Lot." Beth rubbed her back and then pinched her butt.

Lottie pinched Beth's butt back. "You're such a closet taco lover."

"I only love yours." Beth backed away and winked at Lottie.

Lottie wiped a tear that had fallen down her cheek. "I'll see you tomorrow."

"Yes, you will." Beth jumped into her Jeep.

Lottie watched her pull away then climbed into her car, stopping for a moment to look in the mirror, crinkling her nose. She didn't see what Beth could possibly think was beautiful about her, especially with no makeup. "I hate my skin," she muttered as she looked way, buckled up, and put the car in gear.

As she drove out of the parking lot, she could see Grant and Dan walking out of the building together. Grant must've said something funny because Dan doubled over laughing as he tried to put the key in the door. Lottie swerved when she finally peeled her eyes from Grant as she nearly drove up onto the curb. Her face flushed just as red as if she had and they'd noticed.

Lottie drove straight home, determined to cook something healthy for dinner rather than grabbing the fast food she'd been chowing on almost every evening since she started living alone. Week after week she'd bought bags of ready-to-eat salad at the grocery store but had forgone it for a burger and fries, only to throw it away every Saturday morning once the brown juice collected in the corner of bag. "Next week," she'd always promise herself as she plopped it in the trashcan, knowing full well when she put a fresh bag in her cart on Sunday that it would meet the same tragic fate.

Not this week, she told herself. She was going to eat it today. And she was going to start shedding those extra pounds she knew she'd packed on since David walked out. Oh, why couldn't she be one of those people that neglected eating when they were feeling low? But no, she was the opposite. She'd mindlessly filled her face. Not once had she stepped on the scale—but the way her clothes were fitting her, she could guesstimate that she'd gained somewhere between five to ten pounds. Seven. She'd assume she'd gained seven and wouldn't step on the scale again until she knew she'd lost at least ten.

If she stepped on the scale now, she'd probably leap off and head straight for the ice cream section of the supermarket. "Why bother dieting now?" she'd tell herself as she stuffed a sweet, blue spoonful of birthday cake ice cream in her mouth. The thought of it made a drip of drool fall from her lip and onto her lap.

Piglet.

Disgusted, she shook her head and sucked in a deep breath. Determined, Lottie knew she had to get back on a downward weight trajectory if she was ever really going to shake free from the divorce-town slump she was sliding deeper into. The other night as she folded up into her reading chair, without pants—another habit she'd adopted since living alone—the tip of her stomach touched her bare thighs and completely grossed her out. There was no way she'd allow herself to become one of those women whose stomach could sit on their lap. Then it wouldn't be long before her arms would barely reach across her gut to lock around it at the wrists. Or maybe she'd have to buy her shelf-to-trash salads while riding a motorized cart, stomach hanging between widely spread legs, nearly skimming the bottom of the cart.

Lottie shook her head as she drove by the row of fast food restaurants that had pulled her in like Pavlov's dog on regular, after-work basis. She gripped the steering wheel tight, almost as though she were worried her car had become just as programmed as her stomach that grumbled in protest as she rode by. Why did cheap, fattening food have to be so damn delicious? Thank the Lord Jesus above that Happy Donuts was closed. She could go for one of those powdered sugar, custard-filled ones right now.

She straightened her back as she turned off the fast-food laden streets. No, she was going to be a rabbit-food girl now. No Happy Donut or delicious burgers or tacos allowed until that ass was ten pounds lighter and her tummy no longer resembled bread dough.

Lottie pulled in the driveway and walked into the house, her phone buzzing in her purse. Shaking her head, she put the keys in the door. Beth was ready to grill her over Grant sooner than she thought. "Damn, Beth. I'm not even in the door yet," she muttered. Tossing her keys in the bowl on the table near the door, she kicked off her shoes and leaned her tote against the wall.

Turning to the side, she smoothed her stomach as she looked in the hall mirror. "You're not eating until an appropriate dinner time, either." Maybe she'd take Beth up on her offer to join her at the base gym every evening for spin class. She always did enjoy riding bikes. How much different could it be?

She scooped the stack of papers to be graded and her grade book from her tote and headed to the couch, ready to get everything accomplished so she could make it to the spin class that evening. It was worth a try.

After flopping onto the couch, Lottie peeled Grant's number off the inside page of the grade book and stared at his writing. She traced her fingers along his name and number. A smile tugged at the corner of her lips. She stuck it to the arm of the couch and graded the quizzes and homework pages she needed to get to. Once finished, she padded down the hall and changed into her workout clothes, washed her face, and pulled her hair into a ponytail. All her work done, clothes on, she had no excuse not to go to the class tonight.

She fished in her tote for her phone to text Beth back, who was sure to be happy that she was joining her for spin so she could grill her in person. Lottie's heart jumped into her throat when she saw it wasn't Beth who had texted her. It was the number she recognized from the sticky note with a message.

Grant: Hey, Lottie, it's Grant. Just sending you my number in case you lost it.

She hugged the phone to her chest, heart-pounding, now excited to go to spin class. Lottie immediately sent a text to Beth.

Lottie: Joining you for spin tonight. Want me to pick you up?

Chapter Nine

Grant

Grant's stomach flopped. He knew it was something he shouldn't have done—according to the bro code—but he couldn't stop thinking about her.

We're both teachers. It's natural to make sure she has my number in her phone.

He dropped his phone into his lap. Would she think he was pathetic? He texted the moment he pulled into the parking lot of the dentist's office, the place he'd first set eyes on her. He wished it was a better memory and one that cast a more favorable light on him, but he was just happy they'd met at all. She probably wasn't even home yet.

Oh, well. What's done is done.

Before shoving his phone into his bag, he turned the ringer on. If she did text back, he didn't want to miss it. Even though he'd have a mouth full of dental appliances, he still wanted to know if there was a reply.

After his appointment, he drove home. He pulled his keys from the ignition and headed toward the front door. Nana's white hair was visible in the front window. Clearly, she had been watching for him to get home. He turned the knob—which was once again un-locked—and swept inside.

Nana came bursting through the kitchen entrance carrying a cake covered in lit candles. "Happy first day as a school teacher. I'm so proud of you!"

Grant grinned and shook his head.

"Make a wish!"

"Does that work on first-day-of-work cakes?"

"Why shouldn't it?"

"Well, all right then." Grant made a wish and blew out the candles.

Nana smiled and cheered. "You got 'em all. What did ya wish for?"

"I can't tell you or it won't come true."

"You're right, but if you wished for cake before dinner, it's gonna come true. We're gonna eat this cake, then I'm taking you out, my sweet boy." Nana placed the cake on the kitchen counter, licking the frosting from each candle before plunking them into a bowl. She handed him one.

Grant licked the frosting from the candle. "Mmm." Homemade cream cheese frosting. And hers was like no other he'd had since leaving home. He closed his eyes and shook his head. "Another, please."

Nana pulled one out but licked it herself.

"Come on, Nana. Don't hog 'em all."

"What? I made it."

"For me."

Nana pulled out another candle and handed it to him. "It's not like you're not going to eat a whole slice soon, ya know?"

"I could say the same for you." Grant licked the candle and plunked it into the bowl. "Okay, I'm gonna go put my stuff away, and I'll be back for a big slice of that cake." Grant kissed Nana on the side of her head and quickly kicked off his shoes before scooping his bag from the hall floor and heading into his room. Grabbing his phone, he clicked it on to see if he'd missed any messages. Maybe he didn't have the ringer turned up loud enough.

Nothing.

What an idiot. She's going to think I'm desperate and annoying.

Grant padded into the bathroom and stared at himself in the mirror. Did the gray hair at his temples make him look older than he was? Probably. Especially with the wrinkles that peppered the skin around his eyes. He shook his head. Why did he suddenly care so much? He hadn't given his aging looks a thought before, but suddenly, he was seeing everything that she might be seeing when she looked at him. He hardly knew her, yet what she thought mattered more than any of the women he'd been seeing back in Tulsa.

Grant washed his hands, took one more glance at the mirror, and headed out to the dining room. Nana sat at the table with her already half-devoured slice of red velvet cake. One waiting for him sat with what was clearly a finger scoop of frosting stolen from the top. "Oh, come on, Nana, really?'

"You snooze, you lose." She smiled before shoveling another big bite of cake into her mouth.

"I was only gone for a second. Besides, you're the one who always made me wash my hands before dinner when I was a kid."

"This isn't dinner. This is cake, and cake waits for no man." Nana stuck out her finger to steal another swipe of his frosting.

Grant pointed his fork at her. "Don't think I won't stab you. Frosting theft is a serious offense in these parts."

Nana grinned. "So, tell me how your first day went. Did the kids tie you up?"

"Have more faith in me than that." Grant shoved a bite of cake in his mouth. The cocoa sweetness mixed with the cream cheese made him close his eyes for a moment, and childhood memories seemed to rush through him in a flash.

Nana was smiling at him when he opened his eyes. "Good?"

"So good." Grant wrapped his arm around her and squeezed her. "You're an amazing woman, Nana."

"Tell me something I don't know." Nana shoved him in the ribs.

"Here's something you don't know—we've been invited to go for a walk around the reservoir on Saturday afternoon, and I accepted the invitation."

"The reservoir? Well, who invited us?"

"Two of the women I work with. Lottie and Beth."

Nana eyed him for a moment as she chewed a piece of cake. "Would either of them be the one you told me about the other day? From the dentist?"

"Yes. Lottie. And I know what you're going to ask. No. She's not married. Well, she wasn't wearing a ring, and she told me they weren't together anymore. He's living in Hawaii."

Nana tilted her head. "Well, I'm looking forward to meeting this girl. I'll find out the whole story."

"Be nice, Nana. Promise?"

"When did I say I wasn't going to be nice? I'm skilled in the social graces. I know how to find out all the information I want while wearing a smile. And you know, as old as I am, I've learned to trust my gut more than anything when meeting someone new. Besides, it's my job as your nana to make sure she could be deserving of someone as wonderful as you. Now would you pop into the kitchen and get your ol' nana some more milk? I should've just brought it to the table."

"Sure thing." Grant hopped up and scooted around the corner and pulled the milk from the fridge. He returned and filled her glass. "Where'd you want to go for dinner tonight?"

"You know, I thought we might go to Meers. I was thinking about a cheeseburger earlier, and drool actually plopped right off my lip onto my lap. Either I'm really hungry for a burger, or you're going to have to drop me off in one of those nursing homes for drooling old bitties that are in constant need of someone wiping their chin."

"Well, that's definitely not the case. Meers sounds great. It's been a long time since I've had one of their burgers."

Nana placed her fork on her empty plate and gulped down the last of her milk. "Well, my boy, I'm gonna go sleep off a cake coma before dinner. Officially, all I do is eat, sleep, and poop. I'm once again a baby."

"Don't think I'm changing your diapers." Grant winked at her.

She placed her hand on his shoulder to help herself up from the table, cackling at his joke. "You ol' rascal. I better watch what I say, or you really will stick me in one of those homes for helpless Q-tips."

"I'd never do that, Nana."

"I know." She tapped his shoulder and squeezed his cheek before heading off to the bedroom.

Grant finished his cake, put the milk away, cleared the table, and washed the dishes before heading back in his room and checking his phone.

Nothing.

Grant flopped onto the bed, opened his bag, and pulled out the lesson plan that the previous teacher had laid out for rest of the week. He'd actually have to start teaching at some point, but Lottie was right; it was worth it to take the time to get to know the kids today. He was sure he could build the missing lesson into the days remaining.

He tossed the notebook aside, sank down into the pillow, and closed his eyes. A cake coma sounded good. His mind drifted to the shy smile that creeped onto Lottie's face at lunch and the way she'd always tuck her hair behind her ear when her cheeks flushed with a pink that matched her lush lips.

***

Grant's eyes fluttered. He shook his foot. "Brutus, knock it off," he mumbled and rolled over onto his side. A tickling on his foot roused him again. He shuffled his feet and pulled them under the covers. The covers rose up off his foot, he heard a giggle, and something once again tickled his foot. He pushed up onto his elbows. "Brutus!"

Looking around the room that wasn't his Tulsa bedroom, he began to remember he was in Nana's house and that Brutus had been gone for nearly a year. Scratching his head, he looked around the dark room. A giggle spilled up from the end of the bed, and an old hand creeped toward his foot again. "Nana?"

Grant scrambled off the bed and walked around to the end to find the old woman crouched down and struggling to hold in giggles.

"How old are you?" Grant put a hand on his hip and shook his head. A smile spread across his face.

"Not too old to enjoy a little prank but too old to get up off of this floor myself. Give your ol' Nana a hand, would ya?"

"Nah, I think I'll just leave you there and I'll go enjoy some burgers at Meers on my own."

"Boo! Don't be so mean to your ol' nana. I just couldn't help myself. Don't ya remember when you were a little boy and you used to lay on the couch and stick your smelly little feet on my lap to tickle?"

"I was five."

Nana held her hand out once more. "C'mon, help me up."

Grant took her hands and pulled her up off the floor. "I'll get you back for this."

"No need. I'll pay for your burger tonight. Nana's treat."

"Well, you should know that I'm extra hungry and think I'll eat two. Maybe three."

Nana headed for the bedroom door. "I'll give you some time to comb that hair and scrape away that horrible nap breath. I'll grab my purse and wait for you in the living room."

In the bathroom, Grant ran his fingers through his hair and brushed his teeth. He headed into the bedroom and grabbed his phone, checking it quickly for any messages.

Nothing.

Nana was waiting for him in the living room. He helped her up out of the chair and headed toward the front door where they both sat on the bench and slid on their shoes. Grant stood, offering Nana his arm. "M'lady."

She took it, and they headed out. Grant locked the house and opened the truck door for Nana.

"I just love this ol' truck. I remember when your papa first bought it. You really made it look just like new again."

Grant smiled and shut the door. He ran around to the driver's side and jumped in. They headed off toward Meers. Nana talked the whole way about the first time she met Papa Joe, never again mentioning the indiscretion she'd admitted to the other night. No wonder no one ever knew that something like that had ever transpired between them. It seemed that she focused on all the good times, and in the grand scheme of their lives together, Grant figured those must've outweighed any mistakes by far. He smiled as he glanced at Nana and the way her eyes gleamed with happiness and tears when she talked about Papa Joe.

"We used to go to Meers once a month, you know? Your papa loved the peach cobbler, and he'd always overeat. I'd always say, 'Save room, Joe,' but he'd stuff himself silly before the dessert even arrived. But you know, he'd finish every bite, and he'd be in such pain,

I'd always have to drive home, and he'd unbutton his pants in the front seat and lay it way back."

Nana pulled her embroidered handkerchief from her purse and dabbed her eyes. Grant rubbed her shoulder. "I know you miss him."

They pulled into the parking lot of Meers, which was already bustling, a line stretched out the door. "Oh, would you look at all the people."

"You sure you want to stand in line, Nana? We can go somewhere else."

"When I got a Meersburger on my mind, nothing else is gonna do."

Grant helped Nana out of the truck and offered her his arm again. She took it and held on tight; the kitten heels she insisted on wearing clacked along the pavement. "Your Papa Joe always said I had good gams and even a little heel shows them off," Nana said when Grant glanced down at her shoes. Nana was also the only woman over the age of seventy-five who wore skirts that weren't floor length. He remembered her always shaking her head whenever she looked at women in long skirts and saying, "It's hot as hell, and I'm not going to sweat like a pig to hide a few spider veins. Besides, I don't know how anyone can walk in those long skirts without tripping on them and breaking a hip."

The line moved faster than they'd expected, and they were seated in no time. Grant looked at the crowds around them and across the table at Nana. "With so many people in the world, why is it so easy to feel so lonely?"

Nana looked around at all the people and took Grant's hand, holding it in both of hers. "Because numbers don't count, connections do. If you're not connected to anyone, all the people around you may as well be invisible."

Grant reached into his pocket, pulled out his phone, and glanced at it.

Nothing.

The waitress arrived at the table with two waters and a notepad. "Well, hello, Mrs. Ryan. We haven't seen you in a while. I was starting to wonder if you got sick of our burgers."

Nana's eyes welled with tears. She took a deep breath. "Hey, Tiffany. I'm afraid to say that my darling Joe passed." She once again pulled the hanky from her purse and buried her eyes in it momentarily, dabbed them at the corners, and looked up at the waitress who was clutching her chest. "Oh, Mrs. Ryan. Please accept my sincerest condolences. He was such a kind man."

"Thank you, dear girl." Nana stretched out her hand, took Tiffany's, and gave it a squeeze. Then she motioned to Grant. "This is my grandson, Grant. He's moved home to take care of his ol' nana."

Tiffany nodded at him. "Nice to meet you."

"Nice to meet you, too." Grant smiled.

The freckles on Tiffany's cheeks pushed up as she smiled at him. A lock of her red hair spilled down over her eye. She quickly pushed it out of the way and tried to tuck it under a barrette. "I'm sorry." She set her tablet on the table to try to do a better job at tucking her red hair away. "I'm trying to grow my bangs out, but they're still too short to keep pulled back and too long to leave down."

"It looks pretty, doesn't it, Grant?" Nana smiled and winked at him.

"Yes, very pretty." Grant tilted his head at Nana. Did she really bring him to Meers just because she was craving a burger, or did she have other motives? He smiled at Tiffany, who was, indeed, very pretty.

Chapter Ten

Lottie

"Shut up." Lottie repeatedly poked her phone, trying to get the morning alarm to turn off. She groaned when she rolled over and tried to sit up. The pain in her crotch was unreal. She regretted the decision to take the spin class even more than she had when the instructor kept shouting for them to turn the tension up.

"Fuck that," she'd muttered to Beth over and over. Putting her hand on the knob and pretending to give it "another quarter turn." Droplets of sweat covered the floor below her, and she was pretty sure her red head would pop. Beth would giggle, reaching over and pinching the flab of her ass that hung over the seat. "Knock it off, butthole."

As hard as Beth laughed looking over at her, Lottie tried to will her to fall off the bike and onto the floor, making an ass out of herself in front of the whole class. She'd never been so happy as when the class was over. Even at that time, she had no idea of the pain that would scream from her cooter. If she didn't know better, she would've believed gnomes snuck into her room at night and kicked the shit out of her vag.

Lottie got up and waddled into the bathroom. Walking and sitting to pee were both equally painful. She peeled off her clothes and hopped into the shower. And although she had never been a bath person, she considered filling the tub to soak her battered lady parts in some warm, soothing water.

Once out of the shower, she gently patted herself dry, wincing as she stepped into her panties and her skirt. She searched her closet for flats. There was no way she was going to try to balance on any bit of a heel when she was waddling like a duck. Could she call in sick citing cooter pain from spin class as her reason for being out? She considered killing Beth. She'd certainly never told her about the vaginal whooping she'd take. Surely, she'd felt like this her first time.

Lottie finished getting ready and waddled into the kitchen, pulling open the refrigerator before slamming it shut again. She'd much rather starve herself than work out.

You don't have to burn calories you don't eat, right?

She'd eat nothing but lettuce, celery, and carrots for a week if it meant she could skip spin class. And she'd happily walk more. Maybe she'd head to the base track after work. She could change after class and walk a few miles after work every day. And she was certain she'd read somewhere that a glass of red wine in the evening was as good for your heart as an hour workout at the gym. Sure, she preferred beer and had always hated red wine, but she'd rather choke it down than waddle around from such pain all the time. Even though the music at spin class was good, and everyone there seemed to be having fun, she didn't, and she could listen to good, loud music while she ate a salad.

Lottie grabbed her tote, purse, and keys and headed out the door. As she was walking to her car, her old neighbor whizzed by on the red Vespa that should have been hers, and it was the first time she was glad she didn't own it. She couldn't imagine riding that thing all the way to work now. She groaned and lowered herself into her car.

As she arrived at work and parked, Grant pulled up and parked nearby.

"Great." She fumbled to gather her stuff and try to get out of her car before he made his way over and heard her making old lady noises as she tried to climb out. Grabbing her tote and purse, she slammed the car door and tried her best to quickly walk in without looking like she had something shoved up her rear end.

"Lottie!" she heard Grant call after her.

Shit!

"Oh, hey, Grant." Lottie turned and waited for him. "I didn't see you drive in. How are you doing?"

"I'm doin' great. Ready for my second day and maybe getting around to some actual teaching." He smiled.

He had an amazing smile. She was doing her best to match his, but she was worried hers looked fake and plastic. Her cooter screamed with every step. Damn Beth. Why did she have to have a friend that was into exercise? *Note to self: when Beth moves, make a fat friend next.* Her stomach sank as soon as she thought it. She'd exercise every day to keep Beth from moving to another base.

"Can I carry your bag for you? It looks a little heavy." Grant extended his arm.

"Uh, sure." She handed Grant her tote and tucked her hair behind her ear. She felt just like Winnie Cooper in that episode of *The Wonder Years* where Kevin Arnold carries her books. She'd love to be his Winnie Cooper, but she was pretty sure it was more likely that he was going to be hers. Yes, looking at his dark blond hair in the sunlight this morning, she could almost hear the magical Winnie Cooper music playing as he gathered the straps of her tote, carrying it in one hand and his old, worn leather briefcase in the other. Although holding both, he still reached out and opened the door for her.

"Thank you," she said as she passed by.

"You're welcome." Grant walked with her to the teachers' lounge.

Lottie lowered herself onto the farting couch slowly. First, not to hurt her cooter, and second to avoid the fart sound that would surely come if she flopped down too quickly.

Grant placed her tote on the seat next to her. "Can I get you some coffee?"

"I'm not sure I'm desperate enough." Lottie smiled.

"I have some of Nana's coffee in a thermos in my briefcase. I'll pour you a cup. I don't need a whole thermos-full anyway."

"Sure, I'd love that."

"How do you take it?"

"Some half and half, no sugar."

"Gotcha."

Normally, she did take sugar, but she had to start cutting back on calories somewhere, sometime. Grant pulled a long, thin thermos from his briefcase and walked over to the coffee station.

Lottie winced as Beth plopped down on the couch next to her.

"Hey, Lot! What's wrong with you? You look constipated."

"I'm not constipated." Lottie whispered the word constipated. "I'm sore from spin. It feels like someone took a baseball bat to my cooter."

"Oh, yeah. I forgot about that." Beth laughed. "It's been a long time since my first class."

Grant walked over and handed Lottie the cup.

"Just getting you ready for a real pounding," Beth muttered and nudged Lottie in the ribs.

"Would you shut up?" Lottie shook her head and glared at Beth before softening her face and looking up to Grant. "Thank you."

"You're welcome. Would you like some coffee, Beth? I brought some from home."

"Hell, yeah. Anything to skip out on Cooley's crap."

Grant returned to the paper cups.

"Check out that ass," Beth whispered in Lottie's ear.

"You're a pervert. You know that?"

"Oh, right. Like you weren't looking. Like *that* ass isn't the reason you suddenly decided to get *your* ass in better shape."

Grant returned with the coffee, handing it to Beth, who took a sip. "Mmm, Grant. Now this is coffee. I may start swinging by your nana's house instead of the White Buffalo in the morning."

"I'll let her know you said so." Grant smiled as he tightened the cap on his thermos and returned it to his briefcase. He sat in the chair next to Lottie.

Lottie took a sip of the coffee.

"I hope I fixed it okay."

"It's perfect." Lottie smiled. It was. The fact that he'd made it for her made up for the lack of sugar. She could learn to get used to this.

"Welp, I guess we better get our sore asses to class, eh, Lottie?" Beth took another sip from her coffee and extended her hand.

"What are y'all sore from?" Grant picked up Lottie's tote as Beth pulled her from the couch.

She winced. "I went to spin class with Beth last night."

"I forgot to warn her about the pain that comes from getting used to a bike seat." Beth pointed to her ass.

Lottie flushed and shook her head at Beth. "You don't even know him. He doesn't know how gross you are yet."

"Well, he's one of us now, so he better learn. Especially since he's coming to the reservoir with us. I can't be expected to behave all the time."

"You better behave. His nana is coming, remember? Is she coming?" Lottie took a step forward, and the walk out of the teachers' lounge and to her room never seemed longer.

"Yeah. She's looking forward to it. And you don't have to worry about behaving for Nana, Beth. I'm not sure I can promise that she'll behave."

"Awesome. Well, I'm looking forward to meeting her, then." Beth swept out the room and down the hall.

"I can take my tote." Lottie reached out to grab it.

"I don't mind carrying it. I'm headed the same way."

"Thanks." Lottie smiled. He held out his arm for her as they walked through the lounge door and down the hall. Grant placed her tote on her desk as she lowered herself into the seat while wincing.

"That bad, huh? Remind me never to take a spin class." He grinned.

"Sure. As long as you promise to remind me never to take a spin class again."

"Deal. See you at lunch?"

"Sure. I'll see you then." Lottie snuck a peek at Grant's ass as he walked out of the room. He turned before leaving. Had he caught her looking? The grin on his face before he walked out assured her that he probably had.

***

The day was torture. Lottie was what she'd call a bad teacher. A "teach from the desk—here do this word search" teacher. But moving around was misery. Usually, she was on her feet most of the day. At lunch, Grant had brought her some ibuprofen, and that had helped a bit. Beth stopped by, insisting that it was only like that after the first time, but Lottie gave her the side eye, not knowing if she could bring herself to find out. At the end of the day, Grant offered to carry her things and walked her to her car.

Her mind kept flashing back to the thought of him catching her looking at his ass and wondering if he'd really caught her or not. She was seated, after all, so a straight-ahead line of vision would have taken her eyes that way. If he had seen, he didn't seem to mind. He was still talking to her. She wouldn't have minded if she caught him looking at hers.

Lottie climbed into her car. Grant handed her the tote, and she leaned over and put it into the passenger seat.

"See you tomorrow, Lottie."

"Yeah, see ya, Grant."

He closed her door and headed over to his truck. She watched him climb in and back out of his spot. She waved in the rearview as he drove behind. She backed out and followed behind. She once again noticed the I ❤ MY RESCUE magnet on the back of his car. Oh, yeah. He had a dog. Lottie made a mental note to ask him about his dog. She loved dogs and had always wanted one, but David told her it was too hard to move with a dog and never would let her get one.

Lottie's drive took her to the Altus City Animal Control. She'd driven by before but never wanted to go in, worried that she'd fall in love with some furry face that she knew she could never have. After sitting in the parking lot for a little while, Lottie pushed open her door and groaned as she climbed out. It probably would have been a good idea to wait for a different day to go looking at dogs, but she figured that since she was in pain, she wouldn't be lifting and cuddling anyone, lessening her chances of falling in love and taking anyone home.

Walking into the front office, she was a little taken back at the sounds of the barking dogs echoing from the next room.

A gruff-looking woman with bleach blonde hair and 1990s-style bangs smiled at her. "You come to find a friend, darlin?" Her voice was stained with a chain-smoking habit of at least forty years.

"I'm thinking about it. Maybe not today. I mean, I've always wanted a dog."

"You know, I could tell you were a dog person when you came in."

"Really? How?"

"You know, it's a look in the eye. Cat people don't make eye contact when they come in. They seem shier. You look a little shy, but you connected your eyes to mine right away, and there's a brightness behind your eyes that dog people tend to have. I'm not saying cat people are dim, ya got me?" The woman threw her head back and cackled as she pushed her way out from behind the counter. "Were you thinking of a big dog? Little dog? Something in between?"

"I honestly have no idea. I had given up the hope of ever getting a dog a long time ago. I guess I was hoping to look and maybe that would help me decide."

"Oh, yeah. Go on in. Take your time. And honey, when you find the one that's supposed to be your baby, you'll just know." The woman pushed open the door. The sound of the barking intensified. Lottie paused. "They'll calm down in a bit. They're all just really excited for company."

Lottie walked in, and her heart sank. Nearly all the cages were full. Some dogs jumped and barked. One didn't even get out of its bed to give her a second look, as though it were resigned to the fact that this was home and always would be.

Lottie walked down the line, greeting each dog she passed by. A few scared her. Most wagged their tails and seemed to be begging her to play. Then Lottie paused. Beautiful brown eyes peered at her from under of mop of gray and white hair.

"Hello there." Lottie glanced at the sign hanging on the door. "Pickles." She bent down. He leaned against the chain link gate. Lottie let out'an old lady groan, squatted, stuck her fingers through, and scratched him. He panted and grinned. "I shouldn't have come here because I don't want to leave you here."

Lottie sat on the floor, scratching and talking to Pickles until the lady from the front came in and told her they were closing up. She wanted to adopt Pickles then and there, but she decided she better sleep on such a big decision.

"See ya, Pickles." Lottie waved. "Thanks for letting me spend some time with the dogs."

"Oh, sweetheart, the dogs love having visitors. You come back anytime you want."

"I will." Lottie smiled and walked back to her car. She sat a while in the parking lot before picking up her phone. She held it a moment before texting Grant.

Lottie: I noticed your rescue dog magnet on the back of your car. I'm thinking about getting one and I'm wondering if I could ask you about dog ownership.

She hit SEND and squealed.
What a nerd.
She reread her text.
Ask you about dog ownership? Could I be any lamer?

Lottie drove home, embarrassed at the lameness of her text the whole way.

Chapter Eleven

Grant

All week, Grant and Lottie talked about dogs over lunch. He told her all about his rescue dog, Brutus, who was "the oddest-looking dog," as people would always tell him. His head and body looked like a German shepherd but with very short legs, like a basset hound. He'd found Brutus running alongside the I-44 in Tulsa, looking terrified, but as soon as Grant pulled over and swung his truck door open, Brutus jumped right in.

For weeks he hung fliers, contacted all the local shelters, and put Brutus's picture in the local newspapers, Facebook lost and found animal groups, and on Craigslist. Days turned into months with not a word. He figured that Brutus had been dumped along the highway. From the very first day, there was a sense of dread that washed over him every time he got a call from a number he didn't recognize, worried it would be someone calling to claim Brutus. It never was. "How could anyone not want you in their lives?" he'd ask Brutus. Brutus's tongue would flop out of the side of his mouth, and he seemed to be smiling as though saying, "Right!"

Sadly, a year ago, Brutus didn't wake up in the morning. Grant got up and called to Brutus for his walk, but he never came. He searched for him to find him curled up on his bed, unmoving. Tears still readily welled whenever he thought about it, and his heart stung. But he was just happy he'd given Brutus all the love one dog could wish for and that he'd died warm in a soft bed knowing he was loved and wanted.

Grant promised to go to the Altus City Animal Control with Lottie on Saturday afternoon once they'd finish their walk with Nana and Beth around the reservoir. He knew she'd been visiting a little dog called Pickles every day after school that week, but she was nervous about such a big commitment and wanted his opinion. Although it was obvious she had already handed her heart to the little dog. He'd also offered to take her into Lawton to get all the supplies she'd need for her new dog. He was really looking forward to it and was thrilled when she agreed, just as thrilled as he'd been the Tuesday before when she sent him a text asking him if they could discuss dog ownership.

After walking to the door and finding it unlocked, again, he opened it to find himself inside a whirlwind of cleaning. Vinegar stung his nose. Country music was blasting.

"Nana?" Grant called as he kicked off his shoes before heading through the house looking for her. He found her in the bathroom, scrubbing the floor with huge, green rubber gloves on. "What's going on?"

"Oh, I've let this house get out of hand. Time to start cleaning up and make this place shine again."

105

"You've got the cleanest house I know."

"Well, maybe it'd been clean enough for just the two of us but not for company."

"Company?" Grant scratched his head.

"I was having my coffee this morning, and I got a hankering for some pumpernickel bread, so I called up Lorna, and she took me to the grocery store."

"Lorna is still driving?"

"Well, yeah, she's still driving. Just because she's old doesn't mean she shouldn't drive. Anyway, I got the pumpernickel and some of that creamy peanut butter I like, and I ran into Tiffany."

"Who's Tiffany?"

"Tiffany!" Nana's eyebrows knitted together. "You remember. From Meers."

"The waitress?"

"She's not just a waitress. I've known her for years. She's a lovely little thing. Anyway, I invited her over for dinner tonight. I don't want her coming over and thinking I'm a pig, so I've been working to clean this place up. I got so busy that I didn't even eat my pumpernickel."

Grant rubbed the back of his neck. He was feeling a set up, and it wasn't welcomed. That girl Tiffany was pretty enough, but she was just that, a girl. She couldn't have been more than twenty-five, and Grant had dated enough twenty-somethings to know that he wasn't interested, no matter what she looked like.

"Whadya think about that?" Nana paused and looked up at Grant.

"Yeah, great." Grant pursed his lips and did his best to press them into a smile. "Is there anything I can do to help you?"

"Nope. This is the last room I got going on. I may call you in a bit if I can't get myself up off this floor. Why don't you go find something nice to put on?"

"What's wrong with this?" Grant looked down at his school clothes.

"A man should always spiffy up when a lady is coming to dinner. Work clothes aren't gonna do it."

"Yes, ma'am." Grant turned and walked to his room.

Work clothes aren't going to do what exactly?

He sighed as he sat down on the corner of his bed, glancing at himself in the mirror.

How am I going to get out of this one?

Maybe he didn't really need to worry about it anyway. He doubted that a girl that age could be interested in an aging bachelor who worked as a long-term substitute teacher and lived with his grandmother. Sighing, he slouched and shook his head, grinning. Sure. Tiffany had probably been unable to say no to a sweet old lady who had just lost her husband. Surely, she'd feel just as uncomfortable at the prospect of a set up with him. Nothing to worry about.

"Grant, come help your ol' Nana up, would ya?"

Grant scuttled into the bathroom and pulled Nana up from the floor. He dumped the bucket of barely dirty water she'd used to scrub the floor and put it away.

"What time is she supposed to get here?"

"Six-thirty."

"Do you need any help making dinner?"

Nana chuckled. "I've been making dinner so long, I could do it in my sleep. Not to be rude, honey, but you'd just be in my way."

"I'm going to go get some work done if you're sure."

"I'm sure. And don't forget to change your clothes and put on a tie."

"I won't forget."

Grant returned to his room and pulled out his phone, wanting to text Lottie but unable to figure out a reason he might have. He wasn't sure if she liked him more than a friend. He didn't want to scare her off and was determined to play it cool. This was unfamiliar territory for him. Playing it cool had never been difficult. Everything about her made him want to be around her even more. He thought about her way too much. Maybe it wasn't such a bad thing that they were having a guest for dinner. Even though he wasn't interested in Tiffany, she might keep his mind off the urge to text Lottie and ask her to go somewhere, anywhere, with him.

***

The smell of Nana's beef roast wafted in through the door, waking Grant from a nap. He heard a knock at the door and Nana greeting Tiffany.

Fuck!

Grant sat up, catching a glimpse of his hair smashed to his head on one side. He snuck around his bedroom door and slid into the bathroom. He wetted his hand and ran in quickly through his hair. He squirted some toothpaste onto his toothbrush and crammed it in his mouth while he trying to fix his hair. He found it difficult as both hands tried to work the same motion. He'd never been one of those pat your head and rub your stomach success stories as a kid.

Peeing quickly, he suddenly felt like the sound of his stream was thundering so loudly there was no way they weren't hearing it. He reached over and turned the faucet on high. After giving his dick a shake, he flushed and washed his hands.

He slowly twisted the knob and pulled open the door, peeking out into the hall before darting back into his room.

"Grant?" Nana called.

"Yes, Nana." He slowly turned and entered the hallway. Nana and Tiffany were rounding the corner of the dining room.

"Our guest is here."

"Oh, hey there." Grant held up his hand and pressed his lips in a smile.

"Tiffany." The red-haired girl walked toward him, extending her hand.

"Yeah, Tiffany. I remember. From Meers."

"That's right. Gosh, your house is so nice." Tiffany smiled widely and looked around.

"It's not my house. It's Nana's." Grant's voice was curt. He hadn't mean to sound rude, but he knew it came out that way. Nana was shooting daggers right through him. "Sorry, I had fallen asleep. I'm still a big groggy. I apologize."

"I think it's so sweet that you moved back to Altus to live. And you're teaching at Rivers, right?"

"That's right." Grant stifled a yawn.

"Welp, why don't you go out on the patio? It's a really nice night. I'll bring you two some drinks. What would you like Tiffany, dear?"

"I'd love a woo woo if you have it."

Grant raised an eyebrow at Nana, who did her best to wave him away before Tiffany saw.

"What's a woo woo, honey?"

"Oh, it's, like, the most amazing drink. It's vodka, peach schnapps, and cranberry juice."

"I don't think I have any cranberry juice. I do have some orange juice."

"Oooh, a screwdriver. I could go for that. It's just the vodka and orange juice." Tiffany turned to Grant and smiled as though she was waking up on Christmas morning.

He pressed his lips into another smile, turned quickly, and pulled open the door to the patio. "After you?" He held his arm out.

"Thanks." Tiffany brushed past him as she walked by. Close. She didn't need to be that close.

Fuck!

Now he was sure she probably wasn't just being polite when she accepted Nana's dinner invitation. Grant had never been one of those guys that missed the obvious signs that the slightly slutty girls put out. She was into him, and she was making sure he knew it.

"Can I bring you a beer, Grant?" Nana called.

"Bring two!"

Tiffany seated herself on the love seat. She scooted over slightly when he stepped out. He smiled and took a seat in the chair across from her. The air was filled with awkward silence. Grant took a deep breath, smiled, and looked around at the wood privacy fence that lined the backyard.

"Looks like I need to do some repairs on the fence. There's so much to do around here, I'm going to be quite busy for a while with school. No time for much of anything else."

"Oh, I'm sure that's not true." Tiffany held his gaze for a little too long.

He forced a smile once again. "Maybe I should go help Nana with those drinks." Grant stood, and as he opened the door, Nana was right there with a tray.

"Oh, Grant. Good timing."

He took the tray from her. Nana sat in his chair.

Fuck!

He'd have to sit next to Tiffany.

She touched his finger as he handed her the glass and smiled up at him as she did. "Thank you."

"You're welcome."

He handed Nana her drink, set the tray on the table, grabbed his beer, taking a big gulp before sitting down next to Tiffany.

"So, Nana, how long until dinner is ready?" He raised a brow at her.

"It'll be ready soon." Nana waved her hand at him. He knew he was going to get an earful after Tiffany left. She looked at him the exact same way she used to look at him when she caught him dozing off at church. Or like she did the time she caught him tossing little wads of paper into Miss Lorna's gray hair. She took him out to the parking lot and gave him a crack on the ass that time. Certainly, he was too old to be spanked anymore. He straightened in his seat. Best not to assume with Nana.

"So how long have you been working at Meers, Tiffany?" Grant smiled and looked at Nana from the corner of his eye, hoping she'd be pleased with his change in behavior.

"I've been working there since I graduated high school, so six years now."

A waitress for six years. Did Nana really think he'd have anything in common with a twenty-four-year-old girl, let alone be able to have a relationship with one?

"Tiffany goes to Western Oklahoma State College," Nana added, smiling from ear to ear.

"What are you studying?" Grant asked.

"I'm getting my associates degree in early childhood education. I love kids. I'd like to have a bunch of my own someday." Tiffany tilted her head and batted her eyes at Grant.

Fuck! Fuck! Fuuuuuuuuck!

"Do you like kids, Grant?" She looked longingly at him.

Was this girl for real? Grant took a big swig of his beer, looking at Nana long and hard before answering. He wanted to say, "Not with you, crazy," but he thought better of it. "I haven't really thought about it."

"Oh, sure you have, Grant." Nana waved him off. "Welp, dinner should be ready. What's say we go inside and eat?"

"Great idea." Grant hopped up and opened the door for the ladies. "I'll be in there in a minute. Just want to wash my hands." He watched as Nana and Tiffany rounded the corner into the dining room. He slipped into his room and grabbed his cell, quickly texting Dan Cooley to call him in half an hour.

He slid the phone in his pocket and walked to the table. Nana had seated him across from Tiffany. He sat down, relieved. At least it wasn't right next to her.

"Grant, would you say grace?" Nana smiled, folded her hands, and lowered her head. Tiffany did the same.

Grant rolled his eyes. "Dear God. Thanks for the food which we're gonna eat. Amen."

"Amen." Nana and Tiffany began chit chatting about Tiffany's culinary skills and how she'd have to come over and learn this delicious roast recipe from Nana sometime. Grant formulated ways in his mind that he was going to escape this trap they seemed to be setting for him. He eyeballed Nana. What was she doing? He told her how he felt about Lottie.

Thirty minutes passed, and like the good, reliable friend that he was, Dan Cooley called. Grant gave a few "uh-huhs" and "Oh, reallys" as Dan blabbered on, wondering what he needed to be saved from. Grant ended with a "sure, I'll be right there, Dan." He stood and apologized to Tiffany and Nana. "I'm afraid I've got to go. Dan's car broke down, and he's trapped halfway out to Lawton. I've got to go pick him up."

Tiffany's face dropped. Grant would have felt bad, only he didn't at all. It was better she be disappointed now than for her to weave this trap with Nana and still come up empty.

"Well, that's such a shame." Nana's face suddenly brightened. "You know what? We'll just have to make it up over another dinner. Sound good?"

"I'd love to!" Tiffany beamed.

Grant pursed his lips. "Great."

He grabbed his keys and headed out the door.

Chapter Twelve

Lottie

Lottie's eyes sprung open for the first time on a Saturday morning when the alarm squawked at her. She didn't slam it. She didn't tell it to shut up. She didn't even sink her head back into the pillow and think about how an early death caused by obesity was just fine with her. The long dirt nap and lack of exercise no longer sounded as appealing.

Grant was coming along today. Her mind raced. Should she wear some makeup? Maybe a little, but not too much, she decided. Best to try to make it look like she wasn't wearing any. A little light foundation, some brown mascara, and tinted lip balm. Her stomach flipped. Was it excitement, or was she getting the nervous shits that always struck her before she had something important looming?

Her first day teaching, she thought she might miss school. Every time she went to grab her keys and bags, she'd have to dart back down the hallway to squeeze out a fresh batch of diarrhea.

Oh, please don't let me have the cha-chas today.

There was no bathroom at the reservoir, and it wasn't going to be like the one time she had an overwhelming need to pee and Beth convinced her to go pee behind a tree by the side of the path. "Dogs piss wherever they want. It's pee, not toxic waste," Beth had said and promised to be the lookout. Some lookout she was. While Lottie was squatting, a truck came down the path out of nowhere. Beth walked over. "I'll block you," she giggled but bumped her in the shoulder with her hip, knocking her over. Pee pulsed out of her as she screamed at Beth and desperately tried to pull her panties and shorts up before the truck reached them.

"Public indecency! Public indecency!" Beth pointed at her, shouting, as she ran away. Lottie chased her with every intension of punching her in the tit when she reached her. Beth was too fast and gave Lottie plenty of time to cool off before walking back toward her.

Sitting up, Lottie gulped. Worse than being shoved over while peeing at the reservoir would be trying to sneak out a fart and sharting. Then having Beth announce it in front of Grant and his nana. She shook her head. Nah, Beth wouldn't do that to her. She wanted her to hook up with Grant. Letting him know she had shit shorts wouldn't do much for Beth's scheme. Nerves pinched her stomach as she sprinted to the bathroom.

To her relief, it was just a little case of bubble guts and her butt was dookie-free. She brushed her teeth, pulled her hair into a messy bun—the kind that looked effortless but actually required a lot—and carefully put on some—looked like it wasn't even there—makeup. Checking herself over in the mirror, she thought she did quite a good job of looking like she rolled out of bed, naturally beautiful and ready to exercise.

Lottie scampered into the kitchen, grabbed a banana and a glass of water. Her body screamed for coffee, but she knew that if she drank it, the chances of either needing to take a shit or having to pee at the reservoir would pretty much become a certainty.

As she ate her banana, she walked around the house, trying to envision it through the eyes of a guest. Were things out of place? Was dust settled anywhere she hadn't noticed? What if it smelled? People never could smell their own homes, could they? Beth's house always smelled like oranges. She'd been in homes that smelled like garbage. What did her house smell like? Since Grant might be coming over today—if she adopted Pickles—she was mortified at even the thought of him walking in and thinking it was a garbage house rather than an orange house or something like that. She walked over to the trash and flipped open the lid, practically sticking her head inside. It didn't smell good, but it didn't smell bad enough to foul up her entire house.

She pulled the compost container out from under the sink and plopped the banana peel inside. Glancing at the clock, she decided to empty the bin and give it a rinse, just in case. After doing that, she ran into the bathroom and grabbed her homemade air freshener— made of high-proof Military Special vodka and lemon essential oil—and sprayed it all over the house. Better that her house smell like lemon than garbage or something worse. She even sprayed a little on her clothes— just in case she was one of those people who stunk and didn't know it. Her mind flashed back to the last episode of *Hoarders* she watched where a lady had upwards of forty cats living in her house yet insisted that no one knew how she lived. "Right, lady, your house is filled with garbage and mountainous piles of cat poop, but you think no one has any suspicions that you might be a dirty-ass crazy cat lady," Lottie muttered as she ate a bag of chips on the couch, a little drunk from more than one lonely Saturday evening beer.

After taking one more glance in the full-length mirror on her bathroom door, she headed out of the house for the reservoir, making sure to grab the cooler she had packed with extra waters just in case Grant hadn't brought any and his nana got thirsty. While the mornings weren't overwhelmingly hot yet, she suffered the one time she forgot to bring a water and had to share Beth's, who kept telling her not to backwash with every sip.

Beth was, as usual, waiting in her Jeep with the music cranked when Lottie arrived. After parking and getting out of her car, Beth climbed out of her Jeep and serenaded Lottie to the rest of the song playing while using her water bottle as a microphone and trying to swat Lottie on her ass.

"Knock it off, ya dick, or they're gonna pull out as soon as they see what a freak you are and drive away."

"Pull out. That's what you have to remind Grant to do later. Don't wanna get knocked up on your first date."

"God, how old are you? Sometimes you act like a fourteen-year-old boy who just discovered his wiener."

"Wiener? Who's fourteen? Is that what you're going to call it when you ask Grant to put in you?"

Lottie rolled her eyes and shook her head. Words hovered in her throat but refused to participate. Just then, Grant's blue pickup came rolling up. Lottie swatted at Beth to try to get her to stop singing into her water bottle.

"Try to behave. Remember, he brought his nana." Lottie walked over to the truck. "Hey, Grant."

He smiled. "Hey, Lottie." Grant crossed around the front of the truck to the passenger door and opened it up. An old woman climbed out wearing a visor with sunglasses and a long-sleeve shirt and shorts. Shorter than she'd ever seen on a woman that age. Shorter than hers. "This is my Nana Aileen. Nana, this is Beth and Lottie."

Nana smiled. "Ladies. So nice to meet you. Thanks for taking care of Grant his first few days at school. I've heard so much about you both, I feel like I already know you." Lottie shook Nana Aileen's hand, although she wanted to hug her. She reminded her of her own grandma, whom she missed desperately.

"Welp, shall we get going? The calories aren't going to burn themselves." Beth smiled.

Nana clapped her hands. "I'm ready. It's been so long since I've gone out for a walk. Joe and I used to walk around our little neighborhood, but we rarely came out to the reservoir. Oh, we came to feed the ducks a few times but never to just walk."

Beth looked at Lottie and rolled her eyes. Lottie waved her off immediately and mouthed, "Stop," to her. Beth walked forward closer to Nana Aileen. "So, Aileen, have you lived in Altus your whole life?"

Grant slowed, taking a cue from Beth to fall back to talk to Lottie. "So, are you excited about Pickles?"

"Yes! I hope you like him."

"I'm sure I will. I haven't met a dog yet that I didn't like. After the walk, I'll drive Nana home, and I can come pick you up if you want. If you adopt him, we can drive out to Lawton to pick up supplies. My truck is dog friendly."

"Are you sure you don't mind driving me all the way out to Lawton?"

"I don't mind. It'll be fun."

"Okay, but you have to let me give you gas money."

"No way. I was thinking about heading to Lawton this weekend anyway. Get out of Altus for a bit. So I was going to be using the gas anyway."

"Well, can I buy you lunch?"

"Sure. How about Wok and Roll? Have you ever been? They have a drive thru. We can grab it on the way back and eat at your place. I mean, it's been quite a while since I've been there, but I assume it's still good."

Lottie tucked her hair behind her ear and smiled. "That's my favorite place to get Chinese." Lottie's stomach knotted. She was suddenly aware of her thighs rubbing each other as she walked. Stupid thing for a chubby girl to do, talk about how much she loves food.

Grant stopped in his tracks. "Fuck," he muttered.

"What's wrong?" Lottie stopped and turned to him.

But before he could answer, she heard Nana slap her hands together. "Well, Tiffany, my dear. What a surprise running into you here." Nana turned back to

Grant. "Grant, isn't this a wonderful surprise? It's Tiffany."

Grant smiled, but Lottie wasn't sure it was genuine. Lottie glanced at the beautiful, young redhead who was wrapping her arms around Nana Aileen. The red-head walked over and wrapped her arms tightly around Grant after she finished with Nana.

"Well, you know I like to run. I run five miles five times a week as long as my schedule allows, and this is my favorite place to do it." Tiffany straightened her perfectly slicked back ponytail.

"Really?" Beth chimed in. "I'm here all the time, and I've never seen you. I'm sure I would have noticed such beautiful red hair."

"Well, we must miss each other." Tiffany wound a strand of her hair around her finger.

"Tiffany is a waitress at Meers," Nana interjected. "Probably does most of her running while you're in school and then gets to serving up the best burgers in the country while you're out here. You know, I've known Tiffany for years. Joe just adored her. Always said she reminded him of me."

Lottie thought she heard Grant moan.

"Did you say something?" Lottie asked him.

"No, just thirsty. I should have brought a water."

"I have some extras in a cooler in my car if you need one." Lottie smiled.

"Yeah, why don't we get walking back around and I'll get one of those from you? Well, it was nice to see you again, Tiffany." Grant waved and walked on. Lottie followed him.

"Tiffany, sweetie, why don't you join us?" Nana asked.

"Well, I'd love to. I just finished my run, so it'll be nice to walk and cool down." Tiffany turned and quickened her step to catch up with Lottie and Grant.

Beth called out to her. "Wow, did you run five miles? You're not even sweaty. I'm always a sweaty mess when I run."

Lottie tried not to smile, but her mouth kept tugging at the corners. She really did love Beth's courage to call people out on their bullshit. It was obvious that girl hadn't run one lap, let alone five miles.

"Oh, not today. I've already done all my running for the week. I just came out today to get a walk in and enjoy this beautiful day." Tiffany smiled daggers at Beth.

"Tiffany, why don't you come by after the walk and join me and Grant for supper on the patio? I can make some delicious pot roast sandwiches from last night's leftovers, if you'd like. I know you enjoyed the roast." Nana smiled at Grant and then at Tiffany.

"I sure did, and I'd love to."

"Wonderful!" Nana clapped her hands.

"Nana, I told you that I was going with Lottie to the shelter after the walk today. I'm afraid it will just be the two of you." Grant smiled at Lottie.

"Oh, I'm sure her sweet friend Beth here can go with her to get a dog. It's not often we have company over." Nana grabbed Tiffany's hands in hers and patted them.

"We just did yesterday," Grant mumbled.

Nana fanned her hand in front of her face. "Well, I'm really starting to overheat. I think I'm ready to go. I'm sorry to cut our walk short. It's just been a while since I've been out like this."

"I have some waters in my car," Lottie said.

"Oh, that's so sweet of you. I think I just need to go home and sit in the nice cool air conditioning for a while." Nana walked quickly around the rest of the way back to the car. A little too quickly for an old woman that just had to get home and rest.

Lottie pulled open her car door and pulled out two waters, handing them both to Grant. He handed one to Nana.

"Oh, thank you." Nana handed hers to Tiffany. "Here you go, Tiffany, sweetie."

Grant opened his and took a sip. "Why don't you go on home with Tiffany, Nana? I'd like to stay and walk a little more."

Lottie smiled, but it quickly faded.

"Oh, I brought my Vespa." Tiffany shrugged.

"I'm definitely not riding on a Vespa. Come on, Grant, you drive your ol' nana home. You don't mind, do you, girls?" Nana smiled at Lottie.

"I don't mind." Lottie pressed the sweetest smile she could across her face to hide her disappointment.

Grant turned to her. "I'm really sorry."

"It's okay." Lottie waved as he walked Nana around and opened the truck for her, helping her inside.

Tiffany hopped into the bed of his truck. "Give me a ride over to my Vespa?"

"Sure," he said as he climbed in his truck. He rolled down the window and pursed his lips at Lottie. "Call me if you adopt him?"

Lottie nodded and smiled, hoping he'd pull away quickly. She wasn't sure how long she could keep the fake smile pressed across her lips.

The blue truck pulled away. Lottie watched them circle the reservoir to the other side where Tiffany was parked.

Beth wrapped her arm around Lottie's shoulders. "Well, Nana's a fuckin' bitch."

Chapter Thirteen

Lottie

Lottie kicked a pebble around the path, afraid to look up or the tears balancing on the rims of her eyes would tumble down her cheeks. Beth would know just how much she liked Grant then, and she didn't want her level of disappointment to show to anyone.

A dull ache filled her chest. She didn't want to breathe. She only wanted to head home and wrap herself in her burrito of solitude. Beth kept her arm around Lottie as she stood batting the pebble around with the toe of her shoe. A tear dripped from her eye, plummeting straight down and dampening the path near the pebble.

"What do you say we walk a few more laps?" Beth ushered Lottie forward. "We hardly got a good walk in before that fire crotch showed up."

"I just wanna go home." Lottie peeled away from Beth's arm and headed toward her car.

"What about Pickles? You've been talking about adopting this dog all week. I'll go with you and we'll have a fun day. Grant turned out to be a bit of a pansy anyway listening to his little bitch granny and ditching you. If he doesn't have the balls to stand up to that old hag, he certainly doesn't deserve to have them sucked on by you."

"Can you not be gross right now?" Lottie opened her car door and sat inside.

Beth sprinted around the front of the car and climbed inside the passenger door. "Let's go get Pickles, okay? Then you'll have someone to snuggle with when you get home. Okay?"

"You don't have to come with me. I can go on my own."

"Only you won't. Come on, I know you, and I know that droopy lip means you're going to go home, crawl into your bed, and end up eating fast food all weekend. You're finally getting out of your slump. Don't let this ruin it for you now." Beth buckled up and slapped the dashboard. "Now let's go adopt woman's best friend. You've always wanted a dog, and today is going to be the day you get one."

Lottie forced a smile and buckled up. Beth was right. She had always wanted a dog, and she'd always let men stop her from getting one. This wasn't going to be another one of those times. She looked in the mirror and scowled at her messy bun and the fly-away hairs that were escaping at the sides. She pulled out the hair band and let her hair fall around her shoulders. Tiffany had perfect hair and perfect skin. Lottie suddenly felt like a toad. Sighing, she threw the car in gear and headed for the shelter.

Another thing Beth was right about, if Grant really wanted to be with her, he would have been. She churned the thought in her mind over and over. She wasn't going to end up with another David. A man who wants her for his "good enough until I find someone better" girl. If Grant preferred to go spend time with that twenty-something redheaded twit, he could go and do it before they ever got too serious. It was clear that was what his nana had in mind.

"Nana was a fuckin' bitch," Lottie muttered.

"Yeah, she was." Beth laughed. "I guess women don't become any less cunty as they age. You don't need that in your life. I'm lucky my mother-in-law lives across the country. If I had to live anywhere near her, I'm not sure I'd want to be married to Michael. I see that bitch twice a year, and it's all I can do to not to slap her across her wrinkled old face."

"David's mom was always nice to me, but I could tell she thought he could've done better. Did I ever tell you that at our wedding, my aunt overheard her saying to her sister, 'I guess we're too overdressed for *this* wedding?' Ugh, if I ever think about getting married again, I'm going to make sure I find an orphan." Lottie pulled into the shelter parking lot and turned off the engine.

"If I ever have kids, I'm not going to be a bitch of a monster-in-law. I'm going to be sweet as pie, even if my daughter-in-law is a cunt." Beth laughed.

Lottie shook her head and tossed her keys into her purse.

"All righty, let's go see this dog." Beth checked her hair in the mirror before following Lottie inside.

The same older woman was at the front desk. "Back again, eh? Is today the day?"

"I think so." Lottie smiled. "I brought my friend to meet Pickles before I completely decide. Can we hang out with him in the outdoor yard?"

"Sure can. Why don't you two head on out there and I'll get Pickles and bring him on out? I think he's been waiting to see you. I have the feeling he knows what's happening today."

Lottie and Beth walked out into the yard.

Beth crinkled up her nose. "I guess they don't pick up the shit too often out here."

"Well, it's worse inside. You're lucky I asked to come out here."

The door opened, and Pickles ran out into the yard. His white and black fur was a blur as he flashed like lighting across the yard and straight to Lottie. "There he is. There's my boy." Lottie scratched his body as he twisted and turned and rubbed against her legs, almost knocking her over.

"Oh my gosh. That's a cute fuckin' dog. What kind is it?" Beth asked as she moved closer to get a few scratches in.

"Well, he's a rescue, so I can't say for certain, but he looks like a Tibetan terrier to me." The lady lit up a cigarette and started puffing away.

"I thought shelters only had pit bulls and mutts." Beth waved a plume of freshly exhaled smoke away from her face.

"Oh, the majority of what we get are bully breeds of some sort, but occasionally, we get a bunch of pure-breds when a hoarder or puppy mill gets shut down. That's where Pickles came from. He's the last of the bunch."

"Is something wrong with him?" Beth asked.

Lottie covered Pickles's ears. "Beth, don't say that in front of him."

Beth shook her head and looked back at the smoking chimney standing near the doorway, puffing away.

"Nope. He was just the biggest in the bunch. A lot of times people want those tiny lap dogs first. But they missed out. Pickles was the sweetest of them all. He's been a good boy for me. Haven't ya, Pickles?" She pulled out another cigarette, stuck it in her mouth, and lit the end with the one she just finished.

"Well, what do you think?" Lottie smiled at Beth as she continued to pet the dog who was lovingly rubbing up against her, trying to squeeze himself onto her lap.

"I think he's going to knock you over into a pile of shit if you're not careful." Beth grinned. "The two of you obviously love each other. Adopt him and let's get out of here before I end up adopting one."

"Okay, I'd like to adopt him." Lottie smiled and hugged Pickles.

"Welp, let me just finish my ciggie, and we'll head on inside, fill out the paperwork, and take care of the adoption fee." She took a long drag and smiled out the smoke.

"You want come live with me, Pickles?" Lottie scratched behind his black ears. He licked her cheek. She giggled and fell back. She quickly righted herself and looked to Beth to ask if there was shit on her butt without offending the human chimney.

"You're good. Shit free." Beth gave her a thumbs up.

After the lady smoked, Lottie bought an overpriced collar and leash from the shelter lobby, signed the paperwork, and payed the adoption fee. Pickles pranced out the door as though he knew exactly what had just happened. He had a smile stretched across his face that seemed to match Lottie's. Although hers grew by about a mile as they were putting Pickles into the back seat and Grant's truck came pulling into the lot.

"What are you doing here?" She scratched Pickles head as Grant walked over.

"I told Nana and Tiffany that I was going on a beer run. I just didn't tell them that I'd be going to Lawton to get it. You two wanna come along?"

"Give me your keys." Beth stretched out her hand. "I'll drive your car back to my place." Beth unhooked the car key from the chain and threw the rest back to her.

"So, this is Pickles. Hey, boy!" Grant scratched him on the back when Lottie pulled him out of the backseat of the car.

"Yup, this is him. Isn't he cute?"

"He's a handsome boy. Let's get him in the truck and go get him some food and supplies." Grant lifted Pickles into the cab of the truck. He swiftly put his paws on the dashboard and started panting.

Beth jumped into Lottie's car, blew her a kiss, and took off out of the lot. Lottie waved after her.

"Are you sure your nana isn't going to be mad at you?"

"I'm a little upset with her, to tell you the truth. I think she's got it in her head that I need to start a relationship with that girl, and I couldn't be less interested."

"Really?" Lottie tucked her hair behind her ear and looked out the window. "Don't you think she's pretty?"

"I guess she's pretty, but she's pretty annoying, too. I don't know what Nana could possibly think I'd have in common with a girl in her twenties."

"I don't think I'd even want to hang out with my twenty-year-old self."

"Me neither."

Grant pulled out of the lot and headed for 62 East to Lawton.

"Remind me to get beer before we come back so that I'm not a liar." Grant winked.

"I'll try my best." Lottie smiled.

The Wichita Mountains Wildlife Refuge was beautiful out Grant's window. Lottie couldn't help but stare.

Grant smiled. "Wanna take a detour? It's early."

"I don't want you to have to be gone any longer than you need to." Lottie scratched Pickles' ears.

"We can take a quick drive through. See what Pickles thinks of the buffalo? What do you think, Pickles? Should we go?"

Pickles nudged his head under Grant's arm and snuggled up against him before laying his head on his lap.

"I think he might want to go home with you instead." Lottie scratched Pickles' back.

"No way. He's just happy that I'm taking him on a boondoggle. Aren't ya, boy?" Grant scratched Pickles' back. His finger momentarily brushing against Lottie's. A tingle surged through her body. She let her hair fall from behind her ear to hide the excitement that danced behind her eyes. She wanted more of his touch. All she could think about at that moment was kissing him. Tucking her hair back behind her ear, she glanced at him from the corner of her eye. He was looking over at her. Grinning. Perhaps he was thinking the same thing. Something about the look in his eye made her think he was.

As they drove into the Wildlife Refuge, they slowed and watched for buffalo. Pickles once again put his paws on the dash as though he were the lookout. Grant's cell rang. He fished it out of his pocket and groaned. "Nana." He tossed it into the cup holder. "She's always telling me not to talk and drive so I wouldn't want to disobey."

"Are you sure she isn't going to hate me?" Lottie bit her lip.

"Why would she hate you? I told her all week that I was going to help you get Pickles and supplies in Lawton today. And you know as well as I do that it was no coincidence that Tiffany was at the reservoir today." He shook his head.

"But if she's set on you two spending time together, she's not going to like that you were spending time with me today."

"Who says she has to know? I went to get beer. I'm going to get some beer. If she asks if we went together, I'll tell her, but if she doesn't ask, I won't offer the information. Don't worry about it anyway. Nana really is a sweet person. She has no reason to dislike you."

"I hope so. I hate when people don't like me." Lottie tangled her hands around the fur on Pickles' back paw.

"Who could not like you?"

"Somebody." Lottie's mind immediately shifted to David and Veronica. She was sure Veronica didn't like her, not that she did anything to her. Veronica was the one who stole her husband. And every time David

131

talked to her lately, she knew he didn't like her, either. She needed to ship out his clothes. She would ship out his clothes. Tomorrow.

Sitting here with Grant made her feel like she was finally ready to admit that David was never coming home and maybe part of her was finally starting not to care.

Pickles barked and made Lottie jump. She clutched her chest. "That scared me! What a big bark from such a little dog!"

"A buffalo." Grant pointed straight ahead. A buffalo blocked the road. Pickles barked a few more times, looking proud for warning his human companions of the danger ahead. "Good boy!"

The buffalo blocked them for half an hour. "Maybe we'll get stuck here all day and I won't have to go home. Tiffany will be sure to be gone by then." Grant grinned.

"She seemed like a nice person, though."

"Nice? Sure, I guess. But I'm not interested...in her." Grant's eyes locked on Lottie's.

She smiled. They way he'd added the last part "in her" made her cheeks flush and her neck hot. Her eyes teared. She didn't know what to 'say. But she didn't have to say a word. Just then, Pickles farted. It was loud and smelled like rotten egg. Lottie and Grant simultaneously batted the air away from their noses and rolled down their windows, laughing uncontrollably.

"The first thing we have to do when we get to Lawton is get some quality dog food and get this dog's ass under control. Brutus used to stink up my truck worse than this. Then I switched him to a raw diet and, well, he still stunk up the truck, but it wasn't quite as often and wasn't quite as bad."

Lottie laughed. She'd never laughed about farting with David. He told her that there was nothing that turned him off more than a woman who farted. She hid every single one of hers and never mentioned the topic again.

Chapter Fourteen

Grant

Lottie opened the container with the egg rolls and fished one out for Pickles. He gobbled it down in less than two bites.

"That's probably not going to help his farts." Grant smiled at her.

Her cheeks flushed, and she looked out the window. "Yeah, I guess not."

He loved the way she looked when she was a little embarrassed. The pink in her cheeks suddenly matching her lips, lips he couldn't stop thinking about kissing. She let her hair fall forward to hide her face. That was something else he noticed she did when she was embarrassed. He wanted to reach over and tuck her hair behind her ear and stare at her face. Only the fact that he was driving stopped him.

He wasn't ready for their time together to be over, but he knew he had to eat and get back home with the six pack of beer that he would insist he was craving but couldn't find in Altus. Then maybe he'd say how he ran into an old friend while doing so. Okay, part of him didn't want Nana to have any more reason to dislike

Lottie than she already seemed to have. So what if she'd been married? She was free now, and he wasn't interested in faking anything with Tiffany just to please Nana or Papa Joe's memory.

Pickles wagged his tail, patiently waiting for another egg roll. Grant reached over and pulled one from the container. Lottie grinned at him.

"Well, it's adoption day. He needs to celebrate." Grant scratched Pickles behind the ear as he chomped the egg roll down and then stared at the container as though trying to will one of them to fish out another.

"Grant?"

"Yeah?"

"Do you think I should change his name?" Lottie twirled her fingers in Pickles's back hair. "I'm not sure he looks like a Pickle. How did you decide to name Brutus, Brutus?"

"Oh, he looked like a Brutus. Open the glove box. I've got a picture of him in there."

Lottie opened the glove box and pulled out a picture of an odd-looking dog that reminded her of Scrappy-Doo. "You're right. He definitely looks like a Brutus. So handsome."

"He was a good boy. I carry that picture in my truck because I miss having him ride around with me. I know it's not the same, but sometimes I like to get that picture out, when I'm waiting somewhere since I'm usually always early," Grant winked at her, "and just look at it and remember all the good times we had together." Grant did his best not to get teary. He wasn't sure if Lottie was the type of girl that was turned off by a man who cried.

"Do you ever think about getting another dog?"

"I thought about it, but I figure I'll just let another dog find me. Like Brutus did." Grant looked straight ahead. He could hear Lottie sniffle, and he was afraid if he saw any tears in her eyes, he wouldn't be able to stifle his any longer.

"Do you think I should rename him? Or is that mean?" Lottie gently placed Brutus's photo back in the glove box and closed it.

"I don't think it's mean. I'm sure Brutus wasn't always called Brutus. They adapt quick, and I doubt Pickles was at the shelter long enough to grow attached to the name. If you're worried about confusing him, just give him two names for a while and eventually drop the Pickles and just call him by his new name."

Lottie stroked the dog for a while. Grant glanced over at her a few times, lost in thought. She was beautiful. Everything about her was perfect, and he couldn't figure out how anyone could have ever let her go.

"Do you want me to take you to pick up your car before we head back to your place?"

"No, I'll just get it later. Maybe I'll even take Pickles on a walk this evening and we'll pick it up then."

"Okay, then you're going to have to tell me how to get to your house."

Lottie gave Grant directions to her little rental.

"I know where that is." Grant grinned. "My best friend in elementary school lived on your road. Probably just a few doors down."

Once they pulled into the driveway, Grant started to laugh. "Oh yeah. He lived next door. A crazy old man used to live here who always yelled at us for walking too close to his grass on the driveway. We never once stepped foot on his lawn, but we'd walk just as close as we could to hear him yell from the window, 'Get the fuck off my lawn. Fuck kids.'" Grant covered his mouth. "Sorry about the language."

Lottie laughed. "I don't mind. I hear much worse from Beth every day."

She handed the Chinese food bags to Grant, pulled open her purse, and fumbled through for the key. "Beth did give me the key. Right?"

"Yeah. I saw her do it."

Lottie dumped the contents onto her lap, blushing when a tampon tumbled onto the floor. She quickly grabbed it up and slid it under the purse. Grant grinned. Why was she so cute when she was embarrassed?

"Here it is." She held it up and handed it to him. "Knowing me, I'll end up shoving it right back in my purse with the rest of this stuff. I really need to clean this out."

Once everything was back in her purse, Grant handed her the key. She opened the car door, helped Pickles out, and unlocked the house.

"Welcome."

"Nice place." Grant removed his shoes the moment he came inside.

Lottie let go of Pickles's leash, and he promptly scuttled over, hiked his leg, and pissed on the corner of the couch.

"Pickles! No! Bad boy!" Lottie clapped her hands, scooped up his leash, and led him out to the patio. She closed the sliding glass door behind him. "Is adopter's remorse a thing? I didn't think about house training."

"Don't worry." Grant followed her into the kitchen as she got a bucket, soap, and scrub brush from under the sink. "He'll learn. You know what I did with Brutus. I kept him on his leash during the day for two weeks. He went everywhere I went. If he even looked like he was going to hike his leg, I'd make a loud noise and say, 'No!' then I'd take him outside. Every time he peed outside, I made a big deal cheering for him and brought him back inside for a treat."

"Two weeks? What do I do when I'm gone?"

"You can put him in the crate. He'll be okay in there. And once he's house trained, you can let him out for a little longer each time you're gone and see how he does. You might find he goes in the crate anyway while you're out. Brutus always did while I was gone."

"That's not mean? Putting him in the crate while I'm at work all day?"

"Well, call it his den, then. Trust me, it's not mean. He'll be less stressed than if you come home and find pee everywhere and start yelling at him. He won't know why you're mad and it'll just keep happening. I promise it won't take long."

Lottie began scrubbing the carpet. "I hope you're right or my landlord will take one look at stains everywhere and kick us both out."

"Why don't I bring in the supplies and set the crate up while you do that? Then we can eat." Grant stuffed his shoes on and went outside. He brought in all her supplies. "Where do you want the crate?"

"Um. How about in my bedroom? Down the hall to the left." Lottie finished scrubbing the pee out of the carpet, and Grant headed into her bedroom to set up the crate.

He looked around for the best place to put it and noticed a guitar leaned up against the wall near the window. "Do you play guitar?"

"Not well," she called. "I used to take lessons, but I never practiced enough and kind of gave up. Why? Do you play?"

"Only for about the past twenty years." Grant could hear Lottie pouring Pickles's pee water into the toilet and rinsing out the bucket. He moved the guitar aside and set up the crate. Lottie was soon in the room sitting on the bed. He suddenly found himself wanting to kiss her again.

After the crate was assembled, she stood and inspected it. "I guess that doesn't look so bad. You're sure he'll like it?"

"I'm sure he'll be fine. It's got to be better than being in the shelter. And you might never need to use it anyway. You'll figure things out before you know it."

"Ready to eat?" Lottie tucked her hair behind her ear.

"Yeah. Let's eat." Grant followed her into the kitchen, where she handed him a plate and fork. They filled their plates and took them into the dining room. "Hey, would you like a beer? I've got some in the truck."

"No, thanks. Besides, how would you explain to your nana that two were missing when you finally do get back home?"

"I guess I could always tell her I guzzled them in the driveway quick to try to handle spending time with Tiffany." Grant rolled his eyes.

"You wouldn't do that!" Lottie laughed, and a noodle flew out of her mouth. "Oh my god, sorry. I'm so gross." She scooped it up in her napkin.

Grant chuckled and wondered if she had any idea of how cute she was.

After eating, Grant helped Lottie clean up. As she washed the dishes, he grabbed the dishtowel that was hanging on the oven rack, asking her where things went so he could put them away. Since there was only the two of them, it didn't take long before he sighed, realizing he had better get back home.

"I hope Nana isn't too mad at you." Lottie bit her lip as she stood at the door as he pushed on his shoes.

"Don't worry about it. She'll probably be a little upset at me, but I'll just remind her that she had intruded on my plans for the day. Also, that I don't want to spend any more time with Tiffany than I have to." Grant grinned. "See you at work on Monday. Text me if you need anything. I know it can be a little overwhelming with a new pet in the house. Tell Pickles I said goodbye."

"I will." Lottie leaned on the doorframe as Grant stood on the stoop, lingering.

"I had fun with you today," he said as his heart pounded. All he could think about was kissing her. He had a split second before he'd either be able to lean in and go for it or turn and walk away.

"Me too." She smiled, her eyes resting on his in a way that told him he should move in for the kiss.

Grant stepped forward, leaned in, and placed his hand on her face. His lips swept over her warm, sweet lips. She didn't pull away but parted her lips, inviting his tongue inside. He reached around her waist and pulled her close to his body. Her fingers found their way around his neck, grabbing hold and keeping him there.

"Oooooooooooh!" neighbor kids shouted and giggled as they walked by on the sidewalk.

Lottie's face flushed as they laughed at the kids pointing and covering their still-giggling faces. "Fuck kids," Lottie whispered.

Grant laughed and shook his head in agreement. "Maybe that old man wasn't so crazy after all."

Lottie nodded and giggled.

"Can I take you out to dinner on Friday?" he asked.

"I'd like that." Lottie tucked her hair behind her ear.

Grant leaned in and kissed her on the cheek. "I'll see you Monday."

"See ya."

Grant climbed into his truck and drove off toward home, dreading the look of disappointment he was sure to get from Nana and Tiffany, if she was still there. *Please let her not be there.*

Pulling into the driveway, he noticed Tiffany's Vespa parked by the side of the road. He sighed and pulled the six pack from the small space behind the seats. He slowly twisted the doorknob and pushed the door open, hoping to get a hint of the mood inside before entering. Kicking off his shoes, he peeked into the kitchen. No one in there. He pulled one beer from the pack, cracked it open, and guzzled some down, although it was warm. Placing the rest in the fridge, he walked around in through the dining room and noticed Nana and Tiffany out on the patio, chatting.

Fuck.

Grant sucked in a deep breath and slid the patio door open.

"Grant! We were starting to get worried about you. Where have you been?"

"I was craving a particular IPA from Planted Flag, but they didn't have it in town, so I had to drive to Lawton to find it." Grant scratched the back of his neck.

"Planted Flag? I've never heard of that." Tiffany snatched the bottle from his hand.

"They're in Ohio. Best beer I've ever had."

"We have all the best beers at Meers, so I doubt it's better than anything we have there." Tiffany sniffed the beer inside.

Grant crinkled his nose. What did she know about beer? She didn't even look old enough to drink. She should know it's rude to practically shove someone else's bottle of beer up your nose. He'd need more to put up with her the rest of the evening.

"Can you help me get some snacks from inside, Grant?" Nana stretched out her arm to him for help up.

He knew that was code for "I'm going to give you a talking to."

"Yes, ma'am." He took her arm and helped her up, opening the door for her and following her into the kitchen.

Nana pulled open the refrigerator and began arranging some crudités on a plate, encircling a bowl of her homemade ranch dressing. He knew the longer she worked without saying anything directly corresponded to her level of anger at him. She was nearly finished with the snacks and glasses of pink lemonade she poured and placed on a tray before she turned to him, shaking her head.

"Now, Grant. This is the second time you've deserted our guest. It's rude behavior, and I didn't raise you to behave this way. Tiffany is my very dear friend, and I'm going to ask you to stop being so rude to her."

Grant sucked in a deep breath and fought the urge to roll his eyes, wishing he could tell his nana that she needed to stop trying to set him up with the girl. But knowing how fragile she still was after Papa Joe's death, he didn't have the heart to say anything other than "yes, ma'am" and promise himself he'd do his best to behave the rest of the evening. Worse case, he'd just have to be straight with Tiffany and tell her that he wasn't interested in her.

Chapter Fifteen

Lottie

Lottie watched Grant's truck drive off. She closed the door and leaned against it. Resting her fingers on her just-kissed, plump lips, she wished she could taste him again. Now she was sure he liked her. It was a little unimaginable to her that he could possibly want to spend time with—and kiss—her, when he had a twenty-something, redheaded beauty wanting his attention.

A scratching on the patio door glass broke through her daydream. Pickles wanted inside. She sprinted down the hall and opened the door. He ran inside, jumped on the couch, and curled up.

"Hey, that's my spot." Lottie nudged him over and sat next to him. He placed his head on her lap and closed his eyes. "It's been a big day, huh, boy?" Lottie grabbed the remote and flicked on the TV, searching for something to watch. She was excited to take Pickles for a walk and tell Beth all about the kiss and how Grant asked her on a date, but it looked like Pickles wasn't ready to go anywhere any time soon.

She scratched his ears and watched old episodes of *Three's Company* until she woke up with drool dripping down her chin. Pickles was nowhere to be seen. Lottie couldn't see him, but she could hear that he was up to no good. She followed the noise to the kitchen, where, as she suspected, Pickles had knocked over and was nosing through the trash.

She clapped her hands. "Pickles, no! Bad boy." She shooed him out of the kitchen and began picking up the scattered trash when he trotted over to the doorway and pissed on the wall. "Pickles! No! Outside!"

Lottie chased him to the back door and let him out. *Fuck.*

Regret had set in. She didn't know how to train a dog. She certainly didn't want to text Grant already and let him know what a difficult time she was having. Taking a few deep breaths, she returned to the kitchen, finished cleaning up the trash, and cleaned the pee from the wall.

Pickles's leash was hanging on the coat hook in the hallway. She grabbed it and got Pickles from outside. "You and I are going to be hooked together all day from now on, buddy. What do you say we go for walk? We'll figure this out."

Keep a positive mental attitude. It's only going to be rough in the beginning.

She bent down and scratched Pickles behind the ears before stepping outside and locking the door. They headed through the neighborhood, cut through the park, and walked between a few houses to make their way into Beth's development—the one she used to live in. It's where most of the officers who didn't reside on base lived. All the houses were new, brick, and way overpriced for such a small Oklahoma town.

Her old house was two doors down from Beth's, and it always felt so odd to walk by it now. It was almost as if she never lived there. It was like being married to David was only a dream that swiftly turned into a nightmare. Lottie felt a tug on the leash and turned to realize that Pickles was taking a shit. She was grateful that Grant had convinced her to buy the little bone-shaped container of poop bags to hook onto the leash. A man cutting his grass was giving her daggers, watching to make sure she cleaned up after her dog. She pulled out a bag and picked up the poop, trying to avoid eye contact with the man watching her. Even though she was doing the "right" thing, she was mortified over the action of doing it. She closed the bag and scuttled the rest of the way down the street and up Beth's driveway.

She rang the doorbell, and the door opened. Lottie held out the poop bag. "Truffle delivery!"

She jumped when Michael replied, "Uh, no thanks."

"Oh, sorry, Michael, I was expecting Beth to answer."

"That's okay." Michael grinned shaking his head. "You two are weird. I'm used to it. Who's this?" He bent over and scratched Pickles.

"This is Pickles. I just got him today."

"Tibetan Terrier?"

"I think so." Lottie smiled.

"Come on in. I'll take your poop bag unless you really want to give it to Beth."

Lottie handed it to him. "That's okay. Thanks, Michael."

"Sure thing." Michael headed off through the house and out on the patio to throw the bag in the trash.

Beth came out of the hallway from her bedroom. "Hey, Lottie. Hey, Pickles. So how was the trip to Lawton?"

"Can we go out on the patio? I'm worried Pickles will pee in your house."

"Sure."

Michael held the door open for them as they went outside.

"He kissed me!" Lottie could barely hold the words in. She covered her face but peeked at Beth through spread fingers.

Beth grinned and sang, "Finally!"

Lottie giggled and continued hiding her face a bit from Beth, who grabbed her wrist and pried her hands away.

"Look how hard you're blushing. It must have been good! Details!"

Lottie flopped down in the patio chair and covered her face once more.

Beth sat down next to her. "She's speechless. It was that good, huh?"

Lottie nodded, afraid that if she opened her mouth, she'd let out the squeal that had bubbled into her throat.

"I guess now you can stop doubting that he likes you. I told you. You need to listen to me more often."

Lottie nodded in agreement. "He asked me on a date."

"When?" Beth leaned forward, placing her hand on her chin.

"Friday. We're going out for dinner."

"Do you know where you're going yet? The restaurant pickings are slim in Altus."

"I don't know yet. I'm sure we'll decide this week."

"You should invite him to your place for dinner and then have him for dessert." Beth waggled her eyebrows.

"I'm not going to sleep with him on the first date. We just had our first kiss." Lottie shook her head. "Besides, I'm technically still married."

Beth's lip curled. "Right, like David is busy being faithful to you. Fuck him, Lottie. No, fuck Grant; he's hot. We're too old to do that whole waiting game. We are women in our thirties. We have needs!"

"I don't want him to think I'm easy or a whore or something." Lottie tucked her hair behind her ear.

"Well, don't make him wait too long when that Tiffany is wagging her pussy in his face." Beth rolled her eyes.

"He's not interested in her. He told me."

"Honey, he might not be interested in dating her, but that doesn't mean he won't fuck her if he's horny enough."

Lottie frowned and stared at her shoes.

"I'm sorry. I shouldn't have said that. Grant isn't David."

"No, he's not. And I don't want to make the same mistakes with Grant that I did with David. Like sleeping with him too soon." Lottie ran her fingers along the edge of the patio table, averting her eyes from Beth.

"Nothing you did in your relationship with David was wrong. All the wrongs are his. Completely." Beth placed her hand on Lottie's, squeezing it. "You know that, right?"

Lottie shrugged. Tears formed in her eyes. Was she ready for a relationship again? Suddenly, everything seemed a little more terrifying than it had before. Sure, now she knew he definitely liked her, but could she trust a man again?

"I think I'm going to get going." Lottie untangled Pickles's leash from the chair. "I need to feed Pickles, and I want to get David's stuff ready to ship out tomorrow."

"You're finally going to send it?"

"Yeah. I think I was holding myself hostage by hanging onto it and the idea that he was going to want me back."

Beth threw her arms around Lottie and squeezed her tight. "I'm proud of you, and I hope that you're finally going to be able to think about yourself and be happy again."

Lottie nodded. "Me too." She pulled away from Beth's embrace and wiped a tear that had rolled down her cheek. "C'mon, Pickles. Let's go home."

Beth slid open the patio door for Lottie and Pickles. "Let me just grab your key." She raced into the kitchen and fished it off a hook on the wall, handing it to her. "Call me if you want help packing up the last of David's things."

"I will." Lottie smiled and headed out to her car; Pickles jumped inside. She rolled down the windows so he could stick his head out and headed home.

***

Lottie's stomach flipped as she pulled into the school parking lot on Monday morning and saw Grant leaning on his truck, waiting for her. She could feel the heat already filling her cheeks and her pelvis. She desperately wanted to feel his body pressed against hers again. The anticipation overwhelmed her.

After parking, he opened her car door and took her hand. "Good morning."

"Good morning." She smiled.

He took her bags and carried them inside for her. "So how did things go with Pickles?"

"Well, not long after you left, he got into the trash and peed on the wall." Lottie shrugged.

Grant chuckled. "Sounds like it'll be all downhill from here. He's a smart dog. I bet he learns how to behave himself in no time."

"I kept him on the leash all day yesterday, like you told me, and he only tried to pee in the house once before I stopped him. He put his leg down so fast! I almost felt bad and thought he was never going to pee again. But he did as soon as I took him outside to a tree, and then I praised him. I did feel bad putting him in the crate when I left, but he didn't seem to mind."

Grant handed her bags back to her at the classroom door. "See you at lunch?"

"Yeah. See ya." Lottie smiled and watched him walk to his class, sneaking a quick peek at his butt, her cheeks flushing when the thought of seeing him naked passed through her mind. It had been a while since she had sex. And the last sexual encounters she had with David made her feel like dirt. She knew for at least the

150

last six months of their marriage he was also having sex with Veronica. Deep down inside, she knew that he probably wasn't thinking about her during those times and who knew how much beforehand.

Lottie shook those bad thoughts from her head, turned, and walked into the classroom. She stopped short when she noticed a bouquet of pink roses on her desk. She floated over to them, closed her eyes, and sniffed them. Warmth spread throughout her body as she opened her eyes. A card sat perched with her name scrawled across the front. She opened the envelope. "Looking forward to Friday. Grant." Pulling a rose from the vase, she brushed the petals along her lips, unable to remember the last time someone had given her flowers or had looked forward to spending time with her.

The rest of the morning, the grin that had taken hold of her lips could not be erased, no matter what was happening in the classroom. Every time the kids were working silently at her desk, she'd pick up the rose and breathe the fragrance deep into her lungs. Even when one of the boys chewed up some gum and stuck it into a girl's hair, the situation couldn't erase the tingle that radiated up and down her spine.

The smile grew wider when Grant popped his head around the corner, carrying his lunch sack.

"Thank you for the flowers." Although she'd always been embarrassed when given gifts or having someone spend money on her, she wasn't shy accepting them and thanking Grant.

"You're welcome." He smiled. "I hope you like roses. The lady at the flower shop said most women do

151

and that they're non-toxic to dogs. So you don't have to worry if Pickles gets into them."

Tears filled Lottie's eyes, and she felt breathless. Her hands flew to her face to hide the tears that were now threatening to escape.

"Hey, you all right?" Grant placed his hand on her back.

"I'm fine." She waved and wiped away the tears. Grabbing a tissue from the desk, she quickly dabbed her eyes. "It's just really thoughtful."

"Well, it's easy to think of you." Grant kissed her cheek.

Lottie turned and grabbed his face, kissing him fully, tasting his honey-sweet tongue. She wished they weren't at the school as she pulled away, looking around to make sure no one had seen such a passionate kiss taking place in an elementary school classroom.

She pulled open her drawer and took out her lunch, breaking her cookie in two and giving him half.

"So where would you like to go for dinner on Friday night? Do you like Italian? We could go to Roma's." Grant took a bite of the cookie.

"No! I, uh, I don't want to go there." Although her voice was shrill, she was hoping she'd calmed it enough for him not to ask why she'd had such a strong reaction to the place. She just couldn't have her first date with Grant be the place where David had broken her heart. "How about The Plaza?"

"Sounds good to me. What time should I pick you up? Seven?"

"Seven is good. That will give me time to feed Pickles and take him for a walk before we go out."

"You're stickin' with Pickles, then?"

"Yeah. You know, he just seems like a Pickles. I can't imagine changing it now. I guess if I were going to, I should have done it in my head before I spent so much time with him at the shelter."

"True. Brutus showed up in my life with no name assigned." Grant sighed. "I'm jealous of you a bit. I miss Brutus so much."

"Well, you can wait until I'm done cleaning up pee and garbage all the time before you're jealous of me."

"True." Grant chuckled. "I promise it won't take long before he knows all the rules and all you two are doing is enjoying your time together. That's a smart dog. You can tell. The way he worked us for those egg rolls, a dumb dog wouldn't have known how to do that."

Lottie laughed. "I guess you're right. He knows how to look pathetic and like he's never eaten in his whole life. He got half of my egg omelet this morning, and it's not because I wasn't hungry."

Before they knew it, the bell rang. Grant scooped up his containers and shoved them back into his sack. "See you after school?"

"Yeah, see ya." After he walked out, Lottie pulled the rose out the vase again and held it to her chest.

Chapter Sixteen

Lottie

Beth was sprawled out across Lottie's bed, flipping through one of the many magazines she'd brought over for hairstyle ideas for Lottie's date. Even though Lottie had rejected every hairstyle Beth suggested, she kept searching for and suggesting more.

"I think I just want to wear it down. It hides my profile. I hate my profile." Lottie flipped her hair from side to side in the bathroom mirror.

"What the fuck does that mean? You hate your profile?" Beth stared up from the magazine at Lottie.

Lottie ignore Beth's scrunched-face reflection eyeing her in the mirror.

"I hate my nose. It's so pointy, and from the side, I think I look like a witch." Lottie jumped when the magazine came sailing into the bathroom, hitting her in the butt. "That hurt."

"Good!" Beth rolled off the bed and charged into the bathroom. She took Lottie by the shoulders and turned her to the side. "I ought to smack you. You have the world's most perfect nose. They're supposed to be pointy. Do you want it all pushed up like a pig nose?"

"No, but..."

"Besides, witches' noses are crooked." Beth spun Lottie back to face the mirror. "Wear your hair up so he can see your neck and think about how much he wants to kiss it. Then, when you bring him home to fuck him, you can have that magic moment where you let your hair down like a wild lion ready to devour him."

"Female lions don't have manes."

Beth rolled her eyes. "Okay, wear your hair down. It'll hide the marks I'm going to leave from strangling you."

Lottie stomped her foot. "Fine. You can put it up, but don't pick that hairstyle that looked like a peacock, and if I hate it, I'm taking it down."

Beth clapped her hands and jumped up and down slightly. "Yay! Grab the curling iron, your brush, the hairspray, and a few pins and ties and bring them to the dining room." She walked out of room.

"Your arms aren't broken," Lottie muttered as she loaded the hair supplies and her makeup—which she was sure Beth was going to insist she let her do—into a small basket and headed into the dining room.

Beth plugged in the curling iron and pulled out a chair. "Sit down. Oh, good, you brought the makeup!" Beth rubbed her hands together.

"I'm not a doll, you know. Or a whore!" Lottie pointed her finger in Beth's face.

"I'm going to make you look amazing."

"Yeah right. You'll probably leave me looking like the girl gremlin."

"No fuckin' way. I'm a master." Beth picked up the brush and began gently pulling it through Lottie's hair.

She sighed. "I love having my hair brushed."

155

"Oh, I know. Me too. Michael loves to brush my hair."

"Really? David never brushed mine. But I don't think I ever asked him to either."

"You need to be more forward with the things you want. I have a feeling Grant will be very eager to give you anything your little heart desires. He's so smitten with you."

"You really think so?"

Beth pulled Lottie's hair teasingly. "Are you kidding me? He's got the hots for you so bad. Who ignored a horny redhead ready to suck his cock to be with you? Who gave you flowers? Who knocked you off your socks with a kiss that gave you the kind of look I never saw David give you?"

Lottie's face and neck burned with heat. She buried her face in her hands.

"You drive me nuts sometimes with the way you doubt how beautiful you are. You're amazing. I told you before and I'll tell you again, if I was a dyke, you'd be the only pussy for me." Beth picked up the curling iron and began working on Lottie's hair.

"You should really think about writing poetry, you know. You have such a beautiful way with words." Lottie shook her head.

Beth grabbed her head to keep it still. "I know. Now don't move or I'm going to end up putting a burn mark across your face."

"I'm so nervous, Beth. I never thought I'd ever be dating again. I thought I'd be married forever." Lottie sighed.

"I know, sweetie. But if I'm being completely honest with you, I never really liked David, and neither

156

did Michael. He hated whenever he had to fly with David. Everyone in the office called him Douche instead of David behind his back. Hand me a hair pin." Beth held out her hand.

Lottie placed a pin in it. "Why didn't you ever tell me that before?"

"Uh, cuz I'm not an asshole. No one wants to tell their friend that everyone hates their husband and calls him Douche."

"Why didn't you tell me after he left?"

"Because you still had your heart set on him coming back. And what if he did come back and then I'd be the horrible friend that hates your husband and we couldn't be friends anymore?" Beth leaned forward and kissed Lottie on the cheek. "And I am keeping you forever."

"Are you hiding how you really feel about Grant, then?"

"Honey, I think Grant is hot as fuck, and he's absolutely perfect for you. He's the kind of guy you deserve. Another pin."

Lottie handed Beth another pin and thought back to all the First Fridays they'd had at the squadron, never knowing that all the people smiling and chatting with them were secretly thinking of how much they hated her husband and that they all called him Douche.

"Beth, if they called David 'Douche,' did they call me something too?" Lottie pursed her lips and closed her eyes.

"No fuckin' way. Everyone loves you. Michael always asked me what the fuck you were doing with a guy like that, cuz you're so sweet and all. So what did you see in him anyway, besides his looks?"

"I don't know. He's really handsome and maybe part of me always felt that I should be grateful that someone as good looking as him wanted anything to do with me." Lottie sucked in the tearful feelings that bubbled up.

"Oh my god. You need your eyes checked. You're beautiful! David is not out of your league. Seriously, if you add in personality, you're waaaaaaay out of his. Pin."

"You're so good to me, Beth. I never would've made it through David leaving if it wasn't for you, and I probably wouldn't be going out with Grant tonight, either."

"I know, honey. And you wouldn't have this awesome hair, either. Go look in the mirror before I start your makeup!"

Lottie and Beth scampered down the hall and into the bathroom. A large grin overtook Lottie's face when she looked at her hair in the mirror. "I love it!"

"I told you I was good. Now let's go do your makeup."

***

Her hair and makeup done, wearing the dress that Beth lent her, Lottie stood staring at the full-length mirror with Beth grinning and nodding behind her.

"You're a knockout, Lot."

"Thanks to you." Lottie's eyes stayed glued on the mirror. It looked like her. It wasn't like she didn't recognize herself, but she'd never looked into the mirror before unable to find fault somewhere. Her hair, her makeup, the dress, they all seemed to bring out her best features and hide any flaws that would have otherwise grabbed hold of her attention and made every positive quality moot.

"I'd like to be here when Grant comes to check out his expression when he sees you, but I know that would be awkward as fuck. So I'm just going to grab my purse and Pickles and get the hell out of here."

"Thanks for watching him tonight." Lottie hugged Beth. "And thanks for everything."

"Don't you dare start crying and ruin that beautiful makeup job I did." Beth squeezed her tight. "You deserve this."

Beth grabbed Pickles's leash from the key hook and went to the back door. "Pickles! C'mon boy, you're staying the night with Aunt Beth and Uncle Michael." She hooked his leash on when he came tail-wagging to greet Beth, who he'd grown very fond of over the last week.

"Remember to keep him on the leash! He's stopped peeing here, but I don't know if he'll pee in your house since he's somewhere new."

"Oh, don't worry about that. If he pees, I'll make Michael clean it. It'll be payback for all the times I have to clean up piss from around the toilet when he comes home drunk from the o'club." Beth blew a kiss to Lottie and headed out the door.

Lottie closed the door and returned to her mirror. She still had twenty minutes before Grant was supposed to arrive, and she wasn't quite sure what to do with herself. She held her hand over her mouth and nose and huffed to check her breath. It seemed fine, but she decided she better brush again, especially her tongue. She was not planning on sleeping with him like Beth kept insisting would happen, but she sure hoped there'd be kissing. And lots of it.

Lottie wrapped a towel around her neck, paranoid that she'd drip toothpaste on her dress, would have to change at the last minute, and ruin her hair when she pulled on something new.

Happy that she didn't even mess up her lipstick or slop toothpaste down her chin, she smiled at herself in the mirror and gave a little nod. She grabbed the small clutch she borrowed from Beth and put her ID, lip gloss, and wallet inside.

Again, she turned to the full-length mirror and smoothed her hands over her body. The lack of fast food was already making a difference in her body. She could only imagine the changes she could make if she started going to spin and the reservoir with Beth more often. That's when she'd sleep with Grant. When she was just as confident without clothes as she was in them right now. Her face flushed just thinking about sleeping with him, she wanted it. Badly. Her pelvis got warm, and a tingle rushed through her. If she was going to resist him tonight, she was going to have a hard time doing it.

The doorbell rang. Lottie's heart slammed into her stomach. Grant was early. She should have expected it, knowing how much he hated being late. She grabbed her clutch and pulled open the door with a wide grin, excited to see the look on his face when he saw how good she looked.

The smile plummeted to the floor.

David stood on the porch.

"What are you doing here?" Her voice was tipped in anger, and her eyebrows slammed together.

"Great to see you, too." David brushed passed her. "This is your new place?" He shook his head as he looked around.

Lottie burned with anger and felt embarrassed about her meager circumstances at the same time. "What are you doing here?"

"You already asked that. Guess I better answer it. The sims in Hawaii are down for maintenance. I'm deploying, so I've got to get my training done. I leave for Al Udeid on Wednesday. You look pretty. Why do you look like that?"

"How long are you deploying for?" Lottie shifted, hoping he wouldn't ask her where she was going again and hoping she could get rid of him before Grant showed up.

"Forty-five. What's going on? You got a date or something?" David chuckled.

Lottie tucked a loose tendril behind her ear, shrugging.

"Oh." David's brow furrowed. "Who's the guy? Someone from the squadron? Not one of my friends?" His voice deepened near a growl.

"It's no one you know. But he's going to be here soon. I have your stuff all ready to mail out so you can come by and get it tomorrow." Lottie opened the door for David to leave and noticed Grant's truck turning onto her street.

Fuck.

"That's not why I stopped by. I need to talk to you, Lottie." David's attention turned to the door as the headlights appeared in the driveway. "Does he know you're married?"

"Does that matter?" Lottie snapped. "It didn't to you."

The sound of the car door silenced them both. Grant smiled at Lottie through the glass of the storm door. He held a bouquet of daisies. His eyes shifted to David.

Lottie opened the door. Grant handed her the flowers. "Hey, Lottie." He kissed her on the cheek.

David stuck out his hand. "Hey man, I'm Lottie's husband, David."

Grant nodded and shook David's hand.

Lottie shuddered at the awkward feel in the room. Why did David have to show up tonight? Without warning. To fuck up her life once again?

"We're getting divorced." The words flew out of Lottie's mouth so fast, she shocked herself. She'd never really admitted it to herself before, but right now it was all she wanted everyone to know.

David's eyes drifted up and down Grant. "Well, we hadn't actually had that discussion yet."

"You've been living in Hawaii with your girlfriend for months. I'd say it's a discussion we don't need to officially have. What are you even doing here?" Lottie scowled and her fists clenched. Anger bubbled inside her that she wasn't sure she could contain. This wasn't what she wanted Grant to see on their first date. An explosion of anger and her husband.

"Lottie, I told you. The sim is undergoing maintenance at Hickam."

"Not that. Why are you at my house? You could have done your training without stopping by here. I'll mail you your clothes."

"I need to talk to you. It's really important." David turned to Grant. "Can you excuse us for a second, guy?"

"His name is Grant. And he doesn't have to go anywhere. We can talk later." Lottie brushed between them, pushing open the storm door and motioning for David to leave.

"I don't think I'll have much time later. I've got to get all my sim training done, and I'm all jacked up with jet lag. Can't we talk tonight?"

"No. As you can see, I have a date." Lottie's eyes narrowed, and her nostrils flared.

David pressed his hands together in a pleading motion. "Come on, Lottie. I'm sure Grant can take you out tomorrow night instead."

Lottie huffed and crossed her arms, and a few daisy petals fell to the floor.

"Lottie, if you two need to talk, I understand. We can try again some other time."

Glaring at David, Lottie's eyes filled with burning, angry tears. If Grant left her alone with David, she wasn't sure she wouldn't kill him. She turned to Grant. "I guess so. I'm not sure I'd be a good date now anyway."

Grant smiled at her, nodded to David, and walked out the door.

The headlights flashed over their faces as Grant pulled out of the driveway.

Chapter Seventeen

Grant

As Grant backed out of the driveway, his eyes were locked on Lottie's through the glass door. Hers looked like glass. At least she hadn't seemed happy that David was there.

Fuck.

Of course her husband had to look like that. Chiseled jaw, sharp featured, handsome. Grant could practically see his muscles and six pack rippling through his clothes. He looked like a character straight out of *Top Gun*, well, the Air Force version. Fire surged through his body. Didn't Lottie say David lived in Hawaii? What was he doing in Oklahoma? Had he come to reclaim her? From the look in her eyes, if that was the reason, she wasn't exactly receptive.

Grant drove past his road. There was no way he was going to return so quickly and put up with Nana's questions. He knew she didn't approve of the fact that Lottie was still married in the first place. This would be just the type of story that would convince Nana that she needed to steer him away from Lottie even harder.

He drove to Fat Daddy's, went inside, and ordered a farmhouse burger, onion rings, and a beer. At the table, he pulled out his phone and send Dan Cooley a text.

Grant: Date fell through. Up for Woody's?

Dan: What happened?

Grant: I'll tell you later. I'm at Fat Daddy's.

Dan: I'm already at Scooters. Meet me here when you're done.

Grant: Scooters?

Dan: It has the most women.

Grant: Ugh. Fine.

Grant put his phone away and devoured his burger, saving his onion rings for last. He figured he could combat any drunk, desperate skanks with onion breath. He'd do his best to be a good wingman for Dan for the evening. At least it would keep his mind off Lottie and David.

Shoving the last onion ring in his mouth, he chewed it as he grabbed his keys and walked out the door, cursing Dan for making him head to Scooters.

Grant sat in the parking lot listening to the muffled music and watching the tube-top-clad women walking inside in groups of threes and fours. He shook his head and popped open the truck door, sighed, and headed toward the building behind two blondes, one with chicken legs that turned in at the knees and the other trying to wear the same style clothes even though she was six sizes too big to dress in such a way. Why did women let their friends go out looking like such messes? Did they not have the heart to be honest or were they just destroying all competition? His eyes followed the bulges that swayed and giggled over the confines of the way too tight skirt, made of what must have been the toughest denim in all of Oklahoma.

"See something you like, honey?" The chicken-legged blonde eyed him up and down.

Grant shook his head, reached for the door, and held it open for them. He pressed his lips tight, trying not to cringe as the big one gave him a smile that let him know that she was all his if he'd only ask.

"Wanna join us?" Her voice boomed with a manliness that matched the black whiskers that were peeking through the pores of her chin.

Grant felt the bubble of an onion ring burp slide up his throat, so he went with it, letting it out. "No thanks, looking for a friend."

From the look on her face, the burp had traveled through the smell of stale of beer that lingered in the bar and landed directly in her nose. She smiled anyway. "If you change your mind, come find me."

Grant nodded and headed through the crowd.

"I'll save you a dance," she shouted after him.

He nodded again and raised his hand to acknowledge he'd heard her and that she wouldn't need to come find him later—just in case he hadn't heard. Grant slowly waded through the crowds of visiting airmen looking for someone to take home for the evening and the bleach blonde ladies and their chubby friends who were all too eager to fill the roll.

After taking two laps around the place, he pulled out his phone and texted Dan.

Grant: Where are you?

No reply.

I'm going to kill him if he already left with someone.

Grant made his way to the bar. At least with a drink in his hand he'd feel less uncomfortable than he did just standing and staring at people like some kind of perverted weirdo. He ordered a beer and sat down at a table that was miraculously empty.

Halfway through his beer—and a decision to leave when it was done—his phone buzzed in his pocket.

Dan: On the dance floor. Got two babes. Join me.

Grant: No. I'll wait. Got a table.

Grant leaned back, took a drink, and then wrinkled his nose when he noticed the big gal from earlier was now dancing—what was supposed to be seductively—in his eye line. Despite her efforts to make eye contact with him, he deflected it by pulling out his phone and scrolling through Twitter.

Hurry up, Dan.

Every time Grant dared peek up from his phone, his lady large would begin slowly rolling her shoulders and hips, rubbing her body up and down.

I'm gonna need another beer.

167

He chugged down the remainder of his beer and waved for a waitress.

"What can I get ya?" The waitress shouted so loudly he shuddered away from the sound.

"A beer."

"Got ya." She weaved her way through the crowd and over to the bar. When she returned, he paid her, gave a nice tip, and went back to his avoidance cycle of phone, beer, phone.

"Grant!" Dan Cooley slapped him on the back and pulled out a chair next to him. "Ladies, this is Grant. Grant, meet Tiffany and Brittany."

Grant raised a brow at the sounds of their trailer park names then looked up from his phone.

Fuck.

"Hey, Tiffany." Grant painted on the best false smile he could muster. He almost wished he could go back to watching the seductive dance of the water buffalo.

"Hi, Grant. How's Nana?"

"She's doin just fine." Grant took a long sip from his beer.

There goes Nana not finding out he didn't go out with Lottie for the evening. How was he going to explain this?

"Oh, you two know each other?" Dan grinned from ear to ear, obviously beyond three sheets to the wind.

Brittany, a pixie-haired brunette—who Grant wasn't entirely sure wasn't a man at some point—was sitting in Dan's lap with her arms wrapped around his shoulders.

"Tiffany is a friend of Nana's." Grant took another drink of his beer.

"Of Nana's? And yours too, I thought." Tiffany stuck out her bottom lip.

Grant pursed his lips and took another swig.

"Dannyboo, I wanna get shots!" Brittany slobbered as she spoke.

"Yes! Shots!" Tiffany bounced up and down in her seat.

"None for me, thanks." Grant thought about making his exit. He would rather take a nap in the parking lot of the reservoir than do shots with the trailer park twins and his drunk childhood friend.

"Waitress!" Dan waved his hand.

"What can I get ya?" The waitress smiled at Grant.

"We want four blow jobs!" Brittany ran her fingers along Dan's bottom lip.

"And a woo woo!" Tiffany added.

Grant fought the urge to roll his eyes. He held up his beer bottle to the waitress to let her know he'd take another. She nodded and headed to the bar. When she returned, Dan put a shot in front of Grant.

"Blowjob time!" Brittany wailed before leaning over and picking up the shot in her mouth, gulping it back like someone who never has a problem swallowing mouthfuls of various liquids.

Grant pushed the shot away and paid the waitress for his beer. And the shots. And the woo woo.

"Thanks for the drink." Tiffany smiled as she pulled it to her lips.

"You're welcome." Grant figured the sooner they all got drunk and passed out, the sooner they'd get to leave. But he was calling them a ride. There was no way any of them were going to throw up blow jobs in his truck.

"Dannyboo, I wanna dance some more." Brittany stood and pulled Dan to his feet.

"Come on, you two!" Dan motioned for Tiffany and Grant to follow.

"I'm good." Grant sipped his beer and pulled out his phone.

"Yeah, you guys go. I'm gonna sit this one out, too." Tiffany waved and smiled at Grant.

Fuck.

Something about Tiffany made it too easy for him to be rude. Normally, he didn't like to be rude to anyone, but the way she looked at him, like she expected him to adore her and try to talk to her, got on his nerves. Yes, she was pretty, but there didn't seem to be anything else to her.

Tiffany's jaw twitched, and she moved closer to Grant in small increments, like she had something to say but didn't. Grant cocked his head to one side and crossed his arms, looking away from her.

Suddenly, she slid her chair right up next to his.

"Hey, Grant. I can tell you don't like me." Tiffany reached over and took a drink of her woo woo. "And I know why. I mean, I wouldn't like if someone was always trying to set me up either. But I promise, I'm a nice person. And I really like your nana. I don't like to say no and let her down. I'm sorry that I intruded that day at the reservoir and stopped you from going out with your friend."

"I don't dislike you." Grant's eyes widened. He'd been rude enough that she'd noticed, and now he felt like an asshole. He probably was an asshole.

"Well, you dislike being forced to spend time with me. I honestly didn't know that your nana was going to invite me to dinner. She said you two were going to be walking at the reservoir and since she knew I ran, she said she'd love to see me there. I swear that's all. I promise. Then I didn't feel comfortable telling her no when she asked me to lunch." Tears balanced on the rims of Tiffany's eyes. "I'm really not a psycho, or however I may seem."

Grant's stomach sunk. He sighed and rubbed the back of his neck. "Welp, I'm kind of an asshole. Can I make it up to you?"

"Buy me another drink once I finish this one and we'll call it even." Tiffany took a sip of her drink.

"Fine, but you have to tell the waitress your order. There's no way I'm asking for a woo woo." Grant raised an eyebrow and grinned.

Tiffany's hand flew to her face. "Embarrassing, I know. But I don't drink much and it's really good. I wish it had a different name." She pushed her glass toward him. "Here, try a sip."

Grant pursed his lips, picked up the drink, and took a sip. He cocked his head to the side. "You know what, that is good. Not that I'll ever order one. I'll stick with beer." He looked out on the dance floor to see Brittany bent over and Dan practically slamming into her butt. "It's not going to be fun getting those two home tonight."

"As long as we call them a cab, they can take care of each other. When Brittany gets like this, I know there's no way I can talk her out of going home with a guy. Don't get me wrong, I'm not a bad friend, I'll still try, but there's only so much I can do. I worry about her." Tiffany shook her head.

"Well, Dan's a good guy. She'll be all right. Do you come to Scooters often?" Grant rolled his eyes. "I didn't mean for that to sound like a pickup line."

"I'm here almost every Friday night whether I want to be or not. Brittany never gets tired of coming here. Usually, I end up having a pretty good time. I love to dance." Tiffany smiled.

Grant pursed his lips and averted his eyes. "I hope that's not a hint. I don't dance. Especially to music that involves people forcing words to rhyme." He rolled his eyes.

"I'll dance to anything. I took ballet from the time I was three through high school, but I also like hip hop and jazz."

"It looks like everyone on the dance floor here is just dry humping to the beat."

Tiffany looked over to the dance floor and shrugged. "Maybe if you get a few more drinks in you, you'll change your mind?"

"Doubtful."

"We'll see." Tiffany waved the waitress over, ordered another beer for Grant and another woo woo for herself. "He's payin'." She grinned.

Grant smiled. Maybe he'd judged this girl way too harshly. And maybe if a song came on that wasn't completely horrible, he'd ask her dance.

***

A few more beers and a few stolen sips of Tiffany's woo woos later, Grant found himself a little drunk and out on the dance floor. Tiffany was a good dancer, and he found himself drawn in by her moves and her smile.

172

He also admired the way she looked after Brittany, convincing her to switch to water and lay off the shots for the rest of the evening. Grant didn't have as much luck with Dan, who only got more drunk as the night went on.

"You're gonna end up embarrassing yourself with a case of whiskey dick if you keep going this way," he told Dan as he ordered another whiskey and coke.

"I've never had a problem with my cock," Dan shouted over the music a little too loudly. Tiffany giggled and hid her face in Grant's shoulder.

"Okay. Don't say I didn't warn you." Grant held up his hands as he stepped away from the bar.

"You be concerned with your own dick." Dan waved him away and began guzzling his drink without paying.

The bartender raised a brow at Grant, who pulled out some cash and paid.

"It's almost closing time. I don't think I should drive." Grant pulled out his phone to look at the time, also noticing he had no messages from Lottie. Was David still there at 1:30 a.m.? "You know, I don't feel so good."

"Let's all split a ride. Then we can make sure that Dan and Brittany get home okay. I can bring you to get your truck tomorrow." Tiffany smiled.

"Ride on the back of your Vespa?" Grant crinkled his nose.

Tiffany cocked her head and pursed her lips. "I'll let you drive."

"I think I'd rather walk. Oh, and Tiffany, would you keep it to yourself that you saw me here tonight? I don't really want Nana to know."

"Sure thing. Now let's go get those drunks and send for the car before they're flooded with calls at closing time."

"Sounds good." Grant wrangled a very drunk Dan Cooley and a slightly less drunk Brittany to the front door while Tiffany called for a car.

Once they successfully dropped Dan and Brittany off at Dan's house, they went on to Tiffany's.

"Grant, I wasn't completely honest with you."

"About what?"

"Well, I didn't only come because Nana invited me. I also thought you were really cute, and I'm attracted to you."

The car stopped in front of her house. She leaned in and kissed Grant. He opened his mouth and pulled her closer, only stopping when the driver began clearing his throat.

Tiffany kissed him again softly on the lips. "Would you like to come in?"

Chapter Eighteen

Lottie

Lottie glared at David. She didn't have the energy or the will to fake a smile. He didn't deserve it. He was nothing but a crap maker. A make-Lottie's-life-crap maker. And why should she even care that he needed to talk? He was the one that had walked out the door and decided that there was nothing left to be said—with her, anyway.

David made his way into the living room and flopped down on the sofa, putting his boots up on the coffee table as if he lived there. "How long have you been dating that guy?" The words "that guy" were singed with disdain.

Lottie felt the hot ember in her stomach ignite. Hot tears burned down her face, and her throat couldn't contain the fire. "It's none of your fucking business, and get your dirty boots off my coffee table. *My* coffee table. The one I paid for after you had everything in our house packed up and moved to Hawaii! Go put your feet on Veronica's coffee table and get out of my life."

175

David jerked his feet from the table and sat up straight as though she were a general. "Lottie. I didn't mean to make you upset. I just wanted to come over and see if we could smooth things over. I don't like the way things ended between us, and I was hoping we could put the anger behind us."

"Are you kidding me? You busted my heart! You cheated on me and left me for the woman you cheated with. And you left me with nothing. The only reason you've ever called is to get the last few things you left behind in the dresser of the bedroom set—the only thing you left me with. You're a monster. You show up just in time to ruin a date with a man who treats me like you never did. You have no idea how much I want to punch you right now." Lottie's fist balled up and spittle shot from her lips as she spoke.

David stood. "You're right. I know it. I'm a jerk. Go ahead. Hit me." He held out his jaw out and closed his eyes. The tiniest bit of a grin pulled at the corners of his mouth, and before she knew it, Lottie's fist swung straight back and sprang forward again.

Caught off guard, David fell back onto the couch, stunned and gripping his lip, which had busted, blood dripping down his chin.

Lottie gasped and stared, but her body didn't move. Her thoughts scrambled through her mind like a carnival ride. He deserved it! That was awful. Fuck, yeah! Eat that! I'm so sorry. You asked for it! He asked for it. Didn't he ask for it?

Lottie spun on her heels and padded into the kitchen. She yanked a roll of paper towels from the counter and returned, holding them out to David. Still not saying a word, with eyes wide, he took them, wadded a bunch in his free hand, and jerked them free from the roll. He held it to his lip and pulled some more from the roll with his bloodied hand.

Lottie watched. It was all she could bring herself to do. Her hands dropped to her side. But then a giggle suddenly bubbled up her throat. She tried to suppress it but quickly lost the battle. She shook her head and raised her palms as David looked at her with disbelief running through his eyes. The giggle soon turned into a roaring laugh, and Lottie gripped at her aching ribs. Tears flowed down her cheeks.

"I'm sorry, David." The words came out sputtering.

"Yeah, you look really sorry." He pulled away the paper towel to check and see if his lip had stopped bleeding. He ripped off a few fresh pieces and put them on his lip.

"I'll take those." Lottie gathered up the bloody towels and headed into the kitchen. She opened the trash and tossed them in, stopping a moment to stare at David's bright red blood in her trashcan.

She let the lid drop. Most of her felt he deserved what he got, but a tiny piece of her felt bad about what she'd done. In their relationship, neither of them had ever gotten physically violent with the other. And part of her wasn't upset that she'd done it but that he might have the high ground now.

She turned the faucet on and washed her hands with soap and water. The cold water rinsed away some blood that had gotten on her knuckles. Was it his or hers? She wasn't sure. Her knuckles were sore to the touch, but she didn't see any cuts. Gathering two clean dish towels from the drawer, she placed ice in the center of each and wrapped them up. She returned and handed one to David, placing the other on her fist.

"I shouldn't have punched you." She sat in the recliner across from him.

"I shouldn't have done a lot of things to you, Lottie. I deserved it. Do you think you'll ever be able to forgive me?"

"For messing up our marriage or for ruining my date?" Lottie winced. Why did she already have to be so biting back at him when he was trying to apologize? Anger. Yes, she'd been hanging onto a lot of anger hidden behind a layer of hurt. And why should she forgive him anyway?

"Both. If I'd known you had a date, I wouldn't have come by."

Lottie scrunched her face and shrugged. "Maybe you should have called first."

"You're right. I should have, but on the flight here, I was thinking about all my other deployments and how you wrote me a letter every day I was gone. I guess I realized I was going to miss that. I love your letters."

"I'm sure Veronica will write you." Lottie looked away. Saying her name to him was like tasting acid.

"Nah, she's not the letter writing type. I'm sorry I didn't realize how much you loved me and all the special things about you. You really are one of a kind." He dropped the towel from his lip and smiled at her. The look in his eyes was so soft, she felt the icy burning of the frost that had been surrounding her heart melt.

"What are you trying to say, David?" Lottie cocked her head, her eyes now threatening to fill with tears.

"I miss you, Lottie."

"I miss you, too."

"I'm going to be busy while I'm here, getting my training done for the sim, and I know I have no right to ask this, but do you think you'd write to me while I'm deployed?" He put the towel back to his lip and winced.

Lottie stared at him for a moment. Her throat was suddenly dry, and her heart seemed to stand completely still as though it were waiting for her answer as well.

What would be the harm in writing him letters? Maybe it would be a step forward in healing their relationship. It had to be better than punching him. She couldn't say anything but nodded.

David got up and held out his hand to Lottie. She took it, and he pulled her up, wrapping her in a tight hug. It had been so long since she'd felt his body against hers. It was a good feeling, and she didn't want to let go. She wrapped her free arm around him and took a deep breath, trying to hold back tears.

He let go and took a step back, reached in his pocket, and pulled out a piece of paper. "Here's the squadron address. I'll send you a better one when I get there."

"Do you want to have lunch before you deploy on Wednesday?"

"How about tomorrow? My sim schedule probably won't line up with your school lunch."

"Okay. Where?"

"How about Roma's?"

Why would he take her to the place where he broke her heart? Lottie nodded. Maybe she could replace that bad memory with a new, good one. Besides, she'd really been missing their garlic bread.

"I guess. How about one o'clock?"

179

"That sounds good. I'll see you there." David pulled Lottie close. "I'm glad we can start over again." He kissed her softly on the lips.

A fluttering tickled her stomach. "I'm thirsty. Are you thirsty?"

"No, I'm fine. I better get back over to billeting and try to get some rest. My sleep schedule is going to be all fucked up for a while." He handed her the ice-filled towel.

"I'm sorry again about your lip."

"It's okay, Lot." David smiled, walked down the hall, and out the door.

"See you tomorrow," she called to the swinging door. Watching as the headlights of David's rental flashed on and then drove off down the street, the ice in the towel leaked and dripped down her dress. She looked down and realized the dress didn't just have splatters of water on it, there was blood too.

Shit!

Lottie tossed the towels into the kitchen sink and pulled the dress over her head, rinsing the blood spots under cold water. She glanced down at her breasts jiggling in her sheer black bra and realized how much she'd prepared just in case things went well with Grant —despite her protests to Beth. She never thought she'd be wearing her new sexy underwear in her kitchen while scrubbing her husband's blood out of her dress. It was much less of a Monica Lewinsky moment and more of a Rocky Balboa one.

Once she was sure she had all the stains rinsed out of Beth's dress, she hung it to dry over her shower rack, removed her makeup, and crawled into bed, curling up in her burrito of solitude. What exactly did he mean by being glad that they were starting over again? Did he mean as friends? Or did he want her back? He did want her to write to him every day. That's more than friends, wasn't it? And he didn't necessarily seem happy when he mentioned Veronica. Maybe he wasn't happy with her and this was his way of trying to get back together. But what about Grant? Did she even want to get back together with David?

Thoughts raced through her head, and she didn't want them there. She wanted to fall asleep and not deal with any of it now. Poking her arm out of the blanket burrito, she fumbled around on the nightstand until she felt the television remote and flicked it on. *Breakfast at Tiffany's* was on. Holly Golightly's craziness might just be enough to distract her from her thoughts.

Lottie stared at the screen, shaking her head every time her mind flashed to the evening—punching David, hugging David, kissing David. Grant's face upon meeting David and then leaving. No, she didn't want to deal with any of that. Ever. At least for now, she could put it off until the morning. If only she could drift off to sleep but that was the last thing her mind was going to allow her to do.

After the movie, she kicked off the blankets, padded out into the living room, and pulled open her clutch, searching for her cell. Her stomach dropped when she saw she had no messages. Nothing from Grant. He was probably mad. She wouldn't blame him if he never wanted to talk to her again. She could only imagine how she'd feel if she'd went to pick him up for a date and found his wife there. Or Tiffany.

What she felt that day that Tiffany showed up at the reservoir couldn't even feel like a fraction of what he had to be feeling right now. Maybe she should have kicked David out. Why wasn't she a stronger person? She didn't owe David anything and, so far as their relationship had been going, owed Grant more than what he got.

Lottie sent Beth a text.

Lottie: You up?

Beth: Yeah. What the fuck? Is your date over already?

Lottie: It never started. David showed up right before Grant did.

Beth *Emoji with eyes wide open. Poop emoji. Anger emoji*.

Lottie: Grant left. David stayed. I punched him and busted his lip.

Beth: Good. What did the Douche want? Other than to ruin your date.

Lottie: He's deploying and wants me to write him while he's gone. He wants us to start over again.

Beth: No fucking way. What did you say?

Lottie: I'm meeting him tomorrow for lunch. At Roma's *unamused face emoji.*

Beth: What time?

Lottie: One.

Beth: So, he wants you back, just when you find someone who makes you happy?

Lottie: I don't know if he wants me back. I don't want to discuss it all right now. We'll talk it over at the reservoir. Okay?

Beth: Fine. You better show up.

Lottie: I'll be there. I just don't want to talk about it anymore. I'm tired and I want to go to bed.

*Beth: All right. Goodnight, Lottie. *Face blowing a kiss emoji.**

*Lottie: Goodnight. *Face blowing a kiss emoji.**

Lottie tossed her phone on the nightstand and padded into the kitchen. She ripped open her cabinet and riffled through the various vitamins and cold and flu medications until she found the allergy medication that had knocked her out last winter and popped a few capsules. She downed a glass of water, headed back to bed, and resealed herself in her burrito with only her head sticking out enough to breathe and watch television. *Tootsie* was on now. Another good movie to keep her mind off things.

Lottie's phone rang. She kicked herself free and grabbed it. It was Grant.

"Hello?"

There was no answer. A butt-dial.

Lottie squished the phone into her ear harder—as though it would somehow help her hear better—and listen for as long as the call lasted. All she could hear was muffled talking, loud music, and a woman laughing.

A black hole opened in Lottie's stomach, sucking and twisting, pinching and pulling. He had gone out. He probably wasn't even thinking of her. Time seemed to stop. She kept listening until the phone went completely silent and she was left listening to the sound of blood rapidly whooshing in her ears.

The phone flew across the room. Lottie pulled the covers back over her body and stared blankly at the TV screen.

"Life lasts too long," she muttered before the heaviness of the antihistamine took over and she drifted off into black.

Chapter Nineteen

Grant

Grant's head pounded, and his stomach swirled with nausea. The moment his eyes fluttered open, he slammed them shut again. The light from the window stabbed through to his brain. With his eyes still closed, he kneeled on the bed and felt around for the blind strings. Squinting, he grabbed them to try to close the blinds but accidentally opened them completely.

He raced to close them and sat on the edge of the bed, blinking himself fully awake before opening the door and peeking out to see if Nana was up yet. Not hearing a sound, he sprinted around the corner and into the bathroom, locking the door behind him. Grant sat on the toilet and peed. A loud fart escaped him; his stomach felt completely jacked up from the burger, onion rings, multiple beers, sips of woo woos, and a few shots of who knew what.

After flushing, Grant washed his hands and glanced up in the mirror. He looked like death. He was way too old to pull off nights like that. His mind flashed to kissing Tiffany in the car. His hand flew to his face. True, he'd seen a different side of her, but all the work he'd put into letting her know he wasn't interested was now moot. Was he interested? They'd had a lot of fun together, and she was available. It seemed that Lottie might not be.

Grant slipped back into his room and grabbed his balled-up jeans off the floor and pulled his cellphone from the pocket. He opened it to check for messages from Lottie and noticed an outgoing call to her. He must have accidentally dialed her.

Fuck!

What had she heard? What time had he called? Okay, it was before the kiss. She probably just heard music—if anything. His cell was shoved in his pocket most of the night. Grant immediately felt like an asshole. He wanted to call Lottie and explain everything. How he'd just gone to get something to eat, and Dan invited him to Scooters, and how he just happened to run into Tiffany there. But not about the kiss, there would be no benefit to telling her about the kiss.

Coffee. He decided to start everything off with some coffee. His hungover mind probably wasn't the best to be trusting with decisions like this. Grant stumbled into the kitchen and put the coffee into the machine. He padded back into the bathroom and pulled open the medicine cabinet. All Nana had was chewable baby aspirin. Rolling his eyes, Grant poured a few of them into his hand and popped them in his mouth, chewing on his way back to the kitchen.

"Oh, hey, Nana." Grant passed Nana as she opened her bedroom door.

"Good morning. You look like shit." Nana crinkled her nose at him. "I think if we both went out right now, people would think that I was your little sister. I'm guessing that means you either had a good night or a bad one. Didn't hear ya puking, though, so it couldn't have been too bad."

"I just need some coffee." Grant returned to the kitchen to watch the coffee pour through the machine and fill up the carafe.

"And some toast." Nana pulled open the bread and popped them into the toaster.

"I don't feel like eating."

"Of course you don't feel like eating. You're hungover. I'm not too old to see that. You need to get something in your stomach or you're going to feel like shit even longer. Dry toast will do just the thing."

The swirling scents of toast and coffee made Grant's stomach gurgle angry, vomitus threats. He did his best to calm them and remain perched to rush to the bathroom if he needed to. He laid his head on the table; the cool wood calmed his puke sweats.

Nana pushed a plate of toast in front of him and a mug. He lifted his head and grimaced at the string of a teabag hanging over the side. He pushed it away. "I need coffee."

"Peppermint tea will soothe your nausea. Tea, toast, then coffee." Nana sat next to him.

Please don't ask me questions.

He pulled the mug to his lips and sipped the tea and then nibbled on the corner of a piece of toast.

"I guess you and Lottie really hit the drinks last night. I hope she didn't drink as much as you did. Drinking isn't my idea of a first date activity, but I know how things can be when people are awkward around each other and run out of things to say. Sometimes a little alcohol can keep things going."

"We didn't run out of things to say. Lottie didn't even drink. She had an emergency with a friend, so I went out with Dan Cooley afterward."

"Dan Cooley? Well, where did you two go?"

"Scooters."

Nana's eyebrows nearly hit the ceiling. "Scooters? I didn't think anyone without bad intentions for dirty deeds ever stepped foot in that place."

"Well, it wasn't my choice." Grant sipped the tea. Some part of him now wanted to tell Nana that Tiffany was there. Perfect Tiffany. Except that he didn't dislike her anymore so there was no point. Even though they'd kissed—a kiss he'd enjoyed—he would at least like to be friends with her.

"What was the emergency? You know, sometimes women use that ol' excuse to get out of dates. Not that I'm trying to hurt your feelings, but I want you to be realistic with this one."

Grant groaned and took another bite of toast, chewing it to the beat of his headache as he tried to figure out how to shut the Lottie hating down this morning. He just didn't have the energy to paint on a smile and deal with it.

Swallowing, he turned to her. "Or maybe she's just a good friend who is there when her friends need her." His tone was biting. The hangover didn't allow him to tenderize it.

"Well, excuse me for looking out for you."

"Nana," Grant barked, grabbing his head. "I know you don't like Lottie. You don't even know her, yet you don't like her. Well, I do, a lot, and that should be enough for you. You're so set on me being with Tiffany

—who by the way is way too young for me—that you don't want to get to know anything about Lottie."

"Honey, I know. You're right. I just don't want you to get hurt by someone who has already been married. What if you fall for her and you're just an in-between guy?"

"Well, that's my risk to take, isn't it?"

"Why, yes, it is. I'm sorry. But Tiffany isn't too young for you. She's mature for her age, and she's so sweet and beautiful. I know you'd have beautiful children together and a wonderful life. Your Papa Joe would go on and on about her whenever we'd leave Meers. How she'd be just perfect for you." Nana dabbed her eyes with a napkin.

Grant guzzled the rest of his still too hot tea and plunged the rest of the toast into his mouth, rising to head into the kitchen to pour himself some coffee. "I've got a headache. I'm going to go lie down." He kissed Nana on the top of her head before saying anything he'd regret, padded to his room, and closed the door.

***

Lottie

Lottie's alarm screeched at her from across the room. She reached out to its normal spot on the bedside table, not realizing that it wasn't there at first. Angrily kicking the covers off, she rolled herself off the bed like one of the Dukes of Hazzard sliding across the hood of the General Lee.

Snatching the phone from the floor, she turned off the alarm and sighed. She was too angry to try to go back to sleep. Her knuckles throbbed and burned. Memories of punching David flooded back to her. It wasn't just a dream. Or nightmare?

Lottie stumbled into the bathroom and pulled her hair into a quick bun, peed, brushed her teeth, and returned to the bedroom to pull on some clothes. She shook her head as she looked at herself in the mirror. It was quite the different picture from the last time she'd looked herself over. Last night she'd felt more beautiful than she ever had, and today she was back to looking like a complete slob loser. Rolling her eyes, she darted out of the room, grabbed her keys, headed out, and hopped in the car.

Beth was waiting at the reservoir with Pickles. Lottie parked and laid her forehead against the steering wheel. Her car door opened, and Beth was soon pulling on her arm.

"Come on, Lot. You can't stay in there forever. You'll feel better after we talk things over."

"My life is a mess."

"I know it is, babe. Now, come on."

Lottie flung one foot out the door and stomped the ground.

"Oh boy, she's in a mood today."

She looked up at Beth. "You better watch out. Remember, I'm a person that punches people now." Lottie twisted her other foot out of the car and held out the bruised knuckles of her right hand.

"He deserved more than a punch. He needs his dick cut off with bolt cutters. Does he have radar for fucking shit up for you or what?"

"You wouldn't need a bolt cutter for him. A hole punch would work."

Beth screamed and laughed, clutching her sides and doubling over. "Are you telling me that Douche has a small dick?"

Lottie grinned and shrugged. "A skinny one."

"Ew! Skinny dicks are the worst! It's like being fucked with a pencil. Oh, Lottie, please tell me you're not considering taking him back. You need to find a man with some girth, and something tells me Grant is a meaty man."

"I doubt he's going to want anything to do with me now. I was mortified. And I didn't know what to do. I stood there like an idiot. I never know the right things to say until long afterward, and then I just kick myself for the way I acted and replay how awesome my way-too-late response would've been." Lottie climbed out of the car and closed the door with her hip. Beth handed her Pickles's leash.

"Tell me what your perfect response would have been. Let's start walking and burn off some frustration. And don't tell me you don't want to burn calories, too. I know you've finally started noticing a difference in your body in that dress last night."

Lottie stopped in her tracks. "Speaking of the dress. I got blood on it when I punched David. I rinsed it in cold water right away, but I'm worried it'll be stained."

"Casualty of justice and well worth it. I'm sure it's fine. Now walk." Beth charged forward.

Lottie caught up, surprised at how much easier it had become to keep up with Beth just from the small amount of time she'd been exercising more and cutting out the fast food. Although a burger and fries sounded great now. Maybe she could talk David into Fat Daddy's rather than Roma's.

"But seriously, Lottie. You're not going to take him back, are you?"

"I'm not even sure if that's what he wants."

"Well, what did he say exactly?"

"He hugged me and said, 'I'm glad we can start over again,' but I don't know what he meant by that. He wants me to write him while he's deployed. He said Veronica isn't the writing type. But does that mean he misses me and he's disappointed with her?"

Beth growled. "That's cryptic as fuck. It sounds like he wants to get back together with you, but it doesn't sound like they're breaking up or wouldn't he have just said so?"

"I don't know. Maybe I'll find out at lunch."

"Are you going to call Grant before you go?"

"I don't know. You know, he butt-dialed me last night, and it sounded like he was at a club or something. All I could hear was loud music, muffled talking, and a woman laughing. Do you think he went out with someone else instead?"

"Oh, I doubt that. He really likes you."

"He certainly wasn't sitting around thinking about it. Cleary, he went somewhere and had a good time."

Beth stopped, crossed her arms, and cocked her head. "What would you do if you were him? You'd probably call me, and I'd take you out somewhere to get your mind off it and you would go. That doesn't mean you'd forget about him and have fun, right?"

"I guess." Lottie pursed her lips.

"Give him the benefit of the doubt. He's not David —who you are giving the benefit of the doubt to, by the way." Beth began charging forward again.

"I know." Lottie jogged to catch up. "Do you think I should stand him up?" Lottie couldn't help herself from grinning at the thought.

"Oooh, that's so evil of you. I love it." Beth smiled. "But since he already ruined your date last night, you may as well go and find out what the fuck he wants. Otherwise, it'll just drive you—and me—nuts not knowing. But make him pay for your lunch!"

"I can't do that."

"The fuck you can't! Lottie, he left you with practically nothing. The least he can do is buy you some lunch. If for no other reason than the fact that he cheated you out of dinner last night. You know Grant would have paid. He's an old school gentleman. Michael is that way, too. You know, that's one of the things that always turned me on about him most. He always opens doors, takes my hand, and pays for everything. That and how big and manly he is. I love men who are men, ya know? I hate these beta males carrying purses and getting their nails done, pandering to feminists just in the hopes of getting their wieners jiggled. I wanna grab those men and say, 'Look honey, not even these hairy-armpit feminists want to fuck a man like you. In the end, we all want to be fucked by someone with a ball-load of testosterone.'"

Lottie shook her head. She couldn't believe some of the things that came out of Beth's mouth at times, but she was right. Those kinds of men were such a turn off. She never liked when small, thin men would ask her out. Feeling bigger or more masculine than a man never got her in the mood, but it couldn't be the case for all women, could it? Considering every romance novel she'd ever snuck from her mom's room as a teen, she certainly hadn't read any about men like that. The men in those novels were always very masculine and knew how to make a woman feel like a woman. A grin spread across her face as she thought of Grant taking her like one of the women in those novels. Her cheeks flushed.

After walking around the reservoir more times than she could count, discussing what her perfect answer would be to anything that came out of David's mouth, Lottie gave Beth a hug, put Pickles in the car, and headed home to shower and get ready to meet David.

Chapter Twenty

Lottie

Lottie showered, did her best to copy the color palette Beth had used on her face the night before, and carefully curled her hair to make it look as perfect as possible—without looking like she'd spent any time on it.

Her stomach flipped and flopped the whole drive to Roma's, her mind flashing back to the last time they were there together. The way he'd broken her heart had been so easy on his part, so matter of fact. Oh, why was she meeting him there again? She should have punched him straight away when he showed up at her door and threw his box of clothes on his—crumpled up on the doorstep—body. Her punch was so much more powerful when she replayed it over in her mind.

"Asshole," she muttered as she took a quick right down a side road, deciding to turn around and go home instead. As she pulled the car back out on the street toward home, she cursed herself, "coward," when she decided she couldn't live without knowing what it was he wanted to talk about. She quickly pulled into a gas station parking lot and turned around again.

"Stupid," she muttered, unsure if she was talking about herself or David.

Pulling into the driveway, she parked and eyed the cars around her, trying to see if there was a way to tell if one of them was a rental. Although, with as many officers coming in and out of town for training and sims, that wouldn't have meant much anyway. She flipped down the visor and flicked open the mirror, checking for boogers, unblended makeup lines, and lipstick on her teeth. When she was convinced she looked as good as possible, she took a deep breath and charged inside before she lost her nerve.

Lottie held her chin up, and she shoved her way through the door, trying to look more confident on the outside than the rumpled-up mess she was on the inside. Stopping, she looked around and spied him sitting there in his flight suit, waiting for her with an iced tea—no lemon—at her place. She sucked in a deep breath and headed over to him, guilt slapping her when she saw how fat his lip was.

She grimaced as she sat down, not taking her eyes off it. "Oh my goodness. Your lip."

"Looks like shit, right? I told everyone I got into a bar fight with a big, burly dude at Scooters."

Lottie reached out and grabbed the iced tea. Her throat suddenly felt parched. The moment she set it down, the waitress was over, filling it up.

"Thank you." Lottie smiled at her.

"You're welcome. Need a few more minutes here?"

"Yes, please." Lottie scooped up her menu. "Boy, she must have been watching me drink that."

"Someone wants to earn a good tip." David winked. "I should suck mine down and see how quickly she fills it up."

Lottie smiled and waved him away. "Don't." She chuckled. Her eyes flashed down to her menu. "Hmm, I think I'm in the mood for a pizza. You in?"

"Anything you want, Lot."

Lottie cocked her head to the side. It was so uncharacteristic of him to be so agreeable. She wasn't sure she was comfortable with it. Lottie squinted at him and then glanced back at the menu. "The white out?" She knew he loved the supreme pizza best.

"That sounds great." David smiled and waved the waitress over and ordered the pizza. "You want an order of garlic bread? I know how you like it."

"Sure." Lottie took a sip of her tea but kept her narrowed eyes on David.

"And an order of garlic bread." He handed the waitress their menus and grinned at Lottie once his eyes returned to her. "Why are you looking at me like that?"

Lottie shook free from her gaze. "Like what?"

"You were giving me bullshit eyes."

"No, I wasn't." Lottie shook her head.

He cocked his.

"Fine. What's up? You're never this agreeable. You like to get your way and rarely ever gave me mine that easily."

"What?" David's palms turned up, and he shrugged. "I'm just trying to be nice. That's all."

"That's all?"

"Yeah. Stop being so suspicious of me." David took a sip of his tea. "You know, Lottie, I was meaning to tell you how beautiful you looked last night. Wow, I was blown away, really."

Lottie rolled her eyes. "Whatever."

"No, I mean it. I was caught a little off-guard. You took my breath away."

Lottie took another long sip of her tea to cool the heat that was radiating throughout her body. "Thanks."

The waitress brought their garlic bread to the table, and to try to avoid needing to say anymore, Lottie picked a piece up and shoved it in her mouth. The roof of her mouth was scalded by the hot buttery top. Opening her mouth, she did the reverse blow to cool it off.

David watched her, smiling. "Someone's hungry."

Lottie chewed, swallowed, and took a sip of the ice-cold tea. "It's been a while since I've had the bread here. I got a little excited."

David's eyes danced and the corner of his mouth pulled into that sexy lopsided grin that had always let her know he was interested in getting a little action. Lottie quickly looked away. He couldn't possibly be trying to flirt with her, could he? He had his new girl now and they were over, but he had said he wanted to start over with her. Wasn't that what he'd said? Did he really want her back? Too scared to ask, Lottie quietly chewed on her garlic bread until the pizza arrived.

Careful not to burn her mouth this time, she blew on the cheese before putting it into her mouth, quite aware of the way David watched her. If she were currently admitting the truth to anyone, she would have revealed the way it made her pelvis ache to see him watch her with such longing and the way she stretched out each blow just long enough to tease him just a little bit more.

Most of their lunch was quietly spent watching each other. She knew he wanted her as much as she now wanted him. It was awkwardly delicious to feel horny for someone who had been in her so many times. But could she have him now? Really have him? She wanted to find out.

Her eyes locked on his, unblinking, yearning. Lottie licked her lips and smiled. "Do you have to get back right away?"

"I have a sim in half an hour." His eyes drifted down to her breasts then slowly back up to her eyes.

"You could stop by my place for dessert if you're in the mood for something sweet."

"I think I have time for that." David waved the waitress over and asked for the check. He opened his wallet and quickly handed her the cash. "Keep the change."

"Do you all want a box for the leftover pizza?"

"We're good." He waved her off, stood, and reached for Lottie's hand. His flight suit betraying any doubt that he was interested in the kind of dessert that Lottie was offering.

She took his hand, and they headed out the door. "Do you want to follow me?"

"Yeah, I'm in the silver Civic."

Lottie climbed into her car, backed out, and waited for him to follow before pulling out onto the street and heading home.

As she pushed open the door, Pickles growled and barked at David. The hair on his back stood on end like a ridge.

"Pickles, no!" Lottie grabbed him by the collar and put him in her bedroom.

David pulled off his boots and sat on the couch. "You finally got a dog, huh?"

"That's right." Lottie licked her lips as she approached him. Without saying a word, she knelt down between his legs and unzipped the lower zipper in his flight suit, pulling up enough to reach in and free his cock from his boxer briefs and the uniform.

He groaned when her hands touched him. Her eyes flicked up to meet his; she grinned and rubbed him with her hand before pulling him to her lips.

***

Grant

Grant didn't wake up until it was once again dark outside. Muffled voices drifted in with the light under the door. Confused about the time of day, Grant rolled out of bed, rubbed his eyes, and looked around the room for his cell. He found it on the nightstand. It was passed six p.m. He rubbed the back of his neck and sighed, reiterating the thought that he was too old for this shit anymore. Grant's heart skipped when he realized he had notifications for seven text messages. Had Lottie been trying to get a hold of him?

He clicked them open and realized they were all from Tiffany.

How did she get my number?

Her name had been entered into his phone with a little heart emoji after it. Now he vaguely remembered her entering her number into his phone and saying,

"And a heart because we're friends now." And there was the sent text she'd sent to herself to have his number.

He read the texts.

Tiffany: I had a fun night. Hope we can do it again sometime.

Tiffany: Are you up yet?

Tiffany: I'm going to Western Sizzlin' at eleven if you wanna join me. Mac-n-cheese cures hangovers!

Tiffany: Guess you're not up. Headin' to the sizzling, join me there if you want.

Tiffany: Okay, I'm leaving now. Hope you're not mad at me.

Tiffany: I called Nana, she said you're still sleeping. Call me when you wake up.

Tiffany: I'm in your neighborhood. Stopping by with some cherry cobbler from Meers for Nana. I'm not psycho, when I called earlier, she told me how much she was craving it. I figured it was a hint.

Grant shook his head, figuring it was Tiffany and Nana talking in the hallway. He had half a mind to hide in his room and avoid talking to her. True, she turned out to be sweet, but his head still didn't feel like having a conversation with anyone. His bladder, on the other hand, demanded he find his way to the bathroom. He was also curious as to whether Tiffany told Nana about their night last night. He was sure he'd asked her not to, but he had no idea how drunk she was when he asked and if she'd remembered or not.

He pressed his ear to the door to try to figure out if they'd see him slip around the door and go into the bathroom. The door clicked shut when he leaned against it. He'd obviously not closed it the whole way when he'd gone to lie down.

"Oh, I think someone's up." Nana's excited voice came clearly sailing in his direction.

Fuck.

Grant ran his fingers through his hair, scraped the corner of his eyes to relieve them of any eye boogers, and quickly pulled a pair of pajama bottoms out of his drawer and slid them on. He twisted the knob and pulled the door open, squinting into the light that was assaulting his sensitive eyes.

"Hey, Grant, the coroner's here to check for a pulse." Nana waved from her chair.

Tiffany strolled over and threw her arms around him. "He's still warm. Guess you can send the meat wagon back to the morgue."

"Very funny." Grant pulled away from her embrace. "I'll be right back." He turned and headed straight for the bathroom.

Grant let the thunderous piss free from his body, hoping he wouldn't also release a thunderous fart. The last thing he needed were those two finding another reason to tease him. Normally, he wouldn't care whether others had a laugh at his expense, but he didn't want to deal with much of anything at the moment. He cursed his bladder for waking him up in the first place. After washing his hands, Grant returned to the living room, plopping down onto the couch.

"Someone drank a little too much last night, Tiffany." Nana grinned.

"Oh, really?" Tiffany smiled at Nana and then smirked at Grant.

Good, she obviously hadn't told Nana that they'd been together last night. Grant's mind flashed to the kiss in the car and how he'd thought about going inside when she invited him. It was clear she was a bit hurt when he turned her down, but he was glad to see that she didn't seem upset with him.

Grant shrugged. "Is there any coffee, Nana?"

"Oh, you shouldn't be drinking coffee this late. You've slept the day away, and if you want any chance of quickly getting on a normal sleep cycle, you need to skip caffeine. Tea is better. Tiffany brought us some cherry cobbler. Isn't that sweet of her?"

"Very." Grant shook his head.

"I've got it warming in the oven now. Let me go check it and I'll put on a pot of tea." Nana struggled to get out of her recliner.

Tiffany hopped up. "Oh, you relax. I'll do that."

Nana sunk back down into her chair. "Oh, thank you, sweetheart. You're such a thoughtful girl. Isn't she, Grant?"

"Indeed, she is, Nana." Grant rose from the chair. "Don't worry about the tea, Tiffany. I can take care of that myself." He followed her into the kitchen.

"I just got your texts," he told her once they were in the kitchen. "Sorry I didn't see them earlier."

"No problem. I was embarrassed that I sent so many. I must seem like a needy freak."

"Nah, not at all." Grant reached into the cabinet and pulled out the coffee and the small French press that he bought Nana for Christmas one year. She'd never used it, but she always told him how much she loved it.

"Ooh, I'm telling Nana that you're making coffee and not tea." Tiffany made her way to the doorway as though she were going to tell.

Grant grabbed her around the waist and pulled her back into the kitchen. "You better not or I'll breathe in your face with my hangover breath."

Tiffany giggled. "Ugh, not that. I can already smell it from here." She waved her hand in front of her face before grabbing the potholder from a hook on the wall and opening the oven door. "It's nice and bubbly." She pulled it out and placed it on the counter. She then filled the tea pot and placed it on the burner while Grant scooped the coffee into the press.

"Hey, thanks."

"You're welcome. It's the least I can do. I figure I'm partially responsible for that hangover."

"I'd say you're more than partially responsible. I had to get drunk just so I could live with the embarrassment of ordering woo woos." He rolled his eyes.

Tiffany bumped him in the hip. "Oh, shut up. You had more than your fair share of sips of them, though. You know they're good."

Grant grinned at her. "Okay, I'll admit I liked it a little bit."

"Just a little bit?"

"Okay, more than a little bit." He smiled.

She smiled and bit her lip, and he was sure they weren't just talking about woo woos anymore, and if he didn't have dragon breath now, he would have pulled her to him and kissed her again.

Chapter Twenty-One

Lottie

Lottie heard the mail truck drive up, and without even slipping on her shoes, she bolted out the door.

"Wait! Wait! Don't leave yet. I've got a letter." She waved it over her head.

The mail woman smiled and waved, waiting for Lottie. "You haven't missed a day."

"I almost missed today!" Lottie panted, the taste of the envelope seal lingering on her tongue.

"How much longer is he gone?"

"One more week." Lottie smiled.

"I bet you'll be happy to have him home again." The mail woman tucked the letter in her sack, nodded, and drove off.

Lottie watched her drive away, her heart sinking at the speed of truck.

Home again.

The last lunch they'd had together and the few letters she'd gotten from David left her wondering about that. She was no closer to knowing what it was he wanted than she was the night he'd showed up and ruined her date. She wrote David a letter every day, mailing two letters on Monday to make up for Sunday. She'd received three. Beth didn't approve. Whenever she mentioned David, Beth would purse her lips and raise a brow.

"I still can't believe you didn't ask him straight out before he left."

"I wanted to ask, but the timing never seemed right. I guess I was scared."

"You're letting him fuck up your life, again!" Beth shouted.

Lottie had hung up the phone without telling her about the blowjob she'd given David. She convinced herself it was because she didn't need to be judged any more than she already was. But the truth was that she was ashamed of herself. In the moment, she'd felt sexy and powerful. But after he zipped up his flight suit, put on his boots—saying he had better get going or he'd be late for his sim—and left, she felt like a fool. Again.

Beth and Lottie didn't speak until the following Monday morning in the teachers' lounge. Not that they'd had much of a conversation then. Beth came in and put her arm around Lottie and sat quietly until the first bell rang.

And Grant. Grant had been completely wonderful to her. She explained that she just wasn't ready to date until she knew whether she was officially divorced or...what. He said he understood and wanted her to be happy and that he didn't want to make things complicated for her.

Even though he stopped coming to her room for lunch, he always smiled whenever he saw her, and she used that time alone to write letters to David. Her letter writing days were nearing an end, though. It was his last Saturday deployed, and although he wasn't returning to Altus, she was hoping he would ask her to come out to Hawaii to see him and talk it over. School was nearly out for the year, so the timing would work out perfectly for her. That's what this letter contained...all the questions she'd been holding in for thirty-eight days.

Pickles barked and scratched at the glass door. "I'm not going for a walk yet. Mommy's coming back inside."

She shooed him away from the door as she squeezed back inside. "Let's get dressed and go meet Aunt Beth at the reservoir."

Pickles followed her into the bedroom and laid down on the carpet as she threw on her walking clothes. He always went nuts when she pulled her tennis shoes from the closet. "That's a good boy." She scratched his head as she raced into the hallway. Lottie clipped on Pickles's leash and grabbed her keys. He pulled on the leash and jumped around, nearly tripping her. "Calm down, weirdo!"

Once in the car, Pickles put his paws on the dash and panted excitedly. She rolled down the windows and headed for the reservoir. "We're gonna have lots of places to walk in Hawaii." Lottie scratched his back as she pulled in to the parking area. Beth was nowhere to be seen. Lottie climbed out of the car and took Pickles to the water's edge so he could watch the ducks. He pranced in place but never tried to harm them. It was almost as if he was waiting for an invitation to join them for a swim.

Lottie stood for a while then sat in the dirt, careful not to sit on any duck poop. She cursed herself for not bringing her phone. "Well, Pickles, looks like Aunt Beth isn't coming today. I guess it's just us." Lottie dusted off her butt and took Pickles around the reservoir. On lap two and a half, she heard someone jogging up behind her and felt a hard slap on her butt.

"Hey, hot butt!"

"Where have you been? I thought you weren't coming."

"Hey Pickles, baby!" Beth scratched Pickles behind the ears as he jumped up on her for attention.

"Pickles, down." Lottie gave him a little tug on the leash. "No jump."

"Sorry, I'm late babe. I had to run to the drugstore this morning."

"The drugstore? You couldn't do that after?"

"Well, yeah, I could've, but I was a little anxious to find out if I'm pregnant or not."

Lottie froze. "Pregnant?"

"My period just kept not coming, and I couldn't take it anymore. Michael said I was on his last nerve and told me to get a test and take it so I could finally find out."

"So, did you take it?"

"I did." Beth grinned.

"And?"

"And..." Beth pursed her lips and nodded. "I'm knocked up!"

"Oh my God! Congratulations!" Lottie hugged Beth.

"Thanks. I mean, it wasn't planned, but I'm happy about it, and Michael is so happy I almost wonder if he's been harboring a secret wish to have a baby and just never told me."

"That's so amazing. I'm so happy for you. I guess I'll need to throw you a baby shower."

"Ew! No! I can't stand those fuckin' things. Just take me out to dinner with a few of the non-obnoxious people from work instead."

"But with gifts, right?"

"Oh, of course. Or cash." Beth bumped Lottie in the hip. "Let's get walking. Apparently, my body is going to fight even harder to get fat now."

The three of them walked around the reservoir a couple of times. Beth was unusually quiet and kept looking at Lottie, who finally stopped in her tracks and turned to her. "What? Do I have one of those hanging boogers or something?"

"No. It's just..."

"What? You guys didn't get orders, did you?"

"No. It's...well." Beth bit her lip and then sucked in a deep breath. "I saw something this morning, and I've been debating whether I should tell you."

"Okay." Lottie gulped.

"You know that gas station across the street from the drugstore?"

"Yeah."

Beth scratched her head and averted her eyes.

"What?" Lottie shook her head.

"I saw Grant pull in and pump some gas."

"Wow. Exciting news." Lottie rolled her eyes. "I told you a million times it's not awkward between us. He's been great. He's backed off while I try to figure out what's going on with David."

"That redhead we ran into that time they met us here got out of the truck, kissed him, and went inside the gas station."

"Oh. Tiffany. Her name is Tiffany." Lottie's insides crumbled. Her eyes began to water, and her chin trembled.

Beth leaned in to hug her.

"I'm all right. I mean, why shouldn't he date someone? And of course, Tiffany is interested in him and she's so pretty."

Pickles barked at a lone, meandering duck and ran off toward it, the leash slipped from Lottie's fingers. "Pickles! No! Pickles, come back here." She chased after him. Tears spilled down her face; she was barely able to see through her watering eyes. Pickles slowed at the edge of the water, giving Lottie enough time to grab his leash before he waded in. Lottie slid down and sat next to the water, hugging Pickles. "Don't you run away from me, sir."

Beth sat down beside her and put her arm around Lottie's shoulder.

Lottie leaned her head on Beth. "Why does everything in my life have to be such a shit show?"

Beth squeezed her closer and sat with her until the tears stopped leaking out.

David.

She knew Beth was thinking he was the reason—because she was too—but was too good of a friend to say so when she was hurting.

***

Grant

Tiffany came bounding out of the gas station with a small four pack of wine coolers. She held it up for him to see, smiling widely.

"I hope you don't think I'm drinking one of those. I thought you were just going to grab some iced teas." Grant replaced the gas pump handle and sighed.

"This will make our trip a little more fun." She slid into the truck, sitting in the middle seat rather than the window.

"I'm not sure hiking near buffalo while tipsy is a good idea."

"Those buffalo are used to people hiking in the area, and I mean, it's just walking and looking at rocks. I need to spice it up somehow."

Grant raised his brows, shook his head, and pursed his lips while starting the engine and heading out of the gas station toward the Wichita Wildlife Refuge. Tiffany twisted off the top of a wine cooler and guzzled half of it down before holding it out to him.

He waved her off. "I'm driving."

"The road is completely straight, and there isn't that far to go. It won't even hit you before we get there. Quit being such a fuddy-duddy."

"How can I, when that's what I am?" Grant raised a brow at her. For someone who was so interested in dating him, she sure didn't seem to want an older man who didn't make decisions like a frat boy.

Before reaching the refuge, Tiffany had finished two and a half wine coolers. Although they weren't big, the fact that she weighed about one hundred pounds meant that they really didn't have to be. He considered drinking the rest of them just to keep her from doing it. Once they parked, Tiffany hopped out of the truck, letting the empty wine cooler bottles fall to the ground. When she didn't bend down to pick them up, Grant circle around, picked them up, and put them in the bed of the truck, Tiffany oblivious to his grumbling.

He pulled on his backpack, locked the truck, and took Tiffany's hand as they headed off down the trail. "I can't believe you've lived here your whole life and have never hiked these trails."

"I'm not a huge fan of the outdoors. I'm more of an indoor person."

"You might change your mind when you check out the beautiful views here, though." He grinned.

Tiffany's eyes widened, and her lips pursed. "We'll see."

"Okay, tell me what you like to do indoors?"

"I like to watch TV, tweet, and paint designs on my toenails and fingernails. Oh, I also like to make my own jewelry. One day I hope to have my own boutique."

"In Altus?"

"No, probably Oklahoma City or Tulsa. You used to live in Tulsa, right? Do you think you'll move back there?"

"I don't know. I'm kind of happy being back in Altus." That wasn't necessarily true. Grant hadn't really given much thought to what he might do in the future. He was too busy taking care of Nana. Even if he had thought it over, he wasn't sure if he wanted Tiffany

213

seeing him as her ticket out of town. He wasn't quite sure what was going on in her mind. They'd only been dating three weeks, but she was getting a little too close for his comfort. She was a nice girl, but he was sure that she was just way too young for him or, rather, he was too old for her.

Grant jumped from boulder to boulder upwards along the path and quickly realized that Tiffany was nowhere near him. He turned. "Do you need me to give you a hand?"

Shielding the sun from her eyes with one hand, she put her hip on the other. "I'll just wait down here."

"The view from up here is amazing, though. I don't want you to miss it. I'll come down and help you up." Grant made his way back down to Tiffany.

"If I go up there, then can we leave?"

"What? We just got here. We've barely been hiking an hour."

"I know, but we have to go the whole way back, and it'll be two hours. I think I've had enough fresh air for the day. I didn't have enough wine to make this fun."

Grant turned away from Tiffany to look up at the top of the hill. He grimaced and rubbed his face before pressing on a smile and turning back to her. "Sure, here..." Grant dropped his backpack to the ground and squatted down. "Hop on my back and I'll carry you up."

"Really? No. You can't carry me all the way up there. I'm too fat."

Grant rolled his eyes. "Come on. You know you're not fat."

214

Tiffany jumped on his back, he hooked his arm under her leg, picked up the backpack with the other, and started heading back up the hill. Tiffany squeaked every time he leapt from one boulder to the next.

"I promise, I'm not gonna drop you."

Once they reached the top, Grant set her down and took her hand as they walked toward the overlook. Buffalo were grazing down below, and the landscape was rugged and beautiful prairie.

"Wasn't it worth it?" Grant smiled.

Tiffany shrugged. "I guess."

Grant turned to her. "You really don't think so?"

"Well, I mean, it's rocks and grass." Tiffany crinkled her nose and shrugged again. "Oh, but let's take a selfie!" She pulled her phone out of her pocket, wrapped her arm around him, and smiled like she was the happiest person on earth. She took the pic, inspected it, and deleted it. "I don't look good in that one. Let's try again."

Tiffany repeated that process about six more times until she thought she looked great in the photo. He noticed she didn't look that much different in each one.

"I'm gonna put this on my Insta. You think I'll get a signal out here?"

"I don't know. I leave my cell in the truck when I come out here." Grant pulled his backpack onto his shoulders.

"Oh. I got a signal." Tiffany sat on a rock, posting her picture and speaking into her phone, "Hashtag Wichita Wildlife Refuge. Hashtag Oklahoma. Hashtag I love nature. Hashtag nature photography. Hashtag hiking."

Grant scrunched his face when he heard her say, "Hashtag I love nature." An indoor girl who loves nature? His mind flashed back to the one time that he and Lottie had driven through the park on their way to Lawton. He wondered what it would have been like if he'd brought Lottie to this spot. Was she really who she seemed to be as well, or was there an image that everyone presented these days all while being something else completely? Nah, he was pretty sure that Lottie was who she seemed to be.

"Okay, can we head back now?" Tiffany bounced over to him.

"Yeah, let's go."

"Carry me back down?" Tiffany smiled and twisted from side to side while flashing a big smile at him.

Grant slipped out of his backpack, picked up Tiffany, and carried her down to the bottom of the hill. They headed back to the truck. Tiffany finished off the wine coolers on their way back to town and told him how many likes and comments she was already getting on her picture.

Chapter Twenty-Two

Lottie

Lottie rested her chin on her hand and sighed. It was almost as though she'd forgotten what to do on her lunch break, back before she had letters to write or Grant to chat with. Now she was just alone with her thoughts and worries. David hadn't yet arrived back in Hawaii, but sending letters to Al-Udeid would be worthless; they wouldn't make it there before he was gone, and the last letter she sent contained everything she wanted to say.

He would have the long trip back to Hawaii to think about what she said and what it was that he wanted. Her or Veronica. But she hoped he would re-member the way she looked and the way she had pleased him. She wrote him while he was deployed; Veronica didn't. Maybe she wouldn't end up being a divorcee after all. She didn't want to be alone. And Grant had moved on. He seemed happy with Tiffany— at least from what Beth had said.

Just as she was thinking of her, Tiffany waltzed by her door carrying a picnic basket to Grant's room. Lottie rose and hid behind the door to peer out through the crack as Tiffany greeted him with a kiss.

As they left the room together, holding hands, Lottie pressed herself against the wall so hard she knocked her head and ended up with a bruise she didn't realize she had until she laid her head on the pillow that evening. She tried to bring herself to be happy for Grant, he was her friend after all, but jealousy pooled in her stomach and wouldn't let her sleep.

The following day, she again sat alone at lunch with red, tired eyes, wishing a sinkhole would open up beneath her and suck her out of the hell her life had become.

Something in her gut told her that David wasn't going to pick her, but she'd spent the last month and a half analyzing all his actions and all his words, few though they were. She shook her doubts off and decided to believe that she'd be with her husband in Hawaii before the year was out and wouldn't have to see Tiffany smiling as she held Grant's hand anymore. She told herself that the only thing that really upset her about moving to Hawaii to be with David was that she was going to miss out on being there when Beth had her baby. And Pickles. The quarantine requirements for taking him to Hawaii would take six months. She was unsure if she would stay until Pickles could travel or ask Beth to take him in until then. He did love Beth and she loved him, but the thought of making him bounce around from home to home to home after living in the shelter broke her heart. She'd have to quit her job at the school, and how would she ship her things? The military wouldn't pay to pack her up and send all the new furniture she had to buy herself after he left. She figured she could have a large garage sale. There were always new military families moving to town who might need some furniture, and she'd donate the rest.

Lottie pulled her salad out of her sack and sighed. What she wanted was a double bacon burger and a side of fries. She twisted in her seat. Cramps raked up her back. She rested her head on her desks and moaned. The period pimple that was growing near her brow ached. There was no way to get comfortable. Misery poked at her both inside and out.

"Hey, Lottie."

Lottie straightened up quickly. She knew that voice. It was Grant.

"Oh, hey." She tucked her hair behind her ear.

"Are you all right?"

"Yeah, I'm fine. I just didn't get much sleep last night. How are you doing?"

"Well, I'm heading out for lunch."

"Oh." Lottie's stomach sank. He was probably going out to meet Tiffany.

"You wouldn't want to join me, would you? You seem like you could get out of here for a few." He grinned.

"Could we swing by the White Buffalo? I may need an espresso or two to get me through the afternoon."

"Of course we can. I was just going to grab something from Fat Daddy's and head back here to eat it anyway. We can swing by the White Buffalo first."

Lottie smiled and swung her purse over her shoulder. She and Grant quickly walked down the hall. A lump formed in her throat, and her hands were sweaty. She didn't know what to talk about. Surely, she wasn't going to ask how things were going with Tiffany, and she hoped he wouldn't ask how things were with David. She didn't know anyway.

Grant opened the truck door for her, and she climbed in. He closed it and walked around to the other side. It was nice to be in his truck again. Her mind drifted to the last time she was in it, getting Pickles, heading to Lawton, stopping off at the wildlife refuge, and then getting greasy Chinese. She figured he must have been thinking about it, too, when he climbed in, because he turned to her and asked how Pickles was doing.

"He's doing great. And you were right, he was fast to train. He's my smart boy."

"I told ya. I could tell he was smart by the way he conned us into feeding him half of our egg rolls. It's something in the eyes of a dog. You can tell if they've got a lot of thoughts churning behind them or not. I'd like to see him again."

"I think he'd like that, too." Lottie's cheeks flushed. She turned her head to look out the window to avoid him noticing the pink in her cheeks as he backed the truck out of the parking space.

Grant drove directly to the White Buffalo and ordered her two espressos and a large White Buffalo Mocha. "That's bound to get you through the rest of the afternoon." He handed her the first espresso and put the other drinks in homemade, wooden cup holders.

Lottie removed the lid of the first espresso and blew on it as he drove to Fat Daddy's. She took little sips and tried to balance the liquid in the cup every time they hit a bump.

"Why don't I go in and order for us while you enjoy your coffee?" Grant said as he pulled in.

"Sure, thanks." Lottie fumbled through her purse with one hand while holding the espresso in the other.

He held up his hands. "My treat."

"But you paid for my coffee. I can't let you get my lunch, too."

"Sure, you can. It'll be my way of paying you back for being my first friend at the school and putting up with having lunch with me that first week."

Lottie smiled.

"What can I get you?"

Lottie had enough of healthy eating lately and didn't have the will to pretend to eat like a skinny supermodel. "A bacon cheeseburger and a side of fries."

"Sounds good. I'll be right back." Grant climbed out of the truck and went inside.

Lottie sipped her coffee and once again snuck a peek at his butt as he walked in. He stopped and smiled at her before pulling the door open and going inside. She wasn't sure David had ever done a look back. A pain hit her stomach that was hotter than the espresso. Instantly, she knew she'd made the wrong choice.

With David, she was always trying to prove that she belonged with him. With Grant, she just knew that she did. Burning tears filled her eyes. Her chance was blown. Grant could have been hers. She knew it. But now he belonged to Tiffany, and knowing the way that she felt when Veronica interfered in her relationship, she'd never do that to Tiffany. It didn't matter that they hadn't been together long; she wasn't going to do that to anyone—ever.

Lottie sighed and leaned her head against the truck window, glancing over at the keys hanging from the ignition, radio on, air conditioning cooling her face. David always took the keys and left her in silence, not thinking of her comfort, no matter how hot it was.

"You can always feel the truth. Ignore the words," she muttered. That was the advice her grandma had given her when she was dating David, unsure of whether he loved her. She didn't understand then what her grandma was trying to tell her. Never one to inter-fere, her grandma wouldn't have said if she thought David wasn't right for her. It was clear now. Every-thing Grant did showed he cared for her. Everything with David was her trying to earn his love and ap-proval.

Tears slid down Lottie's cheeks. She tried to suck in deep breaths to clear out the aching feeling, but they hitched in her chest, causing more to spill tears over the rims.

As Grant emerged from the restaurant with the bags in his hands and a smile painted across his face, Lottie desperately tried to wipe away her tears, fearful that half of her makeup would end up on her shirt.

Grant's face sunk when he pulled open the door and looked at her. "Lottie, what's wrong?"

He set the bags on the seat between them and climbed inside, turning to her and placing his hand on her shoulder.

The touch of his hand sent another wave of tears pouring out and breaths hitching. She couldn't speak. She could only shrug and shake her head.

He squeezed her shoulder and held onto her. "Take as long as you need." He fumbled through the Fat

Daddy's sack and pulled out some napkins, handing her one.

She wiped her cheeks and nose. "I'm sorry. I'm okay. I'll be okay. We better drive back, or we won't have time to eat." Lottie forced a smile and pulled free the hair that was tucked behind her ear to cover her face.

"Okay. Mind if I come to your room to eat? You don't have to talk about it, but you seem like you could use a friend right now."

Lottie nodded.

The drive back to the school was quiet. Lottie pointed the vent at her face and let the cool air dry her cheeks. Could she really sit and eat with Grant without explaining her meltdown? She refused to tell him it's because she knew she blew her chances with him and wanted to go back to their first week together. Go back to their date before David swept in and ruined it. There was no way to tell him that she felt like a fool for writing David every day and sucking his cock before he left. All the energy she spent on David never got her anything in return. And yet something in her hoped he'd want her. She still wanted him to want her. Nothing about her relationship with David made any sense. What would she say? "I'm crying because I want David to want me to move to Hawaii to be with him, but I also want you to want me and spend time with me and not be with Tiffany. I want everything and nothing. I want never to have been born. I want to disappear."

They pulled into the parking lot, and Grant carried the sacks and extra coffees inside. Lottie followed him, looking up at the clock in her classroom as they sat at the desk. Only ten minutes to eat. She could avoid the topic for ten minutes.

Grant placed her food in front of her and unwrapped his burger and took a bite. Although she now didn't feel like eating, she pulled her burger to her lips and took a big bite. The bacon and burger tasted like junk food magic, lifting her spirits, and she smiled.

"Good, huh?" Grant winked.

"Really good," she mumbled around her bite. Concentrating on her burger and fries, she enjoyed the comfortable silence with Grant.

After eating, he cleaned up their papers, stuffing them into the Fat Daddy's sack, and stood. He bent over and kissed Lottie on the top of head. "If you ever need me, don't hesitate to stop by or give me a call." He took the garbage with him and walked out the door and back to his room.

Lottie stared at the door, resisting the urge to run across the hall and throw herself into his arms. The students began to flow in from their lunch and recess, arguing over who kicked the ball the farthest during their game of kickball. She sucked down the remaining—but now too cold—espresso and forced a smile, feeling a bit refreshed and determined to get through to the end of the day.

When the final bell rang, Lottie scooped up her stuff and scuttled down the hall to Beth's room. She collapsed into one of the seats in the back and stared up at Beth, who was erasing the board. Turning around, Beth jumped. "I thought I was alone. How long have you been there? Did you hear my fart?"

"No." Lottie crinkled her face. "Stay over there then so I don't have to smell it."

"Okay, but you're missing out. Smells like rotten eggs. You know, I hear about pregnant women getting morning sickness and shit, but I have the worse farts of my life. And I want to fart all the time. I crop-dusted a few of the kids today. It's coming in quite handy. When they're not doing their work, it shuts the little chatterboxes right up."

"I'm so glad you're not my teacher." Lottie shook her head.

"Oh, stop. I'm amazing. And don't pretend that you don't have a few kids whose faces you haven't wanted to fill with fart from time to time."

Lottie tilted her head and tapped her chin. "I suppose." She grinned. "So, I had lunch with Grant today."

"Oh?" Beth's eyes widened. "How was that?"

"Horrible. And wonderful."

Beth's eyebrows knitted together. She put the eraser in the tray, walked over, and sat on the desk in front of Lottie. "More info."

"It was so good to be with him. But I started crying. I didn't tell him why and he didn't ask, but I didn't want the lunch to end, even though we were eating and not talking."

"Tell him you want him."

"I can't."

"Why not?"

"I already wrote David and told him I'd like to get back together. And I think I do want that. But I also want to be with Grant. But I'm not going to do to Tiffany what Veronica did to me. And he seems happy with her anyway, so I don't know if he even wants me anyway. I just feel so confused. I'm an idiot." Lottie laid her head on the desk.

Beth stroked Lottie's hair. "You're not an idiot. And I doubt Grant and Tiffany are serious yet. Did you ask him about it?"

"No way!" Lottie sat straight up.

"Do you want me to ask him?"

"No! It's not like he won't know why you're asking, and I'm not sure I want to know. What if he says yes?"

"At least you'll know." Beth shrugged.

"Just promise me you won't. I'm married to David. If he wants to start over with me, I owe him that." Lottie sighed.

Beth shook her head. "You don't owe him anything. The only person you owe anything to is yourself. Do you want to come over for dinner tonight? Michael has a night flight. We can talk."

Lottie shrugged.

"Yes, you're doing it. We'll go to spin and then have some dinner."

"Spin?" Lottie shook her head and scowled.

Beth giggled. "C'mon, it'll be fun. I'll fart and we'll both pretend we don't smell it and watch everyone else's faces."

Lottie laughed and shook her head. "You're sick, you know that?"

"I know."

Chapter Twenty-Three

Grant

Grant climbed into his truck, looking over the empty space that Lottie had occupied earlier in the day. The tears streaming down her face filled his mind. He ached to know what was wrong, but it was obvious that she wasn't ready to tell him. His stomach pinched, and he chastised himself for hoping that she was upset about David. He should be wishing for her happiness, and in a way, he was, but the wish was that she would find happiness with him.

He headed home, hoping not to find Tiffany waiting for him. He liked seeing her, but her friendship with Nana made him far too accessible to her. Perhaps if he had time to miss her, he would. As he drove by his street, he noticed her Vespa parked outside, and he quickly aborted the right-hand turn. He kept driving. Before he spent any time with Tiffany, he needed to get Lottie off his mind, or he knew he'd treat her with contempt that she didn't deserve.

Without purpose, he wound through the streets of town until he ended up at the animal shelter. He parked and walked toward the front door. A woman chain smoked beside it. "You here to find a friend?"

"I'm not sure."

"Go on back. I'll be in in a few."

Grant nodded and pushed his way inside. He followed the sign for **'dogs.'** The moment the door was open, dogs barked and jumped, begging for his attention. He walked down the rows until he stopped in front of the cage of a sad-looking blond border collie huddled in the back corner who didn't give him a second glance or even a first. Her hair was shorter than it should be, and she was emaciated.

"Came in yesterday. Still on stray hold." A raspy, cigarette-coated voice drifted over his shoulder on stale, smoky breath. "Ain't moved from that corner. Won't even eat."

His face sank. The way the dog looked on the outside matched the way he felt on the inside—trapped and lonely. "Mind if I hang out with her a while?"

"Well, I don't feel comfortable letting you inside with her. She ain't been temper tested yet. But you can hang out in here. I'm sure the others will calm their barking after bit." She waved and pushed out through the door.

Grant sat down on the floor and leaned on the gate. "I understand," he muttered, closing his eyes and taking a deep breath. His eyes fluttered open when a fuzzy chin made its way through the chain link and rested on top his hand. Turning his head, he found the Border collie's soft, amber eyes connecting with him. He didn't dare move. While she didn't look completely comfortable, she looked as though she desperately needed to connect with another creature. He needed it, too.

Would he ever be happy? One thing he did know, he was going to make life happy for this dog while he could. He decided then and there that if she was still here when her stray hold was up, he was going to take her home. He'd been missing Brutus for far too long. Heck, he even missed Pickles. It had been nice to have a dog ride in the cab of his truck again.

Grant stayed and told the blond pup all about Lottie and Tiffany, her eyes rising and softening as though she understood every word. When the raspy, walking chimney popped back in to check on them, she was surprised that the dog had approached Grant and had given him a bowl of food to try to get her to eat.

She'd eat one morsel at a time, and he sat there, feeding her the whole dish, one by one, even staying half an hour after the shelter closed.

"I'll be back to see you tomorrow." He rubbed the dog's furry snout through the fence and looked up to the woman who told him he either had to go or get locked in for the night. "Is it okay if I come back tomorrow to check on her?'

"Sure. I'll do some temper testing on her in the morning, and if everything's fine, you can help me brush her and pick all those ticks off of her. I gotta admit, it's the one job that always gives me the heebie jeebies. I gave her a coating with some tick powder, so hopefully most of them will drop off tonight." She began hacking.

Grant tried not to crinkle up his lip as all the tar in her lungs seemed determined to free itself at that very moment. Instead, he spread on smile and said, "I'll see you tomorrow. Both of you." He smiled at the dog, his heart tugging as he began to walk out, as though she were holding it.

It would be a good time to get a dog, he told himself as he climbed in his truck. The school year was almost out, and he'd have time to train her. There was no way Nana was going to be able to train and walk a dog who weighed half her body weight.

His brows knitted together; would Nana be opposed to the idea of getting a dog? She would be good protection for her when she was home alone, he'd tell her. Especially once he started a job in the fire house come fall. He knew Nana liked dogs. She'd always had rough collies when he was growing up, one after the next all named Lassie.

True, this dog wasn't a rough collie but a border collie. That had to be close enough. All the way home, he'd gone over the argument he'd give in his mind and thought about the best time to bring up the subject. No sense in getting Nana's hopes up about the dog if someone claimed her before her stray hold was up, but he had five days to prime Nana about the idea.

Grant grinned when he turned onto the street and saw that Tiffany's Vespa was gone. As he pulled into the driveway, he noticed the grin that was stretched across his lips. He shouldn't be so pleased with the fact that his girlfriend was gone. But the truth was that Tiffany could only make him smile that way for being gone, and Lottie could make him smile that way just thinking of her. And being with Lottie lit him up on the inside like the City of Altus's Christmas in the Park.

As he pushed his way in the unlocked door, he rolled his eyes and groaned. Tiffany should have known to lock the door when she left. "Nana?"

"In the dining room, honey. I'm just setting the table. Be a good boy and come help your nana. You just missed Tiffany. She left here about twenty minutes ago."

"Oh, bummer," Grant mumbled as he kicked off his shoes.

"Oh, goodness, never mind." Nana crinkled up her nose and waved her hand in front of it. "You stink like cigarettes. Did you go to a bar or something after work?"

Not wanting to tell Nana about the dog yet, he shook his head. "Just a quick drink with some folks from work. School's almost out, so we decided to go for a drink. We won't be seeing each other much after that."

"Well, I wish you had called. Tiffany was awfully disappointed that you didn't come home. She sent you messages, but I guess your phone was off?"

Grant reached into his pocket and looked at his phone. Tiffany had left five messages. He fought hard to keep his eyes from rolling. "I forgot to turn it on after classes."

"Well, I'll finish setting the table by myself. Please do me a favor and go take a quick shower and put on some fresh clothes. Just throw those straight into the washing machine when you come out."

"Yes, Nana." Grant spun on his heels and padded into his room. He tossed his cell on his bed and headed out again and slipped into the bathroom.

Placing his hands on the sink, he sighed and studied his face in the mirror. "What are you doing?" The pit of his stomach was hollow, and it ached. He knew he had to break it off with Tiffany. Even if he could never have Lottie, he knew Tiffany wasn't going to make him happy, and he cared about her enough not to want to ruin her chances for happiness with someone else.

A groan escaped him. After his shower, he would talk it over with Nana, who he knew would be just as disappointed as Tiffany. It was as though he'd have to break up with her twice. He pulled off his smoky clothes and threw them into the corner of the bathroom, turned on the water, and climbed inside once the water reached the perfect temperature.

Thoughts of freeing himself from Tiffany soon turned to thoughts of possibly being with Lottie. And thoughts of being with Lottie led him back to thoughts of kissing her. The water raced down his body as his mind did with images of her hands on him. His body reacted. Lathering up his hands with soap, they slid down his body to his cock. He closed his eyes and let the thoughts of Lottie lead him to a great release. Opening his eyes, he longed more than ever to be with Lottie and no one else.

After rinsing off, Grant climbed out of the shower, wrapping a towel around his waist. The steam blocked his view of himself in the mirror, and he knew he'd been in the shower longer than he'd planned. He quickly grabbed his robe from the hook and pulled it around his body, tying it off. Scooping his smoky clothes from the floor, he opened the door, the steam chasing him out as he sprinted around the corner to the laundry closet, tossing his clothes inside the washer and slipping into his room. He pulled on some clean underwear and a set of pajamas and returned to the dining room.

"Well, I said a quick shower." Nana shook her head at him.

"Sorry, Nana. I had some sore muscles in my back." He avoided eye contact with her, sure she could see the guilt spread across his face as though he were thirteen again. Sliding into his seat, he grabbed the glass of water and chugged it down.

Nana took the lid off the pot of stew and ladled it into both bowls. "Any idea what you're going to do this summer for work? I assume you won't be returning to Rivers next year."

"I've already interviewed with the fire department. I start in the fall. I have enough money set aside to be fine for the summer."

Grant frowned. He'd miss seeing Lottie across the hall every day, and it suddenly occurred to him that he wouldn't have a reason to see her anymore once summer began. A frantic, swirling need to tell her how he felt about her filled his stomach. Groaning, he pushed the bowl of stew away.

"Something wrong? You love my beef stew." Nana dropped the spoon she'd almost raised to her lips and rested it back in her bowl, twisting in her seat to look at him more directly.

"I need to break things off with Tiffany. I know you love her, and I think she's a great girl, but we don't have anything in common, and I can't date her for you."

"Date her for me?" Nana sat back in her chair. "Is that the only reason you're seeing her? Because I want you to?"

"Not the only reason. She's beautiful and she's really sweet, but I don't enjoy spending time with her." He took another sip of water. "And I want Lottie."

Nana crossed her arms and leaned back in her chair, not saying a word. Grant couldn't read what she was thinking or feeling. More disapproval for Lottie? Disappointment over Tiffany?

"Nana, I know you disapprove of her, but spending time with her is all I want to do. I think about her, even when I'm with Tiffany. All I do is think how much different things would be if I were with Lottie instead. The school year is coming to an end, and I won't get to see her anymore. I know you don't like that she's officially still married—even though her husband left her and moved to Hawaii with someone else—but I feel like I need to tell her how I feel about her before the school year is over. The thought of not seeing her every day makes me miserable." Grant looked up from the edge of the bowl he'd been staring at and glanced at Nana, who still hadn't moved.

Slowly, her brown-speckled, wrinkled hand made its way across the table. Palm up, she held it out to him. He placed his hand in hers. Her fingers curled around his, squeezing it tight. "I know I pushed you to be with Tiffany, but I also know what it's like to fall in love with someone. I guess it doesn't matter who me or Papa Joe thought would be great for you. The only one you should listen to is your heart."

A smile stretched across Grant's lips. The urge to run over to Lottie's place and tell her how he felt dou-

bled the swirling in his stomach. Remembering her crying in his truck stopped him from doing so. He would
force himself to be patient and give her time to get over
whatever was bugging her, for at least another few
days anyway until the last day of school for teachers,
then he'd have to tell her.

With a plan set in his mind and the loving support
of Nana, he pulled the stew toward him, sniffed in the
delicious heartiness of it, and took a big bite. After devouring the bowl, without even having to reach for
more, Nana put another ladleful in his bowl. He
grinned and continued to eat. After finishing their dinner, they both sat back in their seats, full and satisfied.
Grant felt so relieved to have Nana's support, but the
thought of telling Tiffany ate at him.

"Excuse me, Nana. I'll be right back to help you
clear the dishes. I need to return Tiffany's text and find
some time to sit down with her." He pushed himself
away from the table as Nana pressed her lips into a
smile and nodded. It was obvious that Nana was as
uneasy for Tiffany's impeding heartache as he was. A
tinge of ache pinged in his stomach for Nana as he realized that Nana had enjoyed all the company she'd received from Tiffany while they were dating. That
would surely come to an end.

"Hey, Nana." Grant peeked back around the corner
of the dining room to Nana who sat with a somber
face.

"Yes?"

"Thanks."

A genuine smile spread across Nana's face, and she
winked at him. He smiled, headed to this room, sat on
the corner of his bed, and picked up his phone.

Chapter Twenty-Four

Lottie

Still sweating and giggling over the looks on the faces of everyone who smelled the sulfuric farts leaking from Beth's ass during spin, they climbed into Beth's Jeep and headed to her house.

"Should we order a pizza?" Lottie asked.

"If you let me get green olives on it." Beth wagged her brows.

"Fine but only as long as you don't ask for extra. I can't stand when every bite is overloaded with them."

"Deal." Beth winked as they pulled out the base gate and made the short drive to Beth's place. The night air blew through the Jeep, drying the sweat that had accumulated in Lottie's hair, causing her to shiver. She struggled to pull the hoodie that was tied around her waist up—a difficult task within the constraints of the seatbelt—and push her arms inside.

"Is Michael already flying?" Lottie asked.

"Yeah, and I'm glad. I'm a little mad at him."

"Why? What did he do?" Lottie stared at Beth with wide eyes.

"He told me he was flying with initial quals tonight." Beth's lip crinkled.

"So?"

"I hate when he tells me that. I hate knowing when he's flying with fuckers who don't know dick. I mean, at what point do you determine a landing is bad? And now that I'm pregnant, I don't want any extra stress. I'll fart even more than I already do." Beth pulled into the driveway. "Let's order the pizza. I'm starving. You mind calling? I gotta pee so bad."

"I don't mind." Lottie padded into the kitchen as Beth flew down the hall to the bathroom, clearly not even bothering to close the door.

"Aahhhh." Beth's voice rang out as loud as the pee stream. "Better than an orgasm."

Lottie pulled the drawer of menus open and fished out the pizza one, grinning as she realized that she'd get to control the amount of olives that would end up on the pizza. She dialed and ordered, having them put "extra olives" on half. Why not give a pregnant lady all the olives she's craving?

"I swear this baby is still the size of a booger, but I'm peeing way too often. What's going to happen when it's full size?" Beth wiped her wet hands on Lottie's cheeks.

"Ew! That better not be pee." Lottie scowled and wiped her face with a tea towel.

Beth smirked and raised her eyebrows.

"I can't believe you're going to be responsible for the upbringing of a little human being." Lottie shook her head.

"Well, believe it. But fear not because this kid will have its Auntie Lottie to bore things down."

237

"I'm not boring." Lottie frowned. "And you'll move and leave me. Maybe before you even have the baby."

Silence filled the room. Beth knew Lottie was right. As with all military friendships, they lasted a lifetime, but the togetherness was always short-lived. Tears filled Beth's eyes.

"Are those tears?" Lottie squinted and moved in.

"Oh, shut up. It's the pregnancy. You know I'm not normally like this." Beth turned and hid her face.

Lottie hugged her from behind. Beth let a few tears escape. They landed on Lottie's arms. Lottie hugged her tighter. "We have modern technology. We can video chat all the time. It'll be great."

Beth turned and smiled. "Yeah. We'll always be in each other's lives."

"Always." Lottie smiled, but her stomach sank. She couldn't imagine living in Altus without Beth, and the thought of living in Hawaii with David wasn't bringing her much comfort either. The more she thought about the possibility, the more she wondered exactly what it was she really wanted.

The doorbell rang, causing the two of them to jump.

"Pizza's here." Beth walked to the door. "I'm starved."

"It can't be here that fast," Lottie said, eyebrow crooked.

Beth pulled open the door. Lottie was right behind her.

"Oh, hey, Jeff. What are you doing here? Michael has a night flight." Beth hands flew to her face, and she gasped. "Is something wrong?"

"No," quickly replied Major Jeff Simmons, who stood at the door in his flight suit. "Everything's fine. Sorry to scare you."

Beth clutched her chest. "I should punch you for scaring me. Why are you here?"

"I'm actually here to see Lottie. I stopped by her place, and when she wasn't home, I thought she might be here." Jeff had a solemn look on his face and avoided eye contact with Lottie even though she was now standing right beside Beth.

"Well, here she is." Beth motioned to Lottie.

He unzipped the pocket on the leg of his flight suit and pulled out an envelope. Lifting his eyes, he looked at Lottie for the first time and held out the envelope. "I'm sorry to be the one to do this, Lottie."

Lottie reached out and took the envelope. "What's this?"

"Divorce papers from David." Jeff backed away a few steps. "I'm really sorry." He turned and climbed into his truck and drove away without looking at her again.

Lottie's free hand raised to touch her parted lips as she stared down at the envelope in her hand. Had he really said "divorce papers?" No letter from David? No call. No explanation. What had she done wrong? The pit of her stomach opened up and filled with foolishness for writing him every day, anger for being used, and pain. Vaguely aware of Beth's arms wrapping around her, she stood, unmoving and breathless. Was her heart even beating?

As though someone else were doing it, Lottie robotically opened the envelope and pulled out the papers inside. She couldn't absorb what she was looking at, as though the letter was written in Italian. The letters were familiar but indecipherable to her.

Unsure how long she stood there, she was suddenly aware that Beth had let go of her and was talking to someone new at the door. The pizza delivery person was asking if Lottie was okay and Beth replied that she was, paid, and thanked them for the pizza. She disappeared, returned, and began rubbing Lottie's back.

"Lot, honey. Let's move into the living room and sit down, okay?" Beth guided her into the living room. Lottie nodded the whole way.

She slunk down into the sofa, still staring at the papers. Raising her head, she looked at Beth. "What a dick." The only thought and only words that she could piece together shot out like an arrow.

"He really is." Beth nodded.

"He's not even in Hawaii yet. There's no way he did this while he was deployed. He must have prepared all this before he talked to me—before he asked me to write to him. He knew he was going to send these papers when I was sucking his dick." Lottie threw the papers to the floor.

Beth stared with her mouth gaping. Lottie knew the dick-sucking part was a shock to her. She'd never revealed that pathetic piece of information.

She turned to Beth with shame-filled eyes. "What do I do now?"

Beth shrugged. "Sign 'em and move on."

Tears spilled down Lottie's cheeks. "I'm such a fucking idiot. I can't believe I let him manipulate me, again. I thought he wanted to get back together, but he was just using me. Wasn't he?"

Beth's lips pursed.

"You knew he was using me, didn't you?" Lottie searched Beth's face. "I know, I wouldn't listen. Why do I always cave to him?"

"Because you're a loving person. And sometimes that means you give more than you should to people who don't deserve you. That doesn't mean anything's wrong with you. Something is wrong with him. Don't let him make you feel like an idiot. You're amazing." Beth moved next to Lottie and wrapped her arms around her.

"I want to go home." Lottie stared at the papers, shaking her head.

"Do you want me to wrap up some pizza for you? I can come with you if you want."

"I don't mean home to my place. I mean, I want to go home to Michigan. I don't want to think about any of this." Lottie scooped up the papers, rose, and walked into Beth's kitchen. She pulled out the same junk drawer that contained the menus and riffled through it until she found a pen.

"What are you doing?"

"I'm going to sign the stupid papers."

"I think you have to do that in front of a notary."

"Shit." Lottie tossed the pen back in the drawer and slid it shut. She stuffed the papers back in the envelope and put it in her back pocket.

"You're going back to Michigan for good?"

"I don't think so, but I can't be here right now."

"What about the rest of the school year? It's the students' last day tomorrow."

"I'll be there tomorrow, but I'm going to talk to Dan about not returning after. Can you clean out my classroom for me?"

241

"Of course I can." Beth took Lottie's hands in hers. "I'll do anything you need me to do."

"Thanks. I'm going to go back to my place, call my mom, and pack."

"Do you want me to come and help you?" Beth squeezed her hands.

"No. I think I just want to be alone right now."

"Okay, let me grab my keys and I'll drive you home." Beth reached for the keys on the counter.

"I'm gonna walk."

"Are you sure?"

"Yeah. I need to clear my head a little. A walk will be good." Lottie pulled her hands free from Beth, spun on her heel, and headed out the door. She walked straight home, all the while knowing that if she looked back, she'd see Beth behind her.

Pulling out her keys, she could hear Pickles barking excitedly, happy for her return. "Hey, Pickles." She scratched his ears as she walked in. He rolled over onto his back, awaiting a belly rub, but Lottie just didn't have the energy. She stepped over him and walked into her bedroom, fishing her suitcase from the closet. As though she were a mindless zombie, she began stuffing clothes inside with no purpose or idea of how long she would be gone.

Lottie picked up the phone and called her mom. There was no answer. She wasn't going to leave news like that on an answering machine, so she hung up. Perhaps the news would be better told in person anyway. She decided she'd just show up on her parents' doorstep, bags and dog in hand. That way, her mom wouldn't have time to object to a dog being in her house.

She padded into the kitchen, pulled open the cabinet under the sink, and grabbed a garbage bag. She dumped everything perishable inside—containers and all—and poured the milk down the drain. Dragging the heavy bag outside, she tossed it into the trash bin and pulled it out to the curb. What else would she need to take care of before she left?

A thought washed over her, and she went inside and checked the clock; it was just after seven. She grinned, walked into her bathroom, opened the shower, and scooped her wedding band off the soap dish where she'd left it. She grabbed her keys as she passed through the kitchen.

"Momma will be back in a bit, Pickles." She closed the door and hopped in her car, heading straight for Red River Pawn. Once there, she hopped out of the car and headed straight toward the man on the counter, slamming down the gold band.

"How much will you give me for this?"

The man picked up the ring, inspected it, and then weighed it. "You looking to pawn or sell?"

"Sell."

"I'll give you forty bucks for it."

"That's all?"

"That's all I can give you. I need to make a few bucks off it when I sell it, and it really isn't worth much more than that."

Lottie pursed her lips. "Cheap bastard."

"Well, I'm sorry, ma'am. You're welcome to take it to the other shops in town, but I don't think you're going to get much more than that." The man pushed the ring back over to her.

"I'm sorry. I didn't mean you. I meant my ex-husband."

The man's eyes filled with pity.

Lottie pushed the ring back toward him with her finger. "It's a deal."

After filling out some paperwork, Lottie took her two twenty-dollar bills and stuffed them into her wallet, anxious to spend them and be free of David completely. At least they would help pay for her gas to Michigan. During the drive back to her place, she glanced at the empty space on her finger where the ring used to be, unsure of how she felt knowing it would never be there again. Even though she hadn't worn it in nearly two months, there was always a possibility before.

Back at home, she slowly walked toward the house that never really felt like a home, stopping on the front porch to survey the neighborhood.

"I don't belong here," she muttered before turning, unlocking the door, and heading inside. She kicked off her shoes and let Pickles outside. Her stomach swirled and her body ached. She felt like she'd just taken a beating from the inside. Being awake was painful and breathing was laborious.

She let Pickles back in after he peed and scratched him behind the ears. "It's just you and me from now on, buddy. I don't know what I'd do if I didn't have you to take care of."

Lottie plopped onto the floor and snuggled Pickles. She could tell that he knew she was sad. He snuggled his body tightly to hers. Tears poured down her cheeks, landing on the little dog's head, soaking his fur, but he never moved once. He listened to every word she said with eyes that seemed to understand and speak back to her with comfort.

The sunlight faded, and she soon found herself sitting in a dark room. She scooted out from under a now-sleeping Pickles, padded into the kitchen, and pulled open the cabinet. She popped an antihistamine into her mouth, ripped open the refrigerator, and chased the pill down with an old bottle of Corona that tasted little skunky. She shivered from the aftertaste and headed back to her room, turning off the light, grabbing the remote, and began wrapping herself in her burrito. Pickles darted onto the bed and snuggled up next to her.

"Okay, but just for tonight," she told him before flipping her TV to the channel that always played old black and white films. She emptily stared at the TV while stroking Pickles' fur. His rhythmic breathing mixing with the sound of music, singing, and tap-dancing in the film helped her drift off before any more tears escaped her eyes that evening.

Chapter Twenty-Five

Grant

Grant glanced over at the alarm clock for what felt like the millionth time of the night. Only thirty minutes remained until the alarm would sound. He grumbled and turned it off. There was no point in trying to sleep now. His mind churned all night with thoughts of dumping Tiffany and hopes of being with Lottie. The sooner the better on both accounts.

Rolling out of bed, he grabbed his throbbing head. Either lack of sleep or the rumbling thoughts had brought him one of those headaches that feels like your brain is loose in your head, slamming against the side with the slightest movement. He quietly opened the door and tip-toed into the kitchen to grab another handful of Nana's aspirin. He decided to take a quick shower and head to the White Buffalo for his coffee rather than risking waking Nana early with the sounds of him banging in the kitchen and the heavenly aroma filling the house. He didn't want any extra conversation surrounding the talk he was going to have with Tiffany over dinner that evening.

He knew from their text exchanges that she was completely clueless as to what was coming her way. He'd prepared himself for every possible reaction. A drink in his face. Tears. A public outburst. He'd be ready for them all.

Grant drank two tall glasses of water and headed for the bathroom where he showered quickly and slid into his bedroom to get dressed. Once ready, he slipped out the door, locking it behind him, and drove to the White Buffalo. He ordered two espressos and a white buffalo mocha—Lottie's favorite pick-me-up combo— and guzzled the first espresso while it was still a bit too hot, burning the roof of his mouth and getting one of those little blisters. He quickly rubbed his tongue against it to pop it.

Glancing in the rearview mirror, he grimaced at the haggard-looking guy staring back at him. Puffy, dark circles rested under his eyes, and every wrinkle seemed to be twice as deep. Maybe his rough-looking appearance would be a good thing for breaking up with Tiffany. She might take one look at him and decide that perhaps he was a bit too old for her. He wasn't sure it would be a good look for expressing his love for Lottie, though.

As he pulled into the parking lot at school, he noticed Lottie's car was already there. He walked inside and noticed her in Dan's office. Lottie's back was to him, but he knew something was wrong since Dan was pushing a box of tissues toward her. Once again, he felt guilty for letting his heart skip with the hopes that she was upset about David. Someone didn't cry when they're getting back together with their estranged husband, right?

Grant realized he was staring when some of this white buffalo mocha spilled onto his shoe and the floor.

Shit!

He quietly set the coffee, espresso, and his briefcase on the floor, pulled a handkerchief from his pocket, and mopped up the spilled coffee. He quickly tried to gather them up again but lost his grip on the coffee. It splattered all over the floor and walls. Dan rose from his desk, walked to the door, and closed it while staring at Grant with a "what is up with you" look painted across his face.

Grant scuttled down the hall to the boiler room and called out for Mr. Jones, the janitor.

"Yeah, what can I do for ya?" Mr. Jones asked as he chewed on a big bite of egg McMuffin.

"I'm sorry, but I, uh, spilled a coffee in the commons. It splattered all over the wall. If you'll give me a mop and bucket, I'll get it cleaned up."

"Eh, don't worry about that. I'm on it." Mr. Jones plopped the rest of his egg McMuffin on a work bench and plunked a hose into a mop bucket, filling it up.

"I really don't mind cleaning it up. It's my fault."

"Hey, that's what I get paid the big bucks for." Mr. Jones grinned and handed Grant a *'Caution* **WET FLOOR'** sign. "If you don't mind setting this up for me quick, though, I'd appreciate it."

"No problem. Thanks again."

"Don't mention it, young fellow." Mr. Jones nodded and returned his attention to the filling bucket.

Grant set up the sign and glanced at the still-closed office door before heading to the teachers' lounge to grab a cup of Cooley's crap to go with his remaining espresso. The adrenaline of his clumsiness would fade soon enough, and he knew he'd need to make up for the caffeine he'd spilled across the floor.

The morning went by rather quickly. It was the kids' field day events. Grant went from cheering kids to searching the outdoor field events for signs of Lottie. She sat on the sidelines, cheering for her students with mostly a blank stare on her face. At the picnic lunch outdoors, he desperately wished he could go sit with her and tell her how he felt about her. He wanted to know what was wrong, and he wanted to fix whatever it was for her. The mothers who came to help out with field day were very chatty and kept him at the group. His students were also very excited and talked a mile a minute about their firefighter teacher. Seeing as this was his last day with the students and he wouldn't be returning next year, he felt obligated to spend time with them. Besides, he could wait and talk to Lottie tomorrow, and he'd feel better letting her know that he had broken up with Tiffany, not that he planned to in the future. Then she'd know he was serious and not just another smooth-talking guy filled with promises of tomorrow.

At the day's end, after giving hugs to so many students and shaking the hands of more parents than he could count, Grant made his way to Lottie's room. The lights were off inside, and the door was locked. He peeked in through the window, still hoping he might see her inside, but she wasn't there. He slowed as he walked by Beth's room, but she too was gone.

He thought about asking Dan about the discussion he had with Lottie that morning but knew that it was none of his business, and since he intended to talk to Lottie tomorrow, he'd just wait and ask her. He hopped into his truck and drove to animal control to see if his furry buddy was still there.

The human chimney was outside smoking—as usual.

"Hey, is the border collie still here?"

"Oh yeah, she's still in there. I think she's waiting for ya. I swear every time I go back there, she lifts her head with hope glimmering in those eyes but huffs and puts her head back down when she sees me. 'Ain't I good enough?' I say to her every time, but she just huffs again."

"Okay, if I go back?"

"Sure, it is, darlin'. Maybe you can get her to eat something again. Lord knows she needs some meat on them bones. She looks like a skeleton, and I don't want people to think I ain't treatin' these dogs right. I love my animals. Every single one of them."

"I know you do." Grant pressed his lips into a smile as he walked passed her. He knew her heart was in the right place, but she definitely wasn't doing the best she could for the animals. Their cages were always too full of shit for her to be on top of things. Maybe if she spent a little less time smoking and a little more time cleaning, more people would want to come into the animal control to look at the dogs. He shook his head to try to shake the judgmental thoughts free.

He pushed through the door marked **DOG** and, as the human chimney said, the Border collie raised her head. Only she didn't huff and lower it again. Grant could swear a smile spread across the dog's lips as she slowly rose and approached the fence as he neared.

"Hey, girl," he said as he put his fingers through the chain link and rubbed her snout. He reached over

with his other hand and scooted her dish over, scooping a few morsels from the bowl. "You wanna try to eat
a few of these?" He put a few pieces in his hand. The
dog gently took them and chewed.

Grant sat there feeding her until the bowl was empty.

"You wanna help pick the ticks off her?" the human
chimney asked as soon as she came into the room. She
stretched out her hand to give him a plastic container
and a pair of tweezers.

"Sure." Grant took the items.

"You can take her into the yard. Probably be able to
see them better there, but make sure you put them all
in the plastic container and don't let 'em drop into the
yard."

"Yes, ma'am." Grant opened the gate and looped a
lead around the dog's neck, but she wouldn't come
out. He scooped her up with one arm while balancing
the container and tweezers in his other hand. "Mind
opening the door?" Grant asked as he carried the dog
toward the outside yard.

"Got it." The chimney held the door open. "Happy
pickins." She closed the door behind them.

So much for the idea of helping to pick them off. It
looked like the job was now his alone.

A little nervous about how the dog would react,
Grant started removing the ticks furthest from her
mouth. If the dog was going to snap, he wanted as
much time to react as possible. But the dog never did a
thing. She just lay there and let him pull tick after tick
off her. She winced every now and then, especially
when he got the ones that were deep inside her ear.

"Poor girl." He rubbed her belly. "But I think we got them all. You should feel much better now." He didn't want to let his hopes get up about adopting her, but it was happening anyway. How could such an emaciated dog, covered with so many ticks, belong to anyone? He was sure she'd be his after the stray hold was up, and he was sure the human chimney wouldn't adopt her out to anyone else first. He had it in his mind to ask her to let him take her before the stray hold was up, if anyone had any claim to her, it should certainly be void since she was clearly neglected. She seemed to have a soft spot for animals and didn't seem exactly strict with the rules or the dog's shit would have been cleaned up the moment she saw it needed it. He shook his head. He was judging her again. It was hard for him to want to leave the dog there any longer than he had to. Clearly, he was already attached, whether he wanted to admit it or not.

"I'll be right back, girl," he said before he got up and made his way into the front office. The human chimney was outside smoking. Grant popped his head out the door. "Is there a brush I can use?"

"Oh, sure, darlin. There's one in the groomin' room behind the office. Just go on through and find it."

"Thanks."

She waved her hand and hacked a "you're welcome" before taking another long puff on her cigarette. Grant made his way through the office and into the grooming "room." Closet was more like it. The tub looked like it could use a thorough cleaning. He wasn't sure how anyone could feel clean after being inside it, but he figured the dogs didn't care, and at least it did seem that she was making and attempt to keep them bathed.

He sat back down on the ground next to the Border collie, who laid her head in his lap. He brushed her while talking about Tiffany and Lottie until his phone chirped, indicating that he needed to get home to get ready for his break-up date with Tiffany. He scooped the dog up off the ground when it was clear that she wasn't going to walk on the leash and placed her back in her cage. He cleaned out a few piles of poop that had collected in the corner, emptied her water dish, and filled it up with fresh water.

"I'll be back tomorrow," he said to the dog before he left. On his way through the office, he stopped to talk to the human chimney. "I'd really like to adopt her. I know I can't until the stray hold is up…" Grant paused and watched for any sign she might say waiting wasn't necessary after all, but that didn't happen. "Is there any way that you cannot put her up for adoption before I can get her?"

"Oh, sure, darlin. I'll just keep the status marked as stray hold until you come get her. But I can't wait too long. Just a day or two. I don't want to ruin her chances if you change your mind and another family shows up."

"I understand." Grant smiled. "See you tomorrow!"

"See ya, darlin."

He sailed out the door, feeling calmer after talking his problems out while he improved the life of the sweet dog. She had to be feeling so much better without those parasites in her life, and he would be feeling better once he shook free Tiffany. True, he still dreaded

E.N. BECK

hurting her, but she was young, and he knew she would move on and find someone else quickly. It wasn't fair of him to be wasting her time anyway. Even if Lottie wasn't going to move into the picture, he'd just be using Tiffany for sex anyway. And he didn't want to be that guy anymore. Now he knew he wanted something more.

Grant drove home and made his way inside. Kicking off his shoes, he met Nana coming out of the kitchen. "Hey, Nana. Door was unlocked again."

She waved him off. "You stink like smoke again."

"I'll shower. I've gotta get ready to go meet Tiffany anyway."

Nana frowned.

Grant pursed his lips. "I've got to do this."

"I know, honey," Nana said before she went back into the kitchen and put the teapot on the burner.

Grant grabbed his robe from the bedroom and hopped in the shower, feeling both excited and nervous about ending things with Tiffany. He decided that staying with her when he didn't feel much for her was him being a bad guy, not him being honest with her and setting her free.

After his shower, he scooped up his smoky clothes from the bathroom floor and tossed them into the washing machine. He did his hair and put on some clothes he thought would be suitable for a break up—nothing he didn't mind losing if they ended up covered in the cranberry juice of a woo woo.

Chapter Twenty-Six

Lottie

Lottie walked out of Dan Cooley's office feeling supported and holding new appreciation for the boss that she and Beth had so frequently made fun of.

"I'm so sorry, Lottie," he told her. "Of course you can take off tomorrow, and I'll help Beth clean up your room. But one thing I won't do is hire someone else until you've had time to think it over and are certain you won't be returning to us. It's easy to fill teaching positions, but it won't be easy to get over replacing you if we could have kept you."

"Thanks, Dan." She walked around the desk and gave him a hug before heading to her classroom. As she did, she tried to paint the best fake smile she could across her face. It was field day, after all, and the kids had been so excited about it all month. At least the different events and parents' helpers chatting with her might help get her mind off things.

She hadn't called her parents back yet to let them know she was coming home, and she wasn't quite sure what their reactions would be. It was hard enough to tell them that she and David had separated. She felt like a failure, especially given the fact that they were never that fond of David to begin with and she'd always put so much effort into defending him. Now she'd have to admit that they were right about him all along. There's another element to being a woman who has been cheated on—shame. Every time someone asked what happened to her marriage, she felt complete and utter shame. Shame at not being enough. Not pretty enough, fun enough, smart enough, adventurous enough, or anything else you can think of— enough. She felt damaged and unworthy. Add to that the way she'd messed things up with Grant and she felt like an utter fool.

The day passed by in a haze of clapping and hugging children who won one event or another. When the end came, she swiftly made her retreat with Beth, turning off the lights and locking the door behind her without giving it a second look. Maybe she'd return but what for? Beth wouldn't be here forever, and without being a squadron spouse, she'd never meet incoming spouses. Her life would be empty and alone in the town where she had been left behind by so many.

Beth drove her to the notary where Lottie signed her divorce papers and then mailed them off. Shrugging when it was all over, Lottie hopped back in the Jeep and stared at the town as it whizzed by on the way home.

A fresh start was what she needed. Maybe she and Pickles would begin again in Michigan, or maybe she'd try to reinvent herself in some destination of her choosing, not one she was following someone else to. She could be the star in her own show rather than play a supporting role in someone else's movie.

Lottie hugged Beth, who promised she'd be over as soon as she changed out of her work clothes to help her pack. She padded into the bedroom and promptly told Pickles to get off her bed, again.

"You know Mommy doesn't like you farting near my pillow." She shooed him out of the bedroom and let him outside.

I guess I should make sure I've cleaned up all the dog's shit in the backyard before I leave.

Lottie scratched her head as she watched Pickles make his rounds in the yard to pee on everything he could find. She still wasn't sure if she was going to leave tonight or in the morning. Beth was already trying to talk her into staying one more night and having a sleepover. Lottie suspected Beth might just want more time to talk her into staying. Part of her wanted to stay, but it's hard to scuttle around a town without a shred of hope for a future. Altus was a ghost town for her now. Places only seemed to exist to remind her of her failures and faux pas. Did she want to go on being haunted by pitiful memories?

It wasn't long before there was a knock on the door. Lottie made her way down the hall and opened it. Beth stood there with a six pack of beer.

"You know I'm not going to be doing any drinking." Lottie shook her head.

"Well, I brought it just in case. I'm gonna miss you." Beth puffed her lip out.

"I'm gonna miss you, too. I don't even know how long I'll be gone. I just can't be here right now." Lottie sighed and walked into the kitchen, slumping down onto the recliner. "Part of me doesn't want to go home. I still haven't told my parents."

Beth sat on the couch, placing the six pack on the counter, pulling one out, and cracking it open. She held it out to Lottie. "One won't hurt."

Lottie took it and chugged it back. It was nice and cold. She sighed and smiled.

"See. Better already." Beth blew her a kiss.

"Do you ever think about moving back home?"

"To Florida?"

"Duh."

"Fuck no. I couldn't handle living within a three-state radius of my mother. She'd drive me crazy."

"I never thought I'd be moving back to Michigan. I feel like a loser, returning with my tail tucked between my legs to live with Mommy and Daddy."

"Then don't go." Beth leaned in close to Lottie. "At least don't think about it as moving back. Think of it as a vacation. And for God's sake, take a flight. That's a long-ass drive for you with a dog. And leave Pickles with me. You can take some time to clear your head knowing he's being loved on. You don't want to make a pregnant chick sick with worry over your safety, do you?"

"I'll be fine. I'll stop for the night and rest. I promise."

"No, you won't. I know you; you'll drive straight through, and I'll be worried sick that you'll fall asleep at the wheel. I mean, did you even book ahead with a hotel that takes dogs?"

Lottie pursed her lips and stared down at her feet.

"I knew it! See! And before you say you want to save money by driving, a hotel room and gas would cost you as much as a plane ticket. Especially since Michael and I are going to buy your ticket for you."

Lottie shook her head and opened her mouth to speak, but Beth shot over and covered Lottie's mouth with her hand.

"I love you, and I'm buying you a plane ticket and watching Pickles. When you're ready to come home, you just let me know, and we'll get your ticket back here. There's no rush. If you decide to move for good, you'll need to come back pack up all your stuff and clear this place out anyway. Save yourself all that fucking driving."

Lottie buried her face in her hands. Tears poured from her eyes. "I don't deserve a friend like you."

"Yes, you do, honey. You deserve everything. You're an amazing person who just happened to step in a big pile of shit named David. And I'm gonna help you hose it off. You'll be okay. You'll see."

Lottie wiped her face and wrapped her arms around Beth.

"Don't squeeze too tight or I'll have to pee." Beth hugged her, rubbing her back.

Lottie chuckled and sat back in her chair, taking another sip of her beer. "I guess since I'm not driving, I don't have to worry about how much I drink."

"You don't leave until tomorrow afternoon. I plan on getting you drunk so I can finally take advantage of you." Beth waggled her eyebrows.

Lottie shook her head. "It'll take a lot more than one beer, lady."

"That's why I brought six. Now before you get too drunk, let's get all Pickles' things loaded into my car and make sure you give me the spare key to your house so I can water your plants and check your mail."

259

"You know I already know I'm coming back to dead plants, right?"

"Stop that! The cactus in my bathroom has been alive for a year. I say your plants have a fifty percent chance of making it."

***

Lottie's eyes fluttered open as Beth tapped her shoulder.

"Lot, get your ass up and give me a hug goodbye. I gotta get to work. I have two classrooms to clean." Beth leaned over and kissed Lottie on her head.

Lottie sat up and hugged Beth, who sat on the edge of her bed.

"Michael forwarded your flight confirmation to your email. He's going to pick you up in two hours to drive you to Dallas. I wish I could take you."

"I wish you could too. Thank you, Beth."

"Don't mention it. That's what friends are for." Beth gave Lottie another squeeze and walked out the bedroom door. "C'mon, Pickles. Time to go to Aunt Beth's."

"Bye, Pickles!" Lottie called. She listened to the door close and suddenly felt extra lonely. Normally, she enjoyed her alone time, but she hadn't recently. To keep busy, she hopped up and got in the shower. No point in being a loser and also the stinky person on the flight—and there was always one, wasn't there? The last time she flew from Detroit to Dallas, there was a man who smelled of ass, armpits, and onions so bad that she could barely stand to breathe.

Lottie put her toiletries away as she finished getting ready, wheeled all her things to the front door, and peeked out the window every thirty seconds, waiting for Michael. Did he forget? Was he going to be late? He knew how much she hated being late, and being late to the airport was about the worst it could get. She didn't want to have to rush through security and scramble to her gate. Maybe she should have chosen shoes that she could slide on more easily. But she hated when she wore any shoes besides her tennis shoes on airplanes. It was like her feet swelled up and her toes were mashed together, and she would wiggle them desperately, wanting to free them from an iron maiden.

Where was Michael? Lottie pulled out her cell and looked at the time. He was two minutes late. How long should she wait before she sent him a text? Five minutes? Ten? Definitely not any longer than ten. She paced back and forth between the window and the door. Anxiety bubbled up inside of her like a lava lamp.

She pulled out her phone to text him at the nine-minute mark when she couldn't stand it any longer. Just before she hit "send," he pulled into the driveway. She quickly erased the message and shoved the phone back in her purse, grabbed her suitcase, and headed out the door.

Michael put her bag in the back of his truck and drove her the three and a half hours to Dallas. The ride was quiet but not awkward. Michael turned the radio on, made a little small talk, but didn't bombard her with it the whole way. She never liked small talk. It only served to remind her of how bad she was at it.

Once they arrived at the airport, Michael got her bag out of the truck and gave her a hug. "You know everyone is behind you, Lottie. Beth isn't your only friend, you know?"

"I know. Thanks, Michael." Lottie grabbed her bag, pulled up the handle, and wheeled it into the airport. She checked in at the kiosk, handed over her bag, and headed through security. She made her way to the gate, where she had time to sit and relax before it was time to board.

She looked around at all the people who were to be her fellow passengers, trying to will some of them not to sit anywhere near her. Those included everyone who looked like they should be purchasing two seats and those that look like they hadn't bathed in, well, ever.

She never could figure out why so many young women wore their pajamas on flights. It always struck her as funny that there was so much fuss made over the people of Walmart when the people of United Air were much worse. It just made her wish she lived in a bygone era when people dressed nice for air travel. Suits, dresses, ties, white gloves and pearls. She had never been a fan of cigarette smoke, but she would almost trade some for the horrible smell of tuna-tinged crotch-cheese that seemed to accompany flights in the modern era.

Lottie boarded the plane and was unfortunate enough to sit next to a large woman wearing purple polyester pants. Her large legs spilled under the arm rest and onto Lottie's seat, making her wish she hadn't worn shorts. The woman smiled at her, and Lottie did her best not to show the disdain she felt as the woman's large, moist polyester leg rubbed against her bare skin. She tucked her purse in between the moist blubber and her leg.

She did her best to make polite conversation with the large, foul-breathed woman on the aisle seat who never stopped chatting the whole way. She did her best to ignore her, reading the horrible inflight magazine over and over to try to drop a hint that she didn't want to chat. The man in the window seat slept the whole time. She was jealous of him. What she wouldn't give to be able to sleep on a flight. She'd never been able to, and it wasn't because someone always seemed to want to chat with her. Anxiety was her constant companion on flights. David used to laugh at her and remind her that air travel was safer than riding in a car, but did that really matter to someone who hated the feeling of your stomach dropping out during turbulence or the thought of plummeting to the ground at any given moment?

Once she landed and retrieved her luggage from the baggage claim, she searched in her purse for her phone to call an Uber to take her to the train station. She couldn't find it.

Fuck!

She emptied the entire contents of her purse onto the airport floor. It wasn't there. She knew she had it when she boarded the plane, but now it was gone. She searched the baggage terminal for the fat woman who sat next to her or the sleeping guy on the other side but could find neither. She was sure one of them had stolen her phone.

Fuck!

She asked an old couple who were sitting on a bench if she could use their cell to call her dad. Smiling, they handed it over. She dialed the number on the old flip phone and asked her dad to send an Uber for her, but he insisted on making the one-and-a-half-hour drive from Frankenmuth to Detroit to pick her up. He asked her a million questions on the phone. "Dad, I'm borrowing someone's cell. Mine was stolen, and I need to give it back. I'll explain everything when you get here."

She hung up and handed it back to the old couple, thanking them over and over. Butterflies swirled in her stomach when she thought about exactly what she was going to say to her parents. They'd be surprised to see her, for sure, and probably happy, but it didn't make her feel like any less of a failure that others would rejoice in the fact that her marriage was over.

Chapter Twenty-Seven

Grant

Grant met Tiffany at The Plaza after her shift at Meers. She was seated in the entryway, staring at her phone. He paused a minute to swallow his stomach back down before approaching her.

"Grant!" She jumped up and kissed him on the cheek. He wiped it away and checked his fingers for signs of a bright red lipstick mark. Yup, it smeared his fingers. He fished a handkerchief from his pocket and rubbed his cheek until he was sure it was clean.

"Y'all ready?" The hostess smiled and led them to a quiet booth in the back. Grant was thankful for that. If he was going to get a drink thrown in his face, he'd like to be sheltered from as many prying eyes as he could.

His mind churned. He wasn't sure when he should do it. How he should do it. What he should say. He decided to let her enjoy her meal first and then try his best to break up with her gently at the end. The silence between them was awkward. Grateful when the waitress appeared with chips and salsa, he happily ordered their drinks and began perusing the menu while stuffing chips into his mouth to avoid talking. Luckily,

Tiffany began talking a mile a minute about her day at work and all the comments she'd gotten on her Instagram post from the wildlife refuge.

"Don't you feel weird pretending you like doing something you don't? Isn't that lying to all your followers?" Grant shoved another chip in his mouth.

"I don't think it's lying. It's telling a story. Are writers liars? It's not like I have a genuine interest in these people. They're my fans. Do you think there are any celebrities who care about their fans? They get an exciting story from me, and I get likes and comments from them. It's a win-win." Tiffany took a picture of her margarita as soon as the waitress set it in front of her. "Hashtag worth the calories." She smiled before taking a big long sip and licking her lips.

She was on his nerves. And he decided to strike while the iron was hot. It was best to break up with her before she said something truly sweet and reminded him that she really was a good person. Or worse yet, when she was doing something that made him horny. She was definitely sexy, and he had a hard time resisting her in those moments.

Grant pursed his lips and was about to speak when the waitress returned. "Are we ready to order?"

"Could we have a few more minutes, please?" Grant thought it might be better to do it before they ordered in case Tiffany wanted to storm out now.

"I'm ready to order now." Tiffany interrupted. "I'll have the flautas salad." She handed the waitress her menu. "Oh, and another margarita."

Grant rubbed the back of his neck as he quickly glanced at the menu, ordering the first thing he saw.

"The Santa Fe quesadilla, please." He handed the waitress the menu. She nodded and left.

He shoved another chip in his mouth. He should have ordered a beer. Why didn't he order a beer? And a shot of tequila. He gulped the chip down, which hadn't been chewed nearly enough, and coughed on a sharp edge that stuck in his throat.

"Excuse me." He grabbed his water and took a drink. Tiffany looked at him with knitted brows and a crinkled lip.

"Is something wrong with you tonight? You're acting weird." Her lip remained crinkled.

Now was the best time to do it. She wasn't looking at him with her lovey-eyes but with a tinge of disgust.

"Actually, yeah. Something is wrong. I don't think we should see each other anymore." Grant bit his lip.

"You're breaking up with me?" Tiffany didn't seem able to believe what was happening. She stared at him, unblinking.

"I think the gap in our ages is too much, and we don't really have anything in common. I'm sorry, Tiffany. I think you're a great person. We're just not well-suited for each other."

Tiffany took a long drink of her margarita while her eyes remained locked on him. She set it down and huffed. "This is some fucking bullshit. You're never gonna find someone as hot as me."

Grant pursed his lips and rubbed the back of his neck. He didn't know what to say, so he nodded in agreement.

"You're old," Tiffany added, taking another sip of her margarita.

My point exactly.

He nodded in agreement once again.

"This is fucking bullshit." Tiffany shook her head while she pulled out her phone and took a selfie with a pouting lip. "Hashtag dumped. You know, there are plenty of people in line to date me."

"I'm sure there are." Grant couldn't believe she was looking down at her phone, posting her breakup selfie while she was talking to him.

After she finished posting her Insta breakup photo, she shoved her phone in her purse, stood, smoothed her clothes over her body, and scowled at him. "You were a big waste of my time."

Grant waited for her to pick up the rest of her margarita and throw it in his face, but she just spun on her heel and stormed out of the restaurant. The waitress arrived with the second margarita.

"I'll take that." Grant took it from the waitress. "Would you mind changing that order to-go and bringing the check?"

"Sure thing." The waitress gave him a pity grin and left.

He drank the margarita as he waited for the food and check, his fingers itched to pull out his phone and text Lottie right away, asking if he could come over and talk to her. He decided to drive by her place instead of texting. After the waitress brought him the check and food, he hopped in his truck and headed over to Lottie's. Beth's Jeep was there, and he didn't want to say all he had to say in front of anyone else.

He didn't feel like going to home to deal with Nana either. He didn't have the energy to answer all her questions about the breakup. Too bad Nana didn't have an Instagram account; she could have read all about it for herself. Half of Altus and a good portion of Oklahoma were probably fully aware of the entire evening by now. He missed the days before social media. And the days before cell phones, for that matter. No one could truly get lost anymore, could they?

Grant weaved around town for a while before ending up at the Falcon Road Liquor store, where he grabbed a six pack then headed home. He slid in through the unlocked door and kicked off his shoes. Nana was asleep in the recliner. He covered her with the old orange and green afghan and made his way out onto the patio. He cracked open one of the beers, put his feet up, and thought about what he was going to say to Lottie. He still didn't want to come between her and David, but with the way she'd been crying lately, he was sure that things there had to be over. No one cried that much when they're happy about something.

***

Grant's head pounded with the pulsing of his alarm clock. He'd had one too many beers. Normally he would have cursed the fact that he had to get up, but not today. He would take a handful of Nana's aspirins and drink as much coffee as it took to make the headache go away. If it didn't get rid of it, he didn't care. Seeing Lottie's face was going to be enough to get him through the day. Filled with a bubbling nervous energy, he bounded out of bed and flew into the bathroom to take a shower. He tried to calm himself down, but he was anxious to get ready, get to the school, and see her already. After carrying the weight of Tiffany around on his back, he was suddenly free to move about life the way he wanted. No more chains, no more stopping to post on Insta, no more of Nana heaping on the guilt of who Papa Joe thought would be perfect for him. He was finally free to follow his heart, and his heart was leading him straight to Lottie.

After trimming his beard, checking for nose hairs and boogers, and doing his best to make his hair look like he hadn't spent too much time on it, he dressed and slid into the kitchen like Tom Cruise in Risky Business.

Nana clapped her hands and laughed. "Well, what has gotten into you this morning?"

"I just have a feeling it's going to be a great day." Grant opened the cabinet and grabbed the aspirin.

"Aspirin? Did you pull a muscle sliding in here?"

"No. I've just got a bit of a headache."

"Well, if you want something stronger, I've got some ibuprofen in the cabinet above the refrigerator. Your Papa Joe used it, but I can't reach up there."

Grant put the aspirin back and reached into the cabinet above the refrigerator. He pulled out a bottle of ibuprofen and opened it up. "What is this?" He pulled out a baggie that was stuffed in on top of the pills. "Pot, Nana?"

Nana's cheeks flushed red. "Would you believe it's for my glaucoma?"

Grant grinned and shook his head.

"Fine. Your Papa Joe and I liked to smoke a little grass from time to time. I just thought we were out. Why don't you hand that over to me?"

Grant shook his head and handed her the baggie.

"It's good for you physically and emotionally. Just wait until you get old and we'll see if you'd rather take all that shit the doctor wants to put you on or just smoke a little grass. You'll see. Costs a lot less too."

"No judgement from me, Nana. Just don't hold out on me now that I know about your secret stash." He popped a few ibuprofens in his mouth and swallowed them down. He filled his thermos with coffee and grabbed his lunch off the counter. He stuffed his feet into his shoes, threw his lunch into his briefcase, grabbed his keys, and headed out the door.

On the way to work, he rolled down the windows and cranked the music despite his headache. Nothing could kill his mood. He was a man on a long-overdue mission. Man, he wished he'd punched David in the face the night he showed up at Lottie's and ruined their date.

When he arrived at the school, he was disappointed that he didn't see her car there yet. He guessed she wasn't as concerned about getting there early when there were no classes. He made his way down the hall to his room, but when he passed Lottie's, he found Dan and Beth inside. He turned and popped inside.

"Hey, guys, what's up?"

"Oh, hey, Grant. We're just cleaning. Wanna give us a hand before you start on your room?" Dan grinned.

"Let me just put my things down and I'll be right back." Grant walked over to his room, unlocked the door, and put his thermos and briefcase down. He poured himself some coffee and strolled back across the hall, sipping it slowly. "Do we move from one room to the next? Is it faster that way?"

"No," Dan said. "We're cleaning out Lottie's room because she had to take a personal day."

"What?" Grant dripped some coffee onto the floor. "Shit!" He set the coffee on the counter and grabbed some brown paper towels and tried wiping it up. "Why does the school buy these things? They don't absorb anything?"

"Right? That's what I keep telling him, but he's cheap as fuck." Beth crossed her arms.

"The school does have a budget." Dan waved her off.

Grant tossed the paper towel into the trash. "So, what's that about Lottie taking a personal day?"

"She won't be returning," Dan said.

Beth turned to Grant and frowned. "She's gone home to Michigan. She's flying out of Dallas this afternoon."

"Wait? Gone home? When is she coming back?" Grant lowered himself onto the corner of the desk.

Dan shrugged. "I don't know if she's coming back. I told her I'd hold off on trying to find a replacement for her for at least a month while she thinks things over."

Grant walked over to Beth while Dan went back to washing the smart board. "Hey Beth, can I talk to you alone for a minute?"

"Sure." Beth followed Grant into the hall.

He led her to his room and shut the door. "Is Lottie okay?"

Beth sighed. "She's been better. David served her with divorce papers after she spent all that time writing to him while he was deployed. Basically, the dick used her again and didn't even have the guts to tell her himself."

"What an asshole. I should have punched him." Grant's jaw tensed and his fist balled up.

"You and me both. Anyway, she wanted to go home. I helped her pack last night, and Michael is driving her to the airport right now."

"Is she coming back?"

"Well, she'll probably be back at some point. Pickles is staying with me, and she'll have to get the rest of her stuff. She talked about moving out of Altus, though. She thinks it's too painful to stay here."

"I should have stopped by last night. I'm an idiot." Grant's jaw clenched even tighter. Then his face softened, and he lowered himself into his chair, resting his head in his hands. "I broke up with Tiffany yesterday. Today I was going to ask Lottie if she'd give me another shot. The way she's been crying lately, I figured something happened with David. I couldn't go on dating Tiffany when Lottie is all I think about."

"Well, it's not too late. You should call her. I know she still has feelings for you, Grant."

"Thanks, Beth."

"Sure thing. I better get back to Dan or he'll claim he gets no help around here." She smiled and slid out the door, closing it behind her.

Grant pulled his phone out of his briefcase and called Lottie. There was no answer and it went to voicemail.

"Hey, this is Lottie. I can't answer so leave a message. Or don't leave a message and send a text instead."

"Hey, Lottie. This is Grant. I'm hoping when you get this, you'll give me a call. I want to talk to you, and I want to know if you'd let me take you out on a date

E.N. BECK

when you get back to Altus. Well, give me a call. Okay. Bye."

Chapter Twenty-Eight

Lottie

Lottie stared up at the white ceiling fan twirling around slowly as she lay on her twin-sized childhood bed. The pink flowers that dotted the white ruffles of the comforter reminded her of the pink roses that Grant had left on her desk. A smile tugged at the corners of her mouth.

After the long ride with her dad followed up by a lengthy explanation of her situation with her parents, she had trudged up the stairs, collapsed on the bed, and fallen asleep. She wasn't sure of the time. Judging from the amount of light in the room, it was either evening or early morning. She wasn't even sure of the day. Having been so tired when she collapsed, she'd have believed if someone told her she'd slept for a week straight.

She knew she should get up and call Beth to let her know she'd arrived safely but minus her cell phone. But as much as she urged her body to move, it just didn't. It was as though someone placed a few of those lead, x-ray aprons on her. Completely weighed down, she just watched the ceiling fan twirl.

After this nap, I'm going to make a list of all the things I could possibly do with my life next and where I might want to go.

One thing she knew for sure, she didn't want to talk about it with her parents anymore. She couldn't listen to her mom's smug "I told you about him," or her dad's "you can always move back home with us." Thoughts of moving overseas filled her mind. The big problem with that idea was that she was shy and didn't make friends easily. It felt great to think about moving far away and seeing exotic things, but she knew she'd just end up feeling even more awkward surrounded by people she didn't even share a common language with.

Somewhere in her thoughts, she drifted to sleep, waking up again when it was completely dark. She sat up and rubbed her eyes. She rose and made her way to the door, gently twisting the knob and cracking it open, first peeking down the hall then turning her ear to listen for signs of life in the house. She saw and heard nothing. Lottie tip-toed down the hall then weaved her way down the stairs, careful to avoid the creaking spots she'd memorized as a teen.

Quiet and darkness filled the downstairs rooms. A sigh of relief escaped her. She crept into the kitchen and looked at the microwave clock, which read three forty-five a.m. She pulled open the refrigerator and fished out some deli cold cuts and cheese and nibbled on them as she watched her reflection in the large bay window of the kitchen. There could have been a serial killer standing in the woods watching her and she'd never know it. It was pitch black outside. There was pure nothingness out there, and it mirrored the way she felt inside.

She pulled the fridge back open and searched for something to drink. Her parents had well water and she never could stand it. It had a smell. Water wasn't supposed to have a smell, and it turned everything red. Her mind flashed to the luggage she'd packed. Did she bring anything that would end up with an orange tint by the time she left? Her mind shifted to how long she'd stay. She already felt an anxious ache in her that wanted to leave. She thought it was funny how a house could be your home for such a long time, but once you'd been gone for a bit, you felt like a stranger whenever you returned.

Grinning, she shrugged, figuring she could stay long enough to save enough money to replace her cell phone by eating her mom's groceries. Fuck, that fat ass on the flight! After thinking it over for a while, she knew she was the one who'd stolen it. Probably when she had her head turned to avoid the butthole-breath that kept landing in her face. She'd call the airline to see if her phone was found, just in case it wasn't the butthole-breathed fat ass. What good was a stolen phone anyway these days? Could people do anything with it without the password to open it? Probably. Technology just made you think your shit was secure when you're probably more vulnerable than you'd ever been in the past. She wondered what time she could call the airport.

Lottie made her way into the office. She turned on her parent's dinosaur of a computer and searched for a number to call United about lost items. Instead of a number, she found a form to fill out. That suited the introverted, "I hate speaking to strangers" part of her but also deflated any hope she had that her phone would be found. The form and lack of number basically screamed, "Yeah, this is too much of a waste of time to hire people to deal with."

Lottie clicked open Solitaire, then Mahjong, and finally Free Cell to pass the time before she could call Beth. There was no way she'd call her early on her first day of summer vacation, but she wanted to let her know she lost her phone, or she'd give her an ear-full about not calling. Two hours ticked by and Lottie found herself yawning again.

She decided to wash her face, go back to sleep, and then call Beth as soon as she woke up. Weaving up the stairs, she made her way into the bathroom, cleaned up, and snuck back into her bedroom, where she went back to sleep.

***

Pain from her bladder woke her. Her body felt heavy as she dragged it down the hall to the bathroom. How was it possible to feel crappier after all that sleep? After using the bathroom, she made her way downstairs, where the smell of coffee and bacon greeted her.

"Well, hey, there she is! How ya feeling, sleepy-head?" Lottie's dad raised his coffee cup to her.

"Hey, Dad." Lottie smiled.

"Looks like a little mouse got into my cheese in the middle of the night." Her mom shook a scrambled egg coated spatula at her.

Lottie fought the urge to roll her eyes. She pressed her lips into a smile instead. Making her way over to the coffeemaker, she grabbed mug out of the cabinet, filled it, and added a little half and half. She took a sip and remembered just how horrible her mother's coffee was.

"Is there any sugar?" she asked.

"On the Lazy Susan, hun." Her mom continued stirring the eggs.

Lottie gave it a spin until she saw the old, orange Tupperware sugar container. She popped open the large end and scooped out a spoonful, adding it to the coffee, stirring, and sipping. Ugh, her mom could give Dan a run for his money on a world's crappiest coffee award.

Sitting at the table, she turned to her dad. "Would it be okay if I borrowed your truck after breakfast? I wanna go into town and get myself a new cell."

And a good cup of coffee.

"Why don't I take you? I can run to Kern's while you're getting a phone. I'll pick up some of their Braunschweiger sausage for us to have at lunch. Your mom doesn't like it, but I know you do."

"That sounds good. I haven't had it in a long time."

"Hon, we got any more rye bread or that Mittlescharfer mustard?" he asked her mother as she set eggs, bacon, and toast on the table.

Lottie filled her plate.

"We have the bread, but I'm not sure on the mustard. Check the pantry," she told him as she sat down.

"Well, I wouldn't know where to look."

Huffing, she rose and charged into the pantry. Lottie's dad winked at her. Her mom returned with a jar of mustard, slapping it down on the table. "Happy?"

"Thanks, darling. And you're sure we have the rye?"

"Yes, I'm sure." Her mom glared at him. "Or would you like me to check?"

"Would you mind? I just want to make sure I get it while I'm in town if we're out. It's not often my girl is home to visit," Lottie's dad said as he put his hand on her shoulder, giving it a squeeze.

Her mom huffed, rose, and marched over the bread drawer, pulling it open, reaching inside and pulling out a bag of rye bread. She held it over her head. "Full bag."

"It's not moldy or anything, is it?"

"No, I just bought it." Her mom returned with it to the table. "Check it over if you like. No mold. Nice and fresh."

"Oh, thank you, dear." Lottie's dad picked up the bread and inspected it closely, as though he wasn't willing to take her mom's word for it.

Her mom mumbled under her breath, and her dad had a grin tugging at the corners of his mouth. Lottie shook her head, wondering why her dad always got such a kick out of antagonizing her mom and why her mom put up with it. Surely, she had to see through his little game. Shaking her head, she bit into a slice of bacon, hoping her mom wouldn't bring David up, but no sooner had she went to take a second bite, her mom opened her mouth.

"So, going to get a new phone today, eh? Gonna get a new number so that bastard can't call you?"

"I don't know, Mom. I didn't even think about it." Lottie dropped the bacon onto her plate, her appetite gone.

"Well, I'm not one to stick my nose in where it doesn't belong, but I think it does belong here. I will tell you that David is a complete narcissist, and he's not going to be happy just letting you get on with your life. He'll pop in every now and then just to make sure he can pull you back in and mess things up for you. The only way to get rid of people like that is to go completely no contact. You need to block him from all your social media, get a new phone number and new email addresses."

Lottie rolled her eyes.

"Yeah, I see those eyes rolling. You always stuck up for him, but why are you still doing it now? You couldn't see what was happening to you because you were duped by him. Lottie, I know this is hard to hear, but you didn't see what he was doing because you're a good person and wouldn't expect anyone to act that way. We saw it. He used you. He never loved you. People like that aren't capable of love."

"So what? You're a psychologist now? You know he's a narcissist suddenly?" Lottie crossed her arms and wanted to cry. She felt like she did when she was sixteen and got caught sneaking home after curfew.

"No, I'm not a psychologist, but I know narcissists because my sister is one. I spent years healing from her abuse. They can be the most charming people on earth, but that part of them never lasts because it's not who they really are. It's a mask. After it drops and they discard you, they pull you back in so they can use you and feed off of you. Especially people like you, Lottie.

281

You're so kind, loving, and good. I hate to say it, but you're a perfect target. Now, I'm not trying to hurt you. I'm trying to help you protect yourself. David will return. He will be watching you. He'll seem to know just when you're happy again and he'll swoop in, pull you into his bullshit, and shit all over you again. It'll never end."

Lottie's mind raced back to his last visit. He had made her feel like they were going to get back together. He'd ruined her date with Grant. But he couldn't have known she was happy. That was a coincidence. Although she supposed he could have changed the extent of the way he planned to use her once he saw she was going on a date.

Tears spilled down Lottie's cheeks. Her mother didn't continue. She leaned over and pulled Lottie to her side, rubbing her arm and stroking her hair. Lottie knew her mom was right. She'd been so used to fiercely defending David's behavior over the years that it had become habit or a matter of winning with her mom and not want to be wrong. She felt ashamed for being duped by someone, more than once.

Lottie grabbed a napkin from the table, dabbed her eyes, and blew her nose. "You're right. I'll get a new number. I'm ready to start fresh. I do need to call Beth today though and let her know I'm safe and that I lost my phone."

"You do whatever you need to do, honey. You can use the phone in my office if you want a little privacy. You gonna finish your food?"

"No, I'm not hungry anymore."

Lottie's dad reached across to Lottie's plate, but her mom slapped his hand.

"I'll wrap it up for you and you can have it later if you change your mind. Okay?"

"Okay, Mom. Thanks."

Lottie got up and padded into the office, still sniffling. She took a few deep breaths before picking up the phone to dial Beth.

Fuck!

She searched her clouded mind for Beth's number. When she was a teen, she had all her friends' numbers memorized by heart; now Lottie only knew her parents' number and her own. She lowered herself onto the office chair and searched her mind. She'd seen the number flash up on the screen, but she didn't really call Beth often. She always texted her. What was she going to do? Why had people become so reliant on smartphones that they let themselves become dumb?

Throwing the snot- and tear-coated napkin into the office trash bin, she flipped on the computer to log into her email. She sent Beth a message.

Lottie: I made it to Michigan safe and sound. Unfortunately, my cell did not. Some fart-lard of a bitch stole it. Anyway, I hope you get this. I'll be getting a new phone today. I can't remember your number. Send it as soon as you get this.

Lottie set up a new email address, blocked David from the rest of her scarcely used social media accounts, and logged off the computer.

Chapter Twenty-Nine

Grant

It had been three days since Grant called Lottie. He'd heard nothing back. Maybe she truly wanted to start over completely fresh and he was just another reminder of the life she wanted to put behind her. But he wasn't ready to put things behind him. Not without letting her know how he felt about her first. If she didn't call today, he was going to call Beth and ask her if she knew why Lottie hadn't returned his call.

He pulled out his phone to check it. The volume was up, and his notifications were on, but there were no messages. Scooping his wallet off the dresser, he opened it up and made sure all the cash was inside. He slid it in his back pocket and walked out the bedroom door.

"Nana. I'm going to get her. Are you sure you don't want to come with me to make sure you like her?"

"Oh, I trust your judgment, hon. And the picture you took on your phone, well, I can see she has kind eyes. We're gonna have to fatten her up, though. Once we get her off that damn dog food and on some real food, it'll happen soon enough. You know, when I was growing up, we never fed dogs kibble. They just ate with the family. And that's the way it should be. They are family, after all."

"I'm so glad you're on board with this. I can't believe I was so nervous to ask you. She's a great dog, Nana. I know you'll fall in love with her like I did."

"Well, get out the door and go get her already."

"Yes, ma'am." Grant waved at Nana, grabbed the leash and collar he bought the day before, and drove straight to animal control. The human chimney was in her usual place by the front door, smoking, when he pulled up.

"Well, hey there, Grant. Today's the big day. She's waiting for ya. Gave her a bath and everything. Why don't ya go on back and get her? I'll be inside in just a minute, and we'll fill out the forms."

Grant made his way in and headed straight to the back. "Hey, Freya." He smiled at the blonde Border collie, whose tail had immediately begun to wag the moment she saw him. Freya. It was her name. He had it in the back of his mind but hadn't uttered it out loud until this moment. He'd been so worried he'd come in one day and find she'd been picked up by whatever owners had mistreated her so poorly. Now, it felt safe to say her name and make the connection that she belonged to him and that they were family. "You ready to go home?"

He opened the gate and put the orange collar around the dog's neck. She looked prideful and pranced along with him once he hooked on the leash. It was almost as if she didn't want to let herself believe until this moment either. The pair walked out into the front room, where Grant filled out all the paperwork, handed the human chimney the adoption fee, thanked her, and took Freya out to his truck. The moment he opened the door, she jumped inside. He walked around and opened his door to find Freya sitting in the driver's seat.

"Oh, no, girl. I'm driving. Scooch." She moved over to the passenger seat and panted happily as he climbed in and started the engine. He thought of Lottie and Pickles, wondering if Pickles and Freya would get along and if the four of them could all fit in the truck together.

He put the truck in gear, leaned across Freya to roll down her window, rolled down his, cranked the radio, and drove through town, stopping at McDonald's to get a Freya a ten pack of chicken nuggets and a vanilla ice cream cone to celebrate her new life. Grant drove by Lottie's house. It still looked dark, and her car hadn't appeared to move. He wondered how long she'd be gone and hoped that he'd get to see her when she did return. He had to ask her for a chance. He had to try to convince her to stay. But was that selfish? To ask her to stay in a town just for the sake of dating him? He had to try anyway.

After arriving home, he quickly took Freya inside to meet Nana.

"Oh my goodness. She's even more beautiful in person."

Freya was on her best behavior, no jumping, no crotch sniffing. When Nana bent down to pet her, she just rolled onto her back.

"Someone wants her tummy rubbed." Nana squatted down. "I'm not sure these old bones can bend like this for too long. You'll have to allow her on the furniture, Grant. That's the only way I'm going to be able to rub her tummy for too long."

"Really, Nana? You never let any of your other dogs on the furniture."

"Well, I'm too old to care anymore. We'll spread out some blankets and you can vacuum up the dog hair. Seems like she's a shedder." Nana glanced at the long blonde hair coating her hand.

"I'll take her out on the patio and give her a good brushing."

Grant rifled through the Walmart bag and pulled out the brush he'd purchased the day before. "Come on, Freya. Let's go outside."

"Freya? That's what you named her?" Nana giggled.

"Well, what would you have named her? Lassie?" He grinned.

"What's wrong with Lassie? It's a good name for a dog."

"Freya is the Goddess of Love, and you're not going to find a more loving dog anywhere. I think it's the perfect name for her."

"Maybe you're right. Freya it is." Nana followed the two of them onto the patio and lowered herself into the chair. "Have you heard from your friend yet?"

"No, Nana. I haven't heard anything."

"Why don't you text the other girl, her best friend, and find out when she's coming back to town?"

"I don't want to seem like a stalker." Grant sat on the ground and began brushing Freya, who rolled onto her back. "I'm gonna have to brush more than your tummy, girl."

"Asking a question ain't stalking. When you're done here, you call her friend and find out what's going on. You've been moping around long enough, checking your phone every couple minutes. I'm not too old to see what's going on. You need to find out so you can stop being so miserable."

"All right, Nana. I'll call Beth after dinner tonight."

***

Grant and Nana took Freya on a walk around their small neighborhood after dinner. Clearly, she wasn't a dog Nana could walk. She was so excited she pulled on the leash the whole time.

She's going to need to be trained and walked a lot before you'll be able to handle her, Nana."

"At my age, the only dog that might not be able to knock me over is a teacup Pomeranian. I'll leave the walking to you. I'm good with the tummy scratches and snuggles." Nana smiled.

"She'll need plenty of walks just the same. I don't want to get my arm ripped from the socket every time I walk her. I guess she had to have one fault."

"Don't we all?" Nana wrapped her arm around his and took a deep breath. "It's gonna be getting unbearably hot soon enough. I can't believe summer is almost here. You'll have to get up early to walk her or wait until it's late. This pavement will scorch her paws."

Grant thought about the coming summer months, wondering if he'd get the chance to spend them with Lottie. Would he get to show her Freya? He longed for the chance to meet her every evening to walk Freya and Pickles. He had to know if she was coming back to town, and he had to know when. He wouldn't miss his opportunity again.

The moment they returned home, Grant poured some fresh, cool water into Freya's bowl and headed to his room. He pulled out his phone, wondering what to text Beth so that he wouldn't seem like the kind of pushy asshole Lottie had just freed herself from.

Grant: Hey, Beth. It's Grant. I was wondering if you've heard from Lottie.

He set his phone on the bedside table and headed in the kitchen to grab a beer. When he returned, he was happy to see he already had a text back.

Beth: I got an email from her a couple days ago. Her cell was stolen. Sorry, I should have thought to let you know sooner. My mind is in a cloud with this pregnancy and I just found out Michael is deploying.

Grant: No problem. I'm relieved that she hasn't been ignoring me. I thought she was upset with me. Do you know when she'll be back in town yet?

Beth: She's coming back on Friday. Do you want her new number?

Grant: I don't feel comfortable calling her new number unless I know she wants me to have it. Just don't let her leave town without me getting a chance to talk to her, please.

Beth: I won't. Come to the reservoir on Saturday. I'll make sure she's there.

Grant: Thanks.

Beth: No problem.

Grant turned off his phone and laid back on his bed, relieved that Lottie hadn't been ignored him after all. His mind swirled, wondering if could say anything that could convince her to stay in town a bit longer. Was he being selfish to ask that of her?

He kicked himself for a moment. Maybe he should have taken Lottie's new number from Beth. Surely, she wouldn't have offered if she knew Lottie wouldn't be okay with it. He'd be able to call her or text her, giving her more time to think. Would she feel ambushed if he showed up at the reservoir and laid all his feelings on her when she's already going through so much with David? Was he setting himself up to be a rebound guy, like Nana said? Did he care about being a rebound guy? Any time with Lottie had to be better than no time at all. No, that was silly. If they genuinely cared about each other, the timing of their meeting was irrelevant. He'd never bought into the dating advice from others before. Of course, he'd never felt serious about any of the women he dated before either.

Grant made his way into the living room where Nana was sitting in the couch with Freya curled up next to her watching the evening news.

"So much crime in Lawton. It's spreading to our small town. When I was growing up, we never had to worry about all these break-ins." She shook her head.

"And yet you keep leaving the door unlocked." Grant cocked his head to the side.

"I guess you're right. Maybe I'll have to start locking it. It's a shame, though. It's a real shame. What's this world coming to?" Nana shook her head some more and tsked at the screen.

"Hey, Nana. Can I ask you for some advice?"

"Well, sure, hon." Nana picked up the remote and muted the television.

"Lottie lost her cell phone. That's why she hasn't responded to me. She's coming back into town on Friday, and Beth wants me to come to the reservoir to meet them. But is it selfish of me to tell Lottie how I feel about her and, well, kind of ask her to stay in town? I'd be asking her to stay just to date me. Is that crazy to ask of someone?"

"Isn't love crazy? Nothing about love makes sense. As old as I am, it's not something I've figured out. But the one thing I have learned is that you should always follow your heart. Now, that's advice I still ignore. I pushed you to date Tiffany even though you didn't feel it. I could tell that. It's just that I love you so much and I guess I thought I knew better than you. What I really needed was to step out of your way and let you follow your heart. If you really think this is the girl for you, you need to do everything you can to be with her. Tell her how you feel. Follow your heart. If she doesn't want to stay and she doesn't want to be with you, well, that's because her heart doesn't want you back. But you at least gotta find out."

"You're right. Thanks, Nana. I'm not sure I can live with myself if I don't try. If she doesn't want to stay or she doesn't want me, I'll accept it and leave her alone, but I won't give up until I know that."

"I think you knew the right thing to do all along, Grant. Some obstacles have gotten in your way, but if you love her, it'll all be worth it in the end. Sometimes the struggles make the love sweeter. Your Papa Joe and I had some struggles, but we made it through, and we loved each other that much harder because we know how close we came to losing it all."

Grant reached out and took Nana's hand. He sucked in a deep breath and nodded. "I'm going to put myself out there completely. I'm not going to hold back."

"Sometimes we just need to talk things out with someone else to find the answers hidden in our own hearts." Nana scratched Freya behind the ears and smiled.

He padded into his room and took out a pad of paper and a pen. He wrote and rewrote all the things he wanted to say to Lottie. In two days, he'd be seeing her, and he'd know if he was going to have his heart soar or break.

Chapter Thirty

Lottie

Lottie rode the escalator down to the baggage claim. There she spied Beth holding up a sign that said **'Most beautiful girl in the world.'** Lottie's cheeks blushed as she ran over to hug Beth. "I bet the people waiting with you were disappointed when they saw me after expecting the most beautiful girl in the world."

"Bullshit." An old man smiled and winked at her. "I think the sign is pretty accurate."

"See!" Beth nudged Lottie in the ribs. "We really need to get you to an ophthalmologist to adjust those eyes of yours. Let's go get your bag."

Lottie and Beth headed to the baggage claim with just enough time to squeeze themselves into a gap near the conveyor belt.

"I'm so glad you're back. It was boring as fuck with you gone. I did nothing but binge-watch Netflix. If it wasn't for Pickles getting me out of the house for walks, I'd have a little extra cottage cheese jiggling around my thighs. I ate so many cheeseballs. Those fucking things are addictive."

293

"I couldn't take my parents anymore. I think when I've been gone for a while, I get amnesia and forget what they're like. My dad picked at my mom and my mom preached at me. I know everything she said was right, but who wants to sit and listen to hours of lessons in 'I told you so' when you already feel like complete shit?" Lottie sucked in a deep breath and let it out. "I feel so lost. I don't think I've ever been more confused about what I'm supposed to do next. I had more direction at high school graduation than I do now."

"Stay in Altus. Think about it. Dan is holding your job for a while." Beth looked at Lottie with pleading eyes.

"There's nothing for me in Altus. Just a bunch of horrible memories of David."

"There's nothing? Really? What about me? What about us? And all our great memories. Don't let David have that much power over you. Fuck him, Lottie."

A loud buzzer rang out, and the conveyer belt began to move. Luggage started flowing from the great beyond. Lottie stood in silence as she scanned the bags for the familiar strip of an old bathing suit she tied to the handle of hers. Her stomach churned and sunk for saying that she had nothing. What a selfish dick she was, not thinking of all the good times she'd had with Beth.

After scooping her bag from the belt, she followed Beth through the maze of the parking garage to her Jeep. Once her bag was in and she climbed into the passenger seat, she turned to Beth with tears balancing on the rims of her eyes. "I'm sorry I said that. Of course I know I have you here. But what happens when you leave? I'll just be some sad spinster teacher who sits alone in her house everyday eating Big Macs until I die."

Beth took Lottie's hand. "What happens to me when you leave? I'll just be some pregnant, antisocial cow who sits around eating cheeseballs. You know I hate all the other bitches in town. Michael is deploying and I'll spend the summer completely alone and pregnant."

"Michael is deploying? Why didn't you tell me?"

"I've been busy sulking. Hence my binge-watching and binge-eating. Besides, I didn't want to pile any more shit news on you." Beth turned the Jeep on and backed out of the parking lot. "We've got a three-hour drive back. At least promise me you'll think about staying. Let me imagine that you'll be there when my baby is born."

"You might move before then."

"Then come with us. Be my nanny until you find a job. You're not just my best friend, Lottie. You're like a sister to me. You can start your life over, but you don't have to do it alone."

"I can't follow you guys around when you move. What will Michael think? He'll get sick of me."

"No way. Michael adores you, and I think he'd be happy knowing we had extra help with the baby, especially if he deploys after it's born. And it's not like you'd have to live with us forever. But you'd have support and family until you decide what you want to do."

Lottie nodded. It was nice to feel wanted, and she did love babies. For a moment, she felt fortunate that she hadn't had any with David. She couldn't imagine going through all this with kids in tow.

"Another thing." Beth glanced at Lottie before pulling out onto the interstate. "Grant called you."

"What? He did?"

"He wanted to talk to you on the last day school. He called you. He texted me a few days ago because you never called him back. I forgot to let him know your phone was stolen because I was all wrapped up in the fact that Michael is deploying."

"What did he want?"

Beth cocked her head and squinted at Lottie. "What do you think?"

Lottie's stomach flipped. "What about Tiffany?"

"What about her, Lottie? I don't know. He wants to talk to you. I didn't probe him for everything he's going to say to you or what happened with Tiffany. You'll find out tomorrow. He's coming to the reservoir. You can find out then. I'm pretty sure whatever it is, it's going to be another reason for you to stay in Altus. He cares about you, Lottie. A lot."

A rush slid through Lottie's body but thudded back down into her stomach. "My mom said I'm a target for narcissists. That it's like I have a bullseye on my back and they zero in on me. How do I know I'm not just letting that happen again? I mean, I thought it was too good to be true that David could love me. Why should I believe that Grant isn't the same?"

"Don't make me pull this Jeep over, Charlotte Stephens!" Beth shot Lottie a glare. "Grant is nothing like the douche. He backed off and gave you your space when David slithered back into it. He's always put your needs first. Narcissist don't do that. You can't let David interfere in your life anymore. Don't put up walls for anyone but David."

Opposing emotions swirled through Lottie the whole trip home. She was nervous about seeing Grant yet extremely excited at the same time. She flipped down the passenger side visor and checked in the mirror for the inevitable pimples that emerged every time she travelled by airplane. Should she act like she was surprised to see him there or admit she was expecting him? Would she need to apologize for pushing him aside for David? Did she want him to think he was staying in Altus to give their relationship a try or immediately make sure he knew she was staying for Beth?

Lottie leaned her head on the window and stared out at the cars they passed, wondering if the lives of the people inside were as fucked up as hers.

***

Lottie's heart thumped in her chest as she waited in the doorway for Beth to arrive. Pickles danced around on the leash anxiously. He must have been feeding on her energy. She couldn't calm herself down. Every inch of her skin seemed to be emitting a cold, invisible sweat. She must've sniffed her armpits at least a dozen times, reapplying deodorant occasionally just to be sure she didn't stink.

She glanced into the hall mirror again. How did her breath smell? Wait, was that a booger? No. But a long, protruding nose hair, yes. Where did that come from? It had to have been growing for weeks to get that long. Sure, it was blonde; maybe that's why she'd never noticed it. Oh, goodness, there was a whole forest of blonde nose hairs growing.

Lottie raced into the bathroom, pulling Pickles along with her. "Sorry, boy," she apologized after jerking on the leash a little too hard as she reached into the medicine cabinet to fish out the little cuticle scissors. Pressing her nose back, she clipped the hairs. "I'm so disgusting. I can't believe I almost went like this."

A honk from the driveway blared out. Lottie dropped the scissors in the sink. "C'mon, boy, Aunt Beth is here." She raced to the front door, taking one more look in the hall mirror, sucking in a deep breath, and walked through the door, trying to look like a normal human being and not a nervous tween who was about to be asked to her first school dance.

Scooping Pickles up, she helped him into the back seat of Beth's Jeep and climbed in, buckling up and trying to stifle the smile that refused to leave her face.

Beth winked. "Ready?"

Lottie nodded, and they took off for the reservoir. There was no sign of his truck when they arrived. Lottie tried not to let the sinking in the pit of her stomach consume her. She looked at the clock. They had arrived a little earlier than they normally did.

"Welp, shall we?" Beth climbed out of the Jeep.

Lottie pressed her lips into a smile and nodded. She lifted Pickles out of the Jeep. As they began their walk around the reservoir, Lottie couldn't help looking all around to see if Grant had arrived yet.

"Don't worry, he'll be here," Beth said, patting Lottie on the shoulder.

"What? I'm not—"

"You're turning around every five steps. You don't have to pretend with me."

"I'm really nervous. I feel so stupid for ditching him for David. How can I apologize for that?"

"I don't think he's coming for apologies, Lottie. Just relax."

Lottie nodded, took in a deep breath, and let it out as they continued their walk.

As they rounded the corner, Pickles suddenly darted off, the leash slipping right out of Lottie's hands. She turned to chase him and ran into Grant, who was walking her way. He had a dog with him, who Pickles was sniffing and circling.

"Grant, hey." Lottie stumbled as she untangled Pickles's leash from the one Grant was holding. "Sorry about that."

Grant smiled as he watched Lottie smooth her hair back and straighten her shirt.

"Who is this?" Lottie motioned to the Border collie.

"This is Freya. I just adopted her. We were wondering if you wouldn't mind us joining you on your walk."

Beth had walked up to them during the shuffle. She gave Lottie a side hug. "Hey, Lottie, I think I'm gonna get going if you don't mind. I'm feeling a little sick to my stomach. Pregnancy, you know. Grant, do you mind driving Lottie home?"

"I'd be happy to. I hope you feel better." He smiled at Beth.

"I'm sure I just need to lie down for a bit. See you guys later." Beth blew Lottie a kiss before heading off toward her Jeep.

Lottie's heart pounded.

299

"Shall we?" Grant asked as he motioned to the trail.

Lottie nodded and walked slowly on.

"I was surprised when you weren't at school the last day. I'm sorry things have been hard for you." Grant paused. Lottie got the feeling that he wanted to ask about David but didn't want to intrude.

Lottie tucked a loose hair behind her ear. "I'm sorry, Grant."

"For what?"

"I'm sorry that I stayed with David instead of going out with you that night. I should've told him to get lost. He was just using me, as always. Anyway, I got my divorce papers. I wrote him forty letters, and I got divorce papers in return."

Lottie stopped walking and turned to Grant. "The thing is I thought about you the whole time. I knew I was making the wrong choice, and I did it anyway. I'm messed up. I don't even know why you still want to be my friend." Lottie's eyes burned and filled with tears.

"I want to be more than your friend, Lottie. We all make choices we regret or else I wouldn't have dated Tiffany. Sometimes we do the things we think we should do or we do things to make other people happy. But I want to be happy, and I know the thing that will make me happy is being with you. I know it's selfish of me to ask you to stay in Altus, but I hope you'll stay. I'd really like to spend more time with you."

Tears spilled down Lottie's cheeks. Grant leaned in close to her. Their lips were almost touching when Lottie's arm jerked, pulling her away. They looked over to see Pickles doing his best to hump Freya, who was two times his height. Freya stood there looking bewildered, as though she didn't understand what it was he was trying to do.

Lottie blushed, embarrassed that her dog was trying to hump his. "Pickles, stop that." She tugged on the leash. She covered her face as Pickles continued to hump Freya's leg.

Grant watched her, a smile spreading across his face as she fumbled and tripped over her words. He pulled her in close to him. "I guess you have to stay now. We can't possibly separate Romeo and Juliet here."

"No, we can't separate them." Lottie smiled and placed her hand on Grant's face.

He pulled her close to him, kissing her. She parted her lips, letting his tongue find its way to hers. As they kissed, Lottie realized she didn't need to make any more decisions about her future; she could feel it. She was home.

The End

Thank You for Reading *Distant Spring*!

I hope you enjoyed *Distant Spring* and that it brought a little more joy, love, and hope into your day. As an indie author, your support means the world to me—it's readers like you who make this journey possible.

If you loved the story, it would mean so much if you could leave a quick review on Amazon or Goodreads. Reviews are the lifeblood of indie authors, helping other readers discover books they might enjoy. Even a sentence or two can make a huge difference!

Want to stay in touch? You can sign up for updates at ENBeckBooks.com to hear about new releases, sneak peeks, and other fun surprises. Speaking of new releases, keep an eye out for my next book, *Falling Under the Stars*—a heartfelt and mysterious journey you won't want to miss!

Finally, if you think a friend or fellow reader would enjoy *Distant Spring*, please share it with them! Word of mouth is one of the best ways to help stories like this reach more hearts.

Thank you again for spending your time with my characters. I can't wait to share more adventures with you!

With love and gratitude,
E.N. Beck

E.N. Beck

E.N. Beck loves storytelling, a passion that has been with her since childhood. Her great aunts called her "the storyteller"—and she's been living up to that name ever since. When she's not writing, she's spending time with her kids, husband, dogs, and chickens, or making wine in her quiet, introverted world. A lover of the night sky, animals, and love itself, she's always on a spiritual journey and works to use the gifts she's been given.

www.ingramcontent.com/pod-product-compliance
Lightning Source LLC
Chambersburg PA
CBHW012038190626
46808CB00019B/3110